Find Me ~ Book Two

She'd Find Out what She was Made of

H.H. Rune

Heartfinder Media LLC

Find Me, Book Two-She'd find out what she was made of.

The second in the Extraordinary Life Seeker series by H.H. Rune.

While this work contains shimmers from the autobiographical record of the author, it is brought forth as a work of fiction. If anyone, by chance, "sees" themself in the pages of this work, I encourage them to feel touched that their presence has made enough of a difference in one person's life to be written about and remembered forever.

No real names have been mentioned for the privacy of all. This series is written from one person's perspective - with her often imperfect memory - and no harm is intended. Imparted wisdom is shared only to be a "potential" teaching moment that may help others in navigating their own lives; however, it is not intended to be taken as any sort of "therapy" or an answer to their own problems as such. The author recommends professional therapy to everyone all along their personal journey, as she has found it invaluable herself. Thank you, M.H.

There are some actual places mentioned in this book that may or may not have been visited by the author; they were included to introduce random places to readers to invite them to explore more. Resources are listed in the back.

Original cover by the author utilizing her Canva Pro account and original art on stamp was done by Scott Poole- scottpoole.com

Dedication and Thanks

This book is dedicated to the younger members of *The Ladies' Lounge*. Your wisdom far exceeds your age and has taught your mother so many lessons in this life. It has been a pleasure- no, a joy- to see you both reach for your own goals and seek out extraordinary life experiences the way you do. You both have intrinsically known and reached way beyond what you thought you were capable of and I know 100% that you will go much further than this Mom of yours.
I love your adventurous spirits, your willingness to do hard things and make big decisions for your ultimate betterment. I am in awe of your undying empathy and love for your fellow kind. I am gushingly proud of you both and cannot wait to watch you grow in all the ways that life has in store for you.
My beauties~ inside and out, you are my whole heart walking free of my body.
Thrive

Love, Mom

And many thanks to T.N, J.B, C.Z, K.T, L.T, C.A, E.B, M.C, K.S, R.G, C.B, & T.C, for sensitivity input and more
A huge thanks to my editor R.C.

Triggers & Style

Trigger Warnings:

Contains topics such as Internment camps, amputation, stuttering, war, sexsomnia, Asian Prejudice, slavery mention, Black history, alcoholism, Family Dysfunction, Fire, Homosexuality, Sudden death, loss of loved one, heart attack, death of a pet, religion, divorce, medical emergency, miscarriage, lupus, adoption, fleeing one's country, death during surgery.

Some of these triggers are only touched on, while others are shown more in depth. Some resources are listed at the end of the book.

Out of respect to one's life experiences, H.H. Rune

***

Stylistic Choices: With Indie publishing comes a freedom I wasn't expecting or maybe even wanted. I have no overseer other than the reader, so it is here that I ask for your understanding of all the quirks or stylistic choices you may see in this book. As a newly diagnosed neuro-divergent-(diagnosed at fifty-two,) I have a certain way of thinking and speaking. When I add a comma in a place that some feel is unwarranted, it is because I want the reader to experience a pause.

Cheat code for the Reader

This book uses three different typesets to show the varied viewpoints

Bolded text shows the author's memories that make up the traveling books themselves

Italics- Journal entries from the author over time

Standard text is to show the travels of Book Two

***

The 2 at the top of the excerpts are to show the the change of scene to the traveling books' movements.
Subsequent books will be numbered 3, 4 & 5
***

The books in the Find Me, Extraordinary Life Seeker series are best read in order.

Find Me

Book Two

Dear Reader,

This traveling book is my secret mission to live a more extraordinary life from within the confines of an ordinary one.

Only five copies of this book exist and this has made its way to you; you are now and forever a part of this story.

Inside you will find moments captured from one person's life. Each passage starts with the set of initials of the person with whom I share the connection.

We are all connected on some level; every person you meet leaves a mark on you whether good or bad. Often it is the worst people who *gift* us the best lessons.

It is my hope that this idea spurs you into living in a more extraordinary way; to think bigger and reach beyond what you currently see.

The memories inside may remind you of a time or a person in your own life; may you think of those people today for the good or the lessons you learned from them.

Please read this book then write your name and location in the back before giving it to someone else. Leave it on a bus, give it to a friend, it will only take a few minutes for you to participate and it is wonderful to think of the adventures it may have.

Let's see how small our world really is.

If you, by chance, recognize yourself in here, please bring the book and,

Find me...

H.H.

My curious and eclectic uncle. He also liked to write. The man, the wickedly creative alcoholic who lived his final days in the solitude of a moored boat tethered to a marina, even though there was a woman on shore who would have loved to have him. Even after a lifetime spent chasing the attention of the Hollywood Studios with very little to show, he never gave up on his stories.

Our family is a strange one, especially if I compare us with those pictures or scenes of *"family"* on the small screen. We are a disconnected bunch, even when physically close in proximity. My nuclear family moved away from everyone, out of state, but even the ones left behind didn't gather as some or most families do. We are all scattered everywhere, just flotsam and jetsam in the world, trying to make our own way despite the challenges. Oddly again, we share more similarities than differences, not that we have any time to compare.

When I was a teen, and Mom would talk about you, you always came off as Mr. Prince Charming, so well put together and dashing. Handsome enough to be a movie star yourself back then, you were a real hotshot. Mom thought you were the "cat's pajamas" to use one of Grandma's favorite idioms.

You and your other sister D didn't get along much, but the two of you managed to combine your efforts enough to try to trade my mother, a baby at the time, your youngest sister, to a neighbor in exchange for their miniature donkey. Quite a caper for a couple of usually fighting siblings to team up like that.

It was mostly in photographs that I would see you, except maybe once when we were all down for a family reunion for Grandma's eightieth birthday. You were there with your sons, and everyone played their part in the happy-go-lucky family. It was mostly an act that day, as I would hear later on, your estrangement with your sons was just one part of your internal pain.

On that trip I got to experience all of you a little bit, hear some of the stories that you shared. It was more time than I'd spent with any of you in my life before or after.

It was that day when I discovered that we shared something in common. Something that mattered to us both in a big way. Something that would ultimately become our bond.

After being told by a counselor that I needed to have something for myself, and to not use up all of my energy and effort on my family and risk burnout and resentment, I began to look at the enticing options I had around me. I'd written little stories most of my life and decided to explore writing seriously for the first time in my early twenties. Back then, I focused on what I'd known as a nanny-children's books. I even tried my hand at illustrating them.

Seeing an article in the local paper talking about a small writers group who met every Wednesday night at seven, I was pulled in, believing that the clipping was meant just for me. I pinned it to the refrigerator and it taunted me every time I stepped into the kitchen to get a snack or feed my baby, myself, or my husband.

(When I say the newspaper clipping was pinned to the front of the fridge, I can honestly say that it was because I had glued cork to the front of it to cover up the horrible paint job.)

When I finally went, I met all kinds of people there. From the soft-hearted-but- rough-and-tumble gym owner who shared tales from his stint in the army, to another woman who reminded me of my dad's mother, mixed with a few other women and men all in their mid to late fifties and sixties.

I was the youngest one there and the only one focusing on children's books, but they were all very kind, and listened intently when I read my work.

I tell you this here, because it was in this writers group that brought me to have a special relationship with you, my faraway uncle with whom I had so much in common, but might never have known.

One of the women in the group was writing a novel along with her brother. They had been at it for three years. Trading off chapters every month, they worked to get it ready to publish together. Her brother lived elsewhere, and they sent disks and pages to each other to continue the manuscript. She shared that they spoke initially, formulating characters and a possible main plot, but mostly they just wrote what they felt was the next part based on the other one's entry. It was such a fascinating idea, a way to stay close when they both lived so far from each other. Something they could do together.

I sent a handwritten letter to you asking if you would write a story with me, and you loved the idea. We started with a dream that I had involving a mafia group, a cigar box and a dreamcatcher.

I wrote the first chapter, and you wrote the second, and so on. Our exchange went on for almost a year. At the time we used handwritten pages and diskette drives that we could plug into each of our computers to add to the story.

When my mother read our shared words, she said she couldn't tell when my writing stopped and yours started up. We might have been able to make this partnership work.

But I was in my early twenties, and a brand-new mom struggling to balance everything. I fell away with our correspondence. Ultimately you wrote up a chapter by chapter outline for our shared story and a character study for me to follow whenever we had the chance to pick it up again.

We never did. As my daughter grew, life became more busy. We moved. We had a second child. Writing fell away from me, and as you continued to toil with your own projects, I didn't realize I'd eventually lose my chance.

Being professionally acknowledged in your writing was a pursuit that never quite panned out for you. You took chance after chance with screenplays, and continued to try, hoping that your stories would end up onscreen. You were a creative, cursed in that way similarly to Ernest Hemmingway. Unlike him though, your gift tormented you with a feeling that what you had written was never good enough because it wasn't validated by the outside world. As much as you tried and kept after it, you never saw the reward.

One of his final showdowns was in protest to a film that made it to the screen, one with the same name and an eerily similar premise to the screenplay he had proposed to one of the studios. In the film there was a scene that he believed was taken from his work without payment or permission from him and he reported the infringement to a reporter at *TV Guide*. His objection was penned into an article. It may have been the only time his name was used in the entertainment world, and we all picked up a copy from the grocery store. Alas, his complaint did not yield him the justice and monies he felt he was owed.

As Hemmingway had chosen the bottle as a way to cope, so did you. Maybe it was because of the family legacy with drinkers from both sides, or maybe it was just your chosen potion. We both shared in the idea that we were meant for something bigger, but I had more time left to achieve it.

He died with his greatness tucked inside, as it happens to many. His stories remained unpublished and unread. Creative energy that, despite the hard work and dedication, would never be appreciated; it is a curse of many of the ones who turn life into art.

In our venture together, he gave me a gift. I can take in his thoughts in our shared words- handwritten and stuck in time, just waiting to be attended to again.

I *will* write our story and believe that his presence will be with me on those writing days.

"Don't use that word, try this one," his influence will push through.

Following his lead, and his character maps, I will write our book for *us*, and it will be grand. When the book comes out, I will make sure that his name is right there alongside mine, because we really will have done it together.

Him from one side of the veil, and me on the other.

~

~2~

Iian

I. Davis in Huntsville, Alabama, paid the taxi driver a twenty, and yanked his luggage out of the backseat. He set his suitcase on the curb and rammed his hand into his carry-on bag to find his keys. He had to piss. He found them in a side pocket after fingering literally everything else in his bag, and almost wetting himself.

Everything had felt rushed that day. He had slept through the first two wake up calls at the hotel and then got caught in traffic in the cab. He arrived at the airport with only fifteen minutes before his flight took off. He hadn't had the chance to sit and have a cup of coffee and wake up a little bit at the airport before takeoff. There wasn't time to wake up slow and work through the aftereffects of his partying the night before.

Instead of the low-key morning he had planned on, Iian found himself bolting down the concourse at the Las Vegas airport with his shoes untied and his too long hair flying in every direction. Throwing his boarding pass at the attendant, he darted onto the plane, wheezing, sweating and murmuring to himself like a crazy person before finally sitting down. He had just managed, even with a headache that wouldn't quit. It was a little less than four hours back to Huntsville; thankfully he had booked a direct flight. Even with the nap on the plane, his headache only lessened some.

Still upset at how his morning had gone, Iian tugged his luggage angrily behind him as he entered his apartment lobby. Suddenly getting a whiff of himself, he put his key into his mailbox and found it empty except for a wrinkled up, handwritten note. Squinting through his headache, he gathered that he had let his mailbox get too full, and he would need to go pick up all of his mail from the post office downtown.

"Dammit, just what I need. Today of all days."

It had already been a shit day, and even more crap had piled onto it when he landed and heard the voicemail from his lawyer letting him know that his divorce from Daphne was now final.

He had skipped town to try and forget all that was happening at home. "Home," he bantered in his head, "*What home?*"

Vegas Baby- for the last week, Iian had tried to leave thoughts of his impending divorce behind. He had specifically picked his old college buddy to visit because he knew he was a professional level partier. A guy who never got attached. The confirmed bachelor. If that guy ever did have a girlfriend, it never lasted long. He had joked with Iian that as soon as they got serious, he was outta there.

Iian wanted to see that lifestyle in action. Somehow, up close, it didn't look as pleasurable as he had hoped it would. Going out to a different bar each night. Having to fluff his feathers to a new woman in hopes of getting laid that evening. Another name to memorize and adding telltale notes to help him remember who she was clogging up his phone. His buddy's life didn't seem all that it was cracked up to be.

Iian locked his mailbox and dragged his suitcase out of the lobby and into the apartment parking garage.

Good, there wasn't anyone around. He walked behind the dumpster and unzipped his fly. He looked around and let it all go. Keeping his eyes open for people coming near, he allowed himself to feel the full release of his bladder. He shook himself, and zipped up.

There. Now he could go get his mail, and come back home to drink himself properly into emotional oblivion.

Tossing his luggage in the trunk, he sped off in his early nineties black corvette to pick up the mail. He couldn't wait to get home and get plastered. His thoughts drifted to Daphne as he mindlessly made the turns into town, reaching the post office in ten minutes flat. He slipped his car into a narrow spot out front, and dashed in with the note with only minutes left to spare until closing. After hassling the postal worker for a few minutes about the size of his mailbox (a person who could do nothing about it), he left with all of his mail in a plastic bag and tossed it onto the front seat.

Tears snuck out of the corners of his eyes. It shouldn't have turned out this way. He slammed his fists on the steering wheel, and swore, "What the fuck is wrong with me?" bellowing with a guttural sob and barreling through a yellow light.

Daphne. Daphne had removed herself from the train wreck that was him forever. He remembered feeling the permanence of it all as he watched her turn away in ambivalence as she left the courtroom. She hadn't even looked at him. Her eyes stayed locked on the judge. Her monotone responses, she didn't shed a tear throughout the proceeding. Before he knew it, they were in the waiting period.

Iian wanted so badly to forget about Daphne, and everything else that was going on while on his trip, but had been unable to do so. If anything, he saw shimmers of her everywhere: In the appearance or mannerisms of women sitting at the bar; each little child, a reminder to him that they planned to have their own kids someday; in the older couples playing together in the casinos, he saw Daphne and himself cheering each other on in their games. If he hadn't blown it, that might have been them in their golden years. Iian felt like a dirtbag. He was a dirtbag.

He hadn't wanted the divorce from Daphne, but he understood that his drunken ways and lack of self control had finally driven her to it. He had spent way too many nights out with his co-workers at the local strip clubs upon receiving that promotion to management.

How could he have been so stupid, when he had such a beautiful wife at home? One who really loved him back then. Wanted him. At least until she finally had enough.

Selling cars, he was good at it. With his hours all over the place, he and Daphne rarely had the same day off. With her working in a mortgage office the usual eight-to-five on weekdays, and with him waking up around eleven to work a twelve-to-nine shift, often staying later to iron out another deal, Daphne was winding down for bed. Two ships passing in the night.

The guys in the office started asking him to go out, once or twice a week, to talk about "sales techniques and all it took to succeed in the car business." At first he was hesitant, too embarrassed about where he was spending his time.

In time, Iian found himself going to the strip club even if no one else did. His time there felt like a necessary end of the workday routine to decompress, a place where he could always count on someone to be nice to him. That business kept hours more like his. Rather than coming home to a wife who was in her jammies and heading for bed, he'd eat at the bar, and watch the ladies dance, many of whom came to know his name out of regularity.

With his absence, Daphne grew more angry and, often when Iian did get home, she would lock the bedroom door, forcing him to sleep on the couch. Since he worked weekends too, their schedule made it hard to even find a common time to have a conversation, let alone decide to find a counselor to work on things.

It was just easier to go where people, the women, were happy to see him. They appreciated him and, yes, he was paying them in tips, he supposed, but Iian imagined it was more than that. A friendship. Maybe even more.

The collapse of their marriage had taken about eighteen months from the time he had been hired at the car lot. Professionally, he felt stronger and more successful than ever, but at home he felt like a failure.

Iian arrived home one evening to find that Daphne had stayed home from work that day, her eyes were nearly swollen shut from crying. Before Iian could reach for her, react or say anything, Daphne started in.

"I can't do this anymore. I don't know who you are anymore. Where is the Iian I fell in love with, the one that I shared my dreams with, the one that gave a damn? The man that would hold me and promise we'd have great adventures together. Ever since you started working at the dealership, the money is there, but you, *you are gone*. I can't live like this *one more fucking day*." She pushed him then, the only time she had ever physically handled him in anything other than a loving gesture.

"*Get out!*" She screamed, her voice rupturing the air as he stood shell-shocked before her. Daphne stormed off to the bedroom and slammed the door for the last time. She locked it with one quick motion, having become an expert at it. Iian could hear her sobbing inside, feeling her desperate and wavering blows against the door in futile warning. She shuffled then landed her full back against the door, her body shrinking to the ground in exasperation.

"*Get out!*" She shouted over and over. Those were the last words she would ever utter at him. He stood there for what felt like hours, hearing her beg, "*Get out, Get out, Get out.*"

Her words pierced his chest. He had blown it. If only he could have been a better man, the man Daphne deserved. He was so weak when it came to alcohol and beautiful women, just like his father. Damn his damn role model.

That night he packed a bag full of clothes and another with booze from their liquor cabinet. He ended up in a hotel with an unspecified check out date until he could figure out what to do next. He pounded gin and whiskey alternately that night, and called in sick the next day to go look at apartments after this hangover wore off.

After some discussions with his closest co-workers, he'd picked his apartment because of the pool.

"You can see all the chicks in bikinis," they had told him.

That was about six months ago, but it might as well have been *today*, or *every day* that came after. The pain stayed acutely fresh.

Iian let the tears fall from his eyes, wiping them as they funneled down to fill in the dimple of his chin. He tried to focus, and fumbled with the wiper blades as the sky started to spit rain. Bad weather was coming.

~

Claiming My Extraordinary Life, Me, 2000

*I*t all started with a single epiphany about my life at the ripe old age of thirty. Thirty seems to be the number when you've lived long enough to track what your life is missing and grow ballsy enough to change it.

As I blew out the candles of my non-existent cake, in came the soulful acknowledgment that I had lived my entire life thus far in fear. I'd made my decisions based on what I thought was the worst that could happen. I was an expert at making up horrible scenarios to keep myself from doing things.

I had said no to countless opportunities that had been presented to me. I stayed in the safe little bubble that kept me small and unworldly and I was okay with that- until I wasn't.

I'd been offered the opportunity to go to Paris right out of high school, all expenses paid, but I said, "No, I'm not interested in France."

When my mother was traveling to India and Tibet for a four day long wedding with the Himalayan mountains as the backdrop, I had told her, "No, thank you." I couldn't leave my little suburban life and kids to spend two weeks out of the country. She and my brother went and have countless stories to tell to this day. I am sure it would have been a once-in-a-lifetime adventure.

I'd married a safe man, as stable as they come. He loved routine and things in their place. I had shied away from going back to school because I worried I wouldn't do well. If I didn't try then I couldn't fail.

When Hubby was offered a new job including a fully paid move to the East coast, I pushed to stay where we already lived because, "I didn't want to leave my family behind."

I stayed exactly where I was but wished for things to be different without trying to change them. I kept rigid and didn't push anyone or myself beyond what I already knew.

I can't say I was standing in a certain place or had just heard an empowering story when I finally understood this about myself. I just suddenly knew and held the belief that only I could rewrite my future, just as I knew I could never rewrite the past.

So I started. I started by saying yes more. I looked up now and then from the little place I was so used to and fished around to see what else there was. Any chance I could get to push myself past the immediate, I took. I tried new foods and went to different places to shop. I listened to what my other friends were doing.

I knew that it would be uncomfortable, and it was, but I buffered the change by seeking out a few similarly-minded soul sisters to walk this new path with me.

We would say yes more. We would encourage each other past our reservations. Together we would seek out the extraordinary opportunities that fit into our ordinary lives. We'd do it step-by-step and be there for each other as things got harder. We would cheer each other on.

At first, I didn't do things for anyone but myself, but over time I came to see that my efforts might inspire my daughters to seek out bigger existences themselves.

I tried on new dreams: Running a 5K; and starting a mom-based newsletter in the neighborhood about parenting; I started making lists of things I would love to do if given the chance.

Hiking in the Rocky Mountains with llamas to carry our sleeping bags, spending a month learning to make pasta and speak Italian in Italy. Seriously seeking the Fenn Treasure and perhaps finding it. Finally writing my book.

I proclaimed to as many people as would listen that I wanted to live an extraordinary life. I promised myself to chase the best, most adventurous life that I could from then on, without abandoning my current commitments. I wasn't going to leave my family and run off with some Greek god never to be seen again, but there was plenty of room to expand from where I was.

This set of traveling books might be my greatest adventure yet.

Once the idea popped into my head and out of my mouth to hubby's negation, I kept it quiet, holed up in my heart. With the way he reacted he wouldn't think that I would have even gone through with it. To him it was just another one of my crazy ideas that I'd lose traction on and give up.

The construction of the little memory books took an afternoon, once the memories and people written about inside the books wafted into me on two rainy mornings. The planning and packaging of each spanned only minutes once I had determined (in my own special way) where each would go. A quick search on the "White Pages" on the internet and I had five unsuspecting recipients chosen. I didn't know them, and they didn't know me as of yet. Random, one might say, but they weren't to me.

Waiting to send the other ones was the hardest at the moment. This little secret teasing and waiting in the background of my life, every day and every night as I lived my wife-and-mom-life. It was a hidden part of me, the action being one of the biggest chances I had ever attempted for myself, and I had no one I could tell.

In the pauses of life's busy days, I wondered if one of the books would be returned to me and who it would be who found it. Maybe this was the wildest part?

I do not have a good relationship with patience, I never have. Why had this idea and the waiting that came with it come to me? Would these books be a tortuous tease for the rest of my days, leaving me crazed with longing?

I had secret hopes that the courier would be certain people, ones with which I felt I had unfinished business, but I wasn't going to be picky in this. No way.

Whoever came would be the perfect one to deliver my secret package back to me. God, please let this crazy dream come true. If it did, then my life could be proclaimed as extraordinary. No one could ever disagree.

Five little books, sent out to strangers. Each containing my life, inked out through shared moments with other people. Was my request that the books travel pleading enough? To tug at the hearts of the reader enough that they keep moving the book along until one or more finds its way back to me?

My life feels bigger just by having attempted this gamble, but if nobody else knows, what will this extraordinary life of mine have to show for it?

***

"Life is either a daring adventure, or nothing." ~Helen Keller
~

Sneaking Out Book Two, Me, 2000

*I*t was a family trip to get away and to do something that wasn't out-rageously expensive. The kids were still small and not big enough to go on the wild rides of a larger amusement park, so we picked a small prehis-toric-themed attraction for a long weekend family vacation that summer. It would be the longest car trip with all four of us, and I hoped it would go smoothly. My oldest, aged six, was super excited to see the dinosaur place that had teased her at the end of her favorite show. We had planned the short trip there to include some sight seeing for us grown ups as well. Both girls were susceptible to car sickness so that wrinkle added another layer of worry to my day.

We left early on Friday morning, after a quick cereal breakfast for the kids and husband with scrambled eggs for myself (I had been avoiding cereal since giving up milk while breastfeeding to try to lessen my youngest's tummy troubles- a wisdom nugget shared with me by my neighbor S.S. Her daughter had also struggled with the transfer and once I quit, I had a totally new and surprisingly laid back kid.)

I packed snacks, drinks, and little backpacks full of fun to keep the kids busy for the drive. Oldest dove into her parcel pretty early, and kept herself fairly occupied with the car bingo and coloring books. Youngest fell asleep right away, and slept most of the way up to the Canadian border, which I would discover later was far from a good thing.

At the border, I worked my plan. Having snuck my second little "Find Me" book into my big purse, I asked to stop at the little market before crossing. Our youngest was just waking up so hubby changed her diaper and I went in to use the bathroom and grab some extra snacks. Attached already to my package was my assortment of stamps, enough to see this baby off to Alabama at book rate.

I walked to the counter and was greeted by a young twenty-something. He saw that my package had the stamps on already and asked if I needed anything else.

"I'm all set, thank you," I said, while thinking, "Off you go."

Pleased with myself, I strolled out to keep the family caravan heading North.

I didn't know anyone in Alabama, but I would soon enough. At least in spirit. Or they would know me or some parts of me anyway.

I looked out the window with a cheshire cat grin on my face, keeping turned away to hide my vibrant expression. The kids drifted off again in the back seat, and my husband pressed the scan button on the radio over and over to find a station before finally giving up and shutting it off.

"What were you doing back there, at the border store? You were gone for a while."

"I wanted to pick up some water for us for the trip, then I remembered I needed to send that bill that I had stuck in my purse. I forgot to mail it at home before we left."

"Glad to see you taking an interest in the finances, Hon," he said with a smirk. It was always our joke: he would see the bills piling up and he would then spring it on me, "It's time to pay the bills."

Usually I would feign a stomach ache or scrunch my face, then we would laugh and pay the bills. We used an at-home computer program to help us keep track of the financial things, the portfolio, the nest egg; it was easier than I ever made it out to be.

It made sense, or should I say "cents."

North to Canada for this family trip. I so desperately wanted to see the Butchart Gardens as I had been gardening my brains out back home.

"We will see," he said. "The kids might get bored."

Little does he know, I am secretly indoctrinating the kids to love gardening. Oldest was four years old when we walked past the plants at the nursery. "Mom, that's a foxglove, that's poisonous," she sweetly said to my utter delight within earshot of an older lady who smiled at us. I smiled back.

"Yes, you are right, honey."

I want the kids to love nature the way I do.

Stopping at the next rest area, we decided to wake the kids so they wouldn't be up all night when we stopped at the hotel. Too late for that. Our youngest had slept enough to throw off her schedule. Once we reached our destination we piled into our hotel room, and there was no keeping her still for the rest of us to sleep. Out of exhaustion, we all piled back into the car for a drive, hoping she would be lulled into a slumber. Nope. Hubby and I ended up taking turns staying in the car and playing with her, so as not to disturb the other hotel patrons and our oldest with her crying and busyness.

Grabbing blankets from the hotel, I tried to make ourselves comfortable. Turning the car into a mobile playpen, I remember getting so frustrated that

I wanted to just drive all the way back home. I didn't care what time it was, I didn't care how far it was; I just didn't want to be there anymore.

Finally after two o'clock in the morning, she settled and I took her back into the room and snuggled her in with me. It had been a rough night.

Oddly, both kids woke up happy and ready to go. I was wiped out but still wanted to see the flowers; I asked hopefully if they were interested in going to the Gardens.

"Sure, Mom, that sounds fun. Do they have hot dogs?"

Dinosaurs, gardens, and launching my second little traveling book into the world. What a trip!

~

~2~

Iian was glad to have finished with the errand. He could finally get home and feel sorry for himself. Sit still and watch the incoming storm swirl around him. He parked in his usual spot, and lumbered toward the lobby, bringing all of his load in at once. He would not be making another trip.

Lugging his suitcase, the bag of mail, and a shorty of beer that he had left in his trunk, Iian stomped up the stairs to his apartment on the third floor.

"Stupid elevator is out again?!" he barked at the janitor on the second floor landing, and then swore over and over with every step until he reached his floor.

"Shit, shit, shit."

He fussed with his keys at the door and dropped his mail on the ground while trying to save his beer from falling.

He stepped inside, immediately catching a whiff of something foul. He dropped his suitcase, and placed the beer on the counter before going back out the door to pick up the bag of mail in the hallway.

He tossed the bag on the couch and put the beer into the fridge to cool down before grabbing the last bottle that was in there. He sniffed the air again, curious for a microsecond about the odor. He shrugged, "Oh, well, the cleaning lady is coming tomorrow; she'll find it."

He flicked the twist-off cap at a dying plant in the corner and sat down with a humph to look through his mail. Iian shuffled quickly through the bills, pushing them off to one side, some inadvertently falling off the couch. His hands grabbed at the brown paper package, and he shuddered at the thought of it being his copy of the divorce papers.

Too lazy to get up and turn on some lights, he squinted at the address: Washington. "Weird, I don't know anyone from there," he thought after seeing the origin city postmark. No return name listed either. Strange.

He ripped the package open only to have the book inside go flying across the room. He pulled his feet off the coffee table and accidentally knocked over his beer. Some gurgled onto the floor before he grabbed it and he set the bottle down hard on the table again. The base chipped and he checked for a crack; luckily, nothing. He'd drink it anyway.

Stumbling to get up as his leg had fallen asleep, Iian yiped, "Ouch, ouch, ouch," as he walked. He flipped on the light and picked up the projectile. Searching the torn envelope for a note, he found nothing.

A book, navy blue in color, a spiral binding held it together. It looked new but not mass produced. Golden letters spelled out *Find Me, 2 of 5.* They were the only markings on the outside of the book at all.

He opened to the first page only to see a pleading message asking for his participation, so he closed it again.

"Really? Why me?"

Iian slunk down further into the couch, and chugged the rest of the beer, letting the empty settle into the crevice of his couch. He got up to get another drink, something stronger.

He poured a whiskey, and grabbed the last ice cube from the stale freezer tray and stood looking out the window. His eyes glazed over as he peered beyond the deck railing and down to the pool. The water was gray, reflecting the clouds above. The wind pummeled the glass, and Iian noticed a waviness struggling in the water. Ebbing and jostling, the motion compounded into him, the storm brewing within himself.

Upon opening the sliding door he let in the wind and air to help improve the smell of his place. Plopping back onto the couch, he opened the book to read the rest of the pages of the odd thing that had come his way. Memories, some woman's memories. So weird that this book was sent to him. Who was he to be in a position to help anyone anyway? His life was a fucking joke.

He sat baffled, drinking more and more as the pages fell away. He didn't remember filling his glass each time but somehow it always had more in it.

Iian read along numbly as some of the patterns of behavior from the people mentioned in the stories were mirrored in his own life. He had pressured that girl Becky into having sex with him in high school. What a jerk he had been. He slammed the book down into his lap.

What a jerk he had been with Daphne. He whacked his head with the book.

"*I ruin everything*!"

He staggered up to get another drink. He poked around in the fridge for something to eat, but found mostly condiments. It had been hours since he'd taken a bite. He opened a jar of dill pickles and grabbed a spear, leaving the top off and placing it to the side of the jar, still inside the fridge. He put one in his mouth and whipped his fingers in the air to get the juice off of them before grabbing another beer, and slamming the fridge door shut.

Iian continued reading the mysterious book, finally getting to the end right before his head started spinning from the booze.

He definitely didn't know the author, even though he tried really hard to think of who it might be based on the stories. Maybe he really was a random pick? Still, giving it to someone else was the least he could do for someone after being a total dick to basically everyone who had loved him or tried to be there for him.

Iian scribbled his name in the back of the book, and walked over to close the patio door to get his apartment warmed up again. Grabbing the last three beers out of the fridge, he sat staring into space while listening to the claps of thunder booming outside.

He lay back, dropping the book on the floor next to him. Reaching for his cell phone off the coffee table, he fumbled to dial Daphne's number. He wanted to apologize. Tell her she was right to get rid of him and that she could and would do much better than him.

The phone number was disconnected, the blaring tone announced. He said he was really sorry to the automatic operator and hung up.

He drank the rest of the beers until they were gone, and passed out on his way to the bathroom, wetting himself as he slept.

The cleaning lady came early the next day, checked his pulse and vacuumed around him. Then she left, taking the little traveling book with her.

Number two of five.

~

Entrepreneurial Me, 2001

*L*ife is busy with two little kids. Eldest is in school part time and Youngest is toddling about. In between pickups, I did the grocery shopping, cleaning and other errands. Other moms in the neighborhood and I have set up a schedule to carpool our kids to allow for added time in our schedules and to save gas. The situation gave me an idea.

What would happen, I thought, if, God forbid, I got into an accident with other children on board, those who didn't belong to me? It could happen to anyone at any time.

Maybe a driver was injured enough and couldn't speak about who those children were to get them safely back to their parents? It bothered me, the potential problem kept me up at night and so I invented a product to remedy that issue. It was an idea that grew in my heart out of purpose and need and it became something to keep me busy and give me a new goal to work towards.

My carpool kit had ID badges with clips that could be put on a child in the event of an accident. The ID badges could speak for the children who were too young to verbally give their parent's phone numbers to authorities, and could be reunited much faster than waiting until the child was reported missing.

I thought of everything. A colorful and fun name badge for each child was placed into a pouch that was kept in the glovebox of each car. The pouch had an emblem that would be obvious to emergency crews to look into. A sticker to announce the kit would be placed on the outside of the car to alert responders.

The complete product took shape. I met with vendors to supply all the parts. I would assemble each unit and send them out when orders came in. I set prices and could alert other emergency offices if an order came in from out-of-state.

I developed a logo, and a website with the help of a friend of mine and started marketing my goods. I advertised in local parenting magazines and was interviewed by a few local newspapers. I sold a few units to friends and a few more orders trickled in from the website,

and I sent letters to introduce the new system to all offices of the fire departments, police departments and ambulance services within a five hundred mile radius of any order that came in.

I was energized with the project. I sought out new people to network with. I had goals and professional conversations beyond the house and home for the first time in years. I researched if any other products were out there that did a similar thing. I found none.

In one massive financial gamble, I signed up to sell my kits in a booth at a Christmas bazaar that winter, hoping to make sales and get the product out in force. Five full days of sitting and trying to sell something that had nothing to do with the holidays. Only a few kits sold.

I had ordered hundreds thinking I would sell out at the show, but that did not happen.

Six months into the idea with a large inventory and I was losing steam. Things were getting dropped back home, I was stressed and I didn't know if this was what I wanted to do with my time, my energy?

The worst part was that I was losing precious time with my littlest one. Time that would be forever gone.

Did I really want to do <u>this</u> for a lifetime? I was torn. Any effort towards a "career" <u>had</u> to be so important to me that I would never get sick of it.

Careers were forever. That's what people do, it is what is expected. That kind of black-and-white thinking was all I knew. It was the way my brain worked.

More money had been spent than was ever earned, and to ask my hubby for more to prop up what looked and felt like a lost cause, for something I didn't even really want to do anymore would have been ridiculous.

The choicepoint came: Either throw more effort into the business and potentially more money, or bag it and go back to spending all of my energy on my family. In the end I chose the latter.

The idea and the business fell away with nary a blip on anyone else's radar. It's amazing how easy a business can disappear. The large box in the garage filled with my kits mocks me when I stumble across it. Another failure, true evidence of an idea that didn't work. One more thing I had given up on.

I tried to work through all that by telling myself that I had gone for it. I'd imagined a product and seen the idea through. I could do things if I tried.

In the lapse, I let the domain creep back into the internet and I kept copies of the articles that were written about me, my product and company. News footage from the local TV station about what I was trying to do, was recorded onto a VHS tape for me to look back on anytime I wished, if I ever did.

I suppose that was my five minutes of fame.

***

If I looked into my heart to see something for myself beyond motherhood, to work at as a "career," it would definitely be writing. Children's books, short stories, fiction.

That is where my heart lies, it was what I always went back to.

If only a life spent telling stories was possible.

~

J.R.

You lived at the end of our block and had three sons. You had been married before. You were a very early Mom. Your two youngest sons were born so close to each other you dressed them like twins, and they never knew the difference. Our kids played together in the cul-de-sac for years, riding on their bikes and in their mini jeeps. Once my oldest daughter "married," your second son in a make believe wedding ceremony. So, I guess we might be *"in-laws"* as well as friends.

Your oldest son- a teenager when I met him- always needed extra attention. ADHD mixed with other stuff led to a dependence on drugs. First weed then harder stuff. His addictions remained a noose around his neck and your heart for many years. Seeing him tumble into that life tore you apart but you held strong and ever hopeful for him and resolute for the younger ones. Life would be different for them.

You were forever fighting for your firstborn.

At sixteen, you were a baby yourself when he came, and you did the best you could. Leaving his father was a big step towards saving yourself. You couldn't keep that role model for your son, you couldn't have him treat you that way either. You had grown up too fast.

Somehow even on your hardest days, you managed to smile through the tears that welled in your shadows. Your soft spoken-voice continued to soothe your younger sons, encouraging them to be their best selves.

With your youngest sons, you were supportive, loving, and always there. Same as your oldest but with different results. There was a genetic predisposition for him, one that you hadn't counted on. Even in your frustration, you remained ghostly calm, never raising your voice to anyone. You were just nice all the time.

When my husband and I were having trouble, he developed a little crush on you, one he didn't even try to hide from me. It was not reciprocated by you, I know, and it gave me a look into who he was really after in a spouse.

"Why can't you be like her? she's so sweet and so nice all the time," he would ask me.

It was just another reminder that I wasn't measuring up.

Living with your self-confessed, sex maniac husband who drank a bit, and your addicted oldest son, I often wondered how you were able to hold it all together?

Eventually it must have to bubble up inside of you enough to explode, right? But when? I never saw it; not even a raised eyebrow.

I remember one day when all the kids were outside and you were trying to get them to do something, or not do something. You spoke to the group in your usual kind, loving tone and they ignored you. They weren't meaning to, you just weren't scary enough to get them to mind.

One of the dads came out then, and shouted basically the same thing you had and those kids fell in line in a second flat. You saw and I saw and we somehow knew that even though men easily convey that authority, it is us who carry our children's hearts and dreams. Keeping our kids safe, loved, fed and listened to. Mom's don't want to be scary.

You were always a good friend to me.

I remember that time when I dangled out of our second-story window trying to hang the Christmas lights by myself. You didn't tell me not to; you just stood below talking to me with your phone ready to call 911 if I fell.

Another time your thoughtfulness showed through was the time I'd called you to help me bundle my broken arm in a plastic bag so I could shower. My husband had left for the day and I was hobbled, alone and unable to do it myself. As you wrapped, telling me it was no trouble at all, you left a tab of tape at the end so I could get myself out of it easily after, an act that made me burst into tears. So thoughtful, so loving, so you.

You are good through and through, and your beautiful smile beams out into the world, no matter what chaos and heartache you are dealing with on the inside. A true Libra: always balanced, no matter what.

You are so damn strong.

~

~2~

Angel

Angelita Meyer, successful, independent, professional cleaner completed her work for the day and headed back home. She had been more rushed to get finished with her schedule, and had successfully shaved two hours off of her typical Tuesday.

Her mother's doctor was calling at four o'clock to talk about her mother's condition. Angel was hopeful that her mother would be able to come home and live with the family again. In her speed, she had brought Mr. Davis's garbage home with her, instead of putting it in the apartment dumpster as she usually did. It sat on the car seat next to her.

That poor guy Mr. Davis. He was always a mess. This wasn't the first time she'd seen him passed out in his apartment in her four months of looking after the place.

When he hired her, he had asked her to call him Iian. His strong handshake and wide smile teased of his almost over-the-top arrogance, a trait she assumed helped him sell cars.

Angel felt cautious about being around him. She didn't feel threatened in a physical or sexual way, but there was something. She had seen others who portrayed a successful life on the outside while struggling hard with their inner demons alone. She could tell he was pure havoc in human form and she wasn't at all comfortable calling him Iian. That would make him a friend, and he was too messed up to be friends with. She wondered what his life story was, but not enough to ask.

She stopped suddenly at a red light and lunged for the garbage bag as it flung forward onto the floor of the passenger side. It splayed open and spilled much of the contents including the garbage from his kitchen and the bathroom. In her haste, she had flung everything into the bag without really paying attention to what it might be.

The imprint of a spiral showed through the plastic and she reached behind a banana peel to retrieve it, suddenly worried she had picked up something that he might want back. Something important, maybe. The light turned green, and the car behind her honked twice.

She tossed the book onto the floor in front of her own seat so she wouldn't get any crud on her upholstery. Angel kept her car spotless. She drove towards home, then remembered that her daughter had asked her to pick up some disposable diapers for her. She had just enough time to stop real quick at the mini-mart.

"Ugh!" she grunted, suddenly visualizing her daughter Solana using her good dusting rags on the baby if they were out of wipes again. She bought a container of those, the diapers and also some formula, just in case.

Solana was sweet to her baby, but being almost a baby herself, she just wasn't tracking all of the necessities of being a mother yet.

Angel had also learned about motherhood early. At only seventeen, she gave birth to her first and only child Solana, naming her for the beautiful sunshine of her homeland.

Unlike the light and bright moniker she was named after, Solana was a dark and difficult baby. Almost annoyed at the burden of being so helpless and stuck in her infant body, she cried most of the time. She was only pleasant when she was held upright and felt a part of the action.

There were fleeting moments when the desperate and exhausted Angel considered adopting her away to someone else. Someone who was more situated and stable in the world. Someone patient. A family maybe who could figure out what her problem was. In the end, Angel would look at her sleeping baby and know that she would never let her go.

Angel worked harder and harder at becoming the mother she needed to be to guide her once difficult baby Solana into the young woman she had become. Just as her mother had done for her.

Thank God for her Mima.

Oftentimes, there in the beginning of her motherhood journey, Angel wished that she would have had the chance to go to college. To dream a little bit bigger and find her purpose and date around more.

Even with her rougher-than-some start, Angel had done very well for herself. She owned her own house, and had a nice car to drive. They had plenty of food on the table. Angel had been running her own cleaning business for over fifteen years, and employed two other people. Life was good.

Sometimes in the quiet of the evening, when she looked around, she felt proud of how much she had accomplished. Even with it all, her daughter hadn't escaped the familial legacy of teenage pregnancy that had started with her. It was the only tug of regret in her heart; what could she have done differently?

Late that afternoon, coming up the walkway to her house, Angel saw a young teen boy, half-naked, scurry out of her daughter's bedroom window. He fell into the garden bed, picked up his clothes and took off running.

"Beat it!" she screamed at his pasty white butt cheeks. He looked back in fear, clutching his clothes and serpentining awkwardly down the sidewalk to his car.

Angel opened the front door and slammed it behind her, as the baby started to cry.

"Solana, get out here!"

"Geez, Mom?" she said, holding baby Jacob on her hip while wearing only a t-shirt. "What's the big deal?"

"Solana, when are you going to learn to keep your legs closed? Look at where it has gotten you so far."

"Oh, Mom, don't worry, I'm covered now." Solana tickled her baby's toes.

Baby Jacob reached for Angel, and this annoyed Solana to no end. Her baby had a favorite and it wasn't his own mama.

Angel dropped the baby groceries onto the couch and scooped Jacob away to change his diaper. She barked at Solana to go make him a bottle as she cooed lovingly over him. Solana placed the warm bottle on the edge of the changing table.

"Good, now I can keep him happy while I am on the phone. Go take a shower, mi niña, sheesh!" Angel snapped her fingers.

"Fine," Solana griped, turning on her heel and storming away.

Her snarky attitude mixed with the sharp turn and hair toss reminded Angel of when Solana was little and would throw tantrums. Her great big uncontrollable personality in such a tiny little body. She was more proportionally sized now for her spunk level. Angel didn't want to put *out* her fire, just adjust the heat a little.

She looked down at Jacob and smiled.

"At least you can't get pregnant," she said. She leaned in and nuzzled noses with him. Jacob smiled as milk spilled cutely from the sides of his lips.

The house phone rang, and Angel picked it up on the second ring.

"Hello, yes, it's me. How is Mom doing? Do you think she can come home soon?"

"Ms. Meyers, I am still concerned that some of your mother's needs can't be met at home. With you working all day, she needs someone there if she needs help. Has anything changed on that end?"

"No, not really. What are the things that she needs help with? Maybe I could find someone?"

"Since the stroke, she doesn't have full use and strength in her hands to clean herself after going to the bathroom. She needs help getting up and down to use the toilet. I was hoping she would have gained more mobility back. If she was able to handle that task on her own, she could probably come home. Maybe if she had a cell phone so she could reach you immediately, and you were always nearby if needed. She has to take her meds at very specific times, and she is also more liable to choke when eating, so having someone around at meal time is key. Didn't you say you had a teenage daughter at home? Maybe she can help out?"

Angel frowned. She so badly wanted to answer yes, but she just couldn't see Solana caring not only for her baby son, but her grandmother at the same time. She was mortified to think that Solana might have gentlemen visitors over who jumped out of windows with Mima at home. Maybe with a little more time, Solana would grow into the responsible person Angel knew she could be.

"Unfortunately my daughter already has her hands full with her baby son. I guess we will have Mom stay there for the time being, and continue with her physical and occupational therapy to try to gain back more strength. I will also look at arranging my days differently so I can be home more, maybe that will help?"

"Maybe if there was a set schedule and we could arrange for some in-home healthcare assistance, that might do the trick. Stay positive, Angel, your mom is doing very well for having had as serious of a stroke as she did. I think we have her on the right meds to avoid another one, and thankfully, her mental capacities were spared, as you already know."

Angel could hear his smile over the phone.

"Yes, thank God. Thank you doctor. Should we schedule another call next month, for her next assessment?"

"Yes, I will have my office set up an appointment. Enjoy the rest of your week."

Angel hung up the phone, and looked down at her now sleeping grandson. The bottle had knocked him out. She settled him down in his crib, and went to retrieve the book and the bag of trash from the car.

Solana asked if she could go out that night with some friends, and Angel agreed to babysit. She loved Jacob, and he was most likely conked out for the night.

"Sure, honey, go ahead," she put her arms around her daughter who squirmed for a moment then settled in and squeezed her back. Oh, how she loved this girl.

"Be smart," Angel called as her daughter held up the peace sign before the door closed.

Angel sat down and rubbed the cover of the stowaway book with a nearby tissue. Strange, it wasn't like a real book from a store. She read the cover: "Find Me."

She opened the front, and read the imploring message inside. Easily reading the stories, she found herself reading them over and over again, searching deeper each time for a possible connection to the author.

But no. Some of the stories were close to her own experiences, or ones she could have imagined if she hadn't gotten pregnant in high school by that beanpole Chris Meyers.

He had married her only because his parents made him, and the soon-to-be parents thought it might work out. They were only married for two years when Chris announced that he was joining the Army. He left for boot camp in Oklahoma and never came back. Divorce papers were mailed to her a year later, and she happily signed so as not to remain in limbo any longer.

Chris was an Army mechanic at the Fort Sill Base in Oklahoma. He had only come to see Solana a few times since she was born. His support checks came in though, every month, and for that Angel was thankful. With her doing as well as she was with her business, she had been depositing them into a savings account for the last three years. She wanted Solana to have a good start at community college. At least, that was before Jacob showed up and altered the plan.

"Things don't always happen the way you picture they will," Angel sighed looking out her sliding glass door into her serene and magical back-yard. It was supposed to be a place for her mother to enjoy retirement and start painting.

Banana trees flanked the entire perimeter of the yard. They managed to give her a few bananas each year, but she wasn't keeping track. In the gaps between the trees, yellow and bright pink canna flowers with their equally enthralling zebra-striped leaves gave a beautiful backdrop to the multicolored coleus displays up front. Angel didn't mind replanting those each year as they were worth the effort, time, and money spent.

The moonflower that she planted last year perfectly punctuated the straight lines of the gazebo she had commissioned to be built. Angel had paid extra for the elaborate fretwork, a nod to the pre revolutionary Havana heyday of her homeland. The woodwork was blanketed in thick white paint with its carved panels below anchored in a Mediterranean sea blue.

The hand-sized blooms of the moonflower fell in random trumpets punctuating the dark of the evening. In the daytime, Angel could see that the heart-shaped green leaves and runners of the unruly vine had taken over. With all of the changes, Angel had let the yard go a bit, but everything was still as beautiful as it could be. Every view was one to be painted or taken in.

Angel picked up the baby monitor and clipped it to her blue jeans. She stepped out the back door to feel the cool twilight air. Strolling romantically over to the gazebo, she ran her hands up the handrails as she ascended the steps like a heroine in an old movie. She'd designed this place with Mom in mind; she hadn't thought to use it herself.

Angel scooted away some fallen leaves and spent blossoms from the yellow-painted wicker sofa and sat down, fully taking in the space for the first time.

The large canvas that she had placed on the easel still sat waiting for the artist. Everything was staged and set up, biding its time for her mother's pictorial touch. Each leg of the stand was encircled with leafy tendrils. Tea saucer-sized flowers and brambles had reached beyond the columns and up onto the canvas, producing Mother Nature's own masterpiece.

A hand-painted Talavera sideways pot sat on a rod iron table waiting to be filled with water to clean her mother's set of handmade horse hair paint brushes. Angel took a picture of the scene in her mind to describe to her mother when she saw her next. Maybe it would inspire her to get better and get back home.

Her mother had worked hard all of her life. Angel had wanted her mother Adelma to be able to enjoy her golden years- finally. The new hobby might have helped her take it easy and heal, while calmly seeing the beauty around her for once. The hard stuff was supposed to be over.

That was before Mom's latest stroke, and before little Jacob's arrival into the household. He was unexpected, yes, but still a blessing.

She closed her eyes and imagined her mother back home again, sitting here amongst the flowers, painting the pictures she might hold in her mind of the beautiful days of her childhood tropical wonderland.

Angel fell asleep, and awoke to her daughter whispering in her ear.

"Mom, are you okay? Maybe come in now. I'm home. I'm safe."

Angel roused and lifted herself up to follow her daughter back into the house. She locked the door behind her and flipped off the lamp in the living room, picking up the book that had inspired so much thinking about her own journey that evening.

Angel often found herself on the couch in the morning waiting up for her Solana as her mother had waited up for her in her teens.

Solana still had a lot to learn, but she knew that with the legacy of strong women in this family she would be okay.

Angel was anxious to share the little book with her mother Adelma at the retirement facility over the weekend.

~

Marriage Counseling Again, Me, 2001

I haven't written for a while. So much has happened. I have been wandering and trying to find myself. I am feeling pushed to figure out what it is that I want to do professionally in my life. I think of things but they all require a lot of education, and I cave at the thought. I need more time to finish my book, the one I started with my Uncle; I have to get back into it. I have the outline, I have his character concepts, but I blew my chance to work with him, because now he's gone.

I still volunteer weekly at the girls' schools. There are parties to plan and help with, and sometimes they are sick. Who would take them to the doctor? I like doing this, this being a mom. I'm good at it.

Maybe I'm not the best housecleaner, or cook, but I am a good Mom. Somehow this is not considered a job or work, as if I am goofing off all day while at home.

It's crap. I cannot think of a single job on earth that has as major of a role or impact on humanity as being a parent. We are growing a whole person from scratch. That person will walk the world in a certain way, buoyed or burdened by their upbringing, treating others as life has treated them.

As parents we help them feel safe, we encourage hidden talents to sprout and become some of the things they love about themselves. Parenting affects the way they act in future relationships, and the way they relate to all of the people around them. I'd challenge that in actuality it's the most important job in the world.

But because our society does not value the role in any kind of a financial way, I will need to choose something other than that to call my profession. I could take in other children and start a daycare, but then it's a business and I'm not sure I want to go down that road right now. I wanted to flip houses with hubby, maybe even at the coast, but he pooh-poohed that idea, too.

So I can only pick a career that he approves of or that makes sense to him. Good God, will I ever be enough?

~

~2~

Adelma

Adelma Fredrick sat in her wheelchair outside the Sunny Days residence for seniors watching and waiting for her daughter, Angel, and hopefully the kids. Every visit, Angel would bring something with her: either a nostalgic memento of Adelma's or something new to delight her. Thinking the move was temporary, Angel had held back most of her mother's belongings. Adelma's small studio apartment was sparse and she missed the colors and history of her favorite pieces, but Angel would often take them back home with her so as not to crowd Adelma's limited space.

What would her precious Angel be bringing with her today?

It was always the simple things that brought her the most joy: a bag of oranges to remind Adelma of her yearly visits back to Florida before having the strokes; the palm tree patterned cotton tablecloth that they used for birthday celebrations; or her lamp with a flamboyance of flamingos skirting around the base with a kitsch seashell-adorned lampshade.

There was the black-and-white photo of the two of them, holding hands and carrying their few belongings to start their new life in America. That photo was laminated in plastic, along with a newspaper clipping from *The Miami News*, circa October 1980.

She'd chased a newspaper tumbling in the wind after disembarking in Key West for emigration processing. It described the Mariel Boat Lift Operation, the mass exodus of refugees from Havana, Cuba, to the United States.

Adelma had kept that token with her in the small space to help her remember all that she and Angel had been through. It was a reminder that even though they came with nothing, their brazen desire and hard work had gained them freedom and a new life together.

Adelma was often overcome with gratitude at the thoughtfulness and caring of her only child. Even with Angel's tougher life circumstances and difficulties, she had made it. Like Adelma, Angel was a single mother who gave birth to a strong-willed daughter. Only in her thirties, but she was a grandmother now as well. Adelma never knew such pride and love as when she had watched *her* Angelita care for her daughter Solana.

Like her name, Angel was an angel in real life, taking Adelma, Solana and the baby under her vibrant and bright wings, shielding them all against the world. Angel had been paying for her mother to stay in this assisted living home.

Adelma waited patiently on the front veranda, soaking up the sunshine. Her straw hat tipped down over her eyes, but her lips still felt the warm kiss of the *sol*. She wore a short-sleeved shirt to allow her arms to gobble up the rays of her forever-bronzed beautiful Cuban- born skin. The trademark smoker's wrinkles around her lips added an extra intensity to her face when she tried to smile. Her once strong cheekbones had sagged a bit, and the fall was more pronounced on her right side. Adelma would look in the mirror each day and grin praying that side would perk up, but every day it lay dead.

Sunny Days was a nice place, given what it was. The final destination for many of the residents. A place to put old people that was out of the way. Or sometimes it felt like that for some. She would hear the sadness and lonesome cries from those who rarely had visitors.

She knew it was expensive, although Angel never bothered Adelma with how much. Her Angel was so responsible, and dependable. She had to be.

Adelma squirmed in her seat when she saw the older red mustang pull into the parking lot. Angel piled out, then Solana and the baby. Adelma's eyes sparkled at the view. She *loved* to see the baby. This would be a good visit.

"Mima!" Angel declared from across the parking lot.

"Hi, mi Angelita. You brought the kids; thank you, mi vida," Adelma answered back waving.

"Hi, Gram," Solana said, whisking over casually and lifting the brim of her grandmother's hat to plant a kiss on her cheek, "You look beautiful today."

"So do you, my dear." she winked.

Adelma reached her one strong arm up for Jacob, and he leaned towards her. Solana placed her son on her grandmother's lap, and stood nearby in case he teetered.

"Let's go inside; everyone always likes to see visitors and I am always so proud to show off my family."

The baby sat remarkably still in Adelma's lap and looked up and around as they rolled inside. His innocent questioning eyes and crinkled nose gave Adelma a boost. The tyke somehow knew to hold on tight, and was content riding with his great-grandmother as Angel pushed Adelma into the visiting lounge.

"This sweet boy; it's about time we had a handsome man around the house," Adelma said, giving him an extra snuggle and nuzzling into his freshly washed dark hair.

The majority of the residents at Sunny Days were much older than Adelma. Her first stroke came at the age of fifty-five but, against the doctor's wishes, she continued to smoke. The second one was much worse and took the strength and faculty from her right side, just after her sixty-first birthday. Adelma wished she had given up the cigarettes when she was told to.

Starting at age thirteen, the bad habit had been unkind to her. She was happy that her mind had been spared in this last event. She saw the Alzheimer's patients in the residence and felt lucky for herself as well as sad for them and their families.

The family chit-chatted about work and what Adelma had been eating at the cafeteria, when Jacob started to fuss.

"Mom, I'm going to take Jake out for a walk. Can you give me the keys so I can get the stroller out of the car?" Solana asked.

Solana didn't love the smell of the old folks' home, and was happy to be able to escape for a while. She was sad that her grandmother was stuck there.

Angel tossed the keys to her daughter and gave her a pointed look as if to say, "Don't you dare take the car anywhere."

Solana rolled her eyes and nodded in quiet recognition.

"Mima, I want to show you what I brought you this time. It's not really something from *your* memories, but from *someone else's*."

Angel took a book out of the diaper bag. The little blue traveling book.

"Here, take a look at this," she held the book out to her mother. Adelma pulled the book in with her left hand and set it on her lap.

"Where did you get it?"

"I picked it up while cleaning, in my rush. I thought it was trash. After looking at it though, I realized it would be fine for me to keep it and share it with you. I want you to read it and maybe pass it around in here."

Adelma angled her bifocals to look at the cover, seeking the author's name. There was none. The small title felt like an appeal.

She opened and scanned the first page, happy with the spiral binding so that she wouldn't have to fight to hold it open.

"Strange, I've never seen anything like this; it's almost like one of those chain letters people used to do, but not exactly. So interesting. I'll read it for sure."

Angel went on to tell her mother about how reading the book made her think of things in her own life. How much they had been through together.

"Mima, I want Solana to visit next week, just the two of you. Can you tell her about how we came to this country together, rushed in the dark of night leaving everything behind? And about how you had to switch careers, after losing your voice? I want her to hear about our family's resilience and changing course. You have always taught me that, whether you knew it or not."

Adelma held her daughter's hand as tears welled in her eyes. "Yes, we have been through so much, my little Niña. I am so proud of the woman you have become. I will talk with her; it is a story that needs to be told."

The warm sunshine was calling the two and they moved outside to enjoy it. They wondered together if the author would ever be found.

"It makes you think that anyone on the street could be the writer, with all those memories and feelings, just hiding their secret dream inside. Only five books." Angel frowned.

"Not very good odds," Adelma agreed.

Solana came back with a fussy baby and saw her mom and grandmother sitting near the front door.

"Jacob is hungry and I forgot to pack a bottle. Can we go now? Really sorry, Gram."

"You two go," Adelma sighed. "Feed that sweet baby. I have some homework to do anyway." She gave Angel a wink.

The four generations hugged on the front veranda and said their goodbyes.

The following Sunday there would be a grandmother and granddaughter date where the full telling of the Fredrick family would be shared.

~

D.O.M.

You cupped my non-existent nine-year-old breasts at the local amusement park arcade. I am sure you would have done more given time.

You were feeding my young male family friend some change to stay focused on playing asteroids while you held me tightly against you, just out of my friend's view. I was not equipped to handle the situation. No one had warned me about such things.

That old men frequented arcades to victimize children. I didn't know to be aware or to not trust others.

I was lucky I escaped never to see you again. I avoided that park forever after, never saying why it was that I didn't want to go.

You made no threats against my family, but I felt the shame and hid it just the same.

I wonder how many other children you grabbed, took advantage of and plunged into your sick and twisted world. You took my innocence. My trust in others was gone.

I take some satisfaction in the fact that you must be dead now.

Dead of the body, although I am sure you live on in your deeds.

How many other children did you fondle, touch and forever traumatize for your sick thrills?

Why didn't anyone question you being in the arcade by yourself with no kid in tow? Why wasn't anyone paying attention?

The stain of your touch continues to alter my life.

Many years later, in a vulnerable state, I shared the secret with my father explaining that I believe the incident had caused me to harbor extra weight on my body in an effort to protect myself from men's unwanted attention.

That the extra weight made me feel a little bit safer.

He looked at me with sadness and said what was probably the most profound thing I had ever heard come from his lips.

"If you live your whole life in a certain way because of what that man did to you, you are giving your entire life to that man."

It was true. My entire life had been affected by a few moments in time.

I didn't want to give you any more space in my life than you had already stolen. You don't deserve even a second in my life or one brain cell of my memory.

Fuck you.

Rot in hell, you Dirty Old Man.

~

~2~

Adelma rolled her wheelchair down the corridor of the fourth floor of the Sunny Days senior residence. Mrs. Turner, her neighbor across the hall, sat outside her door in her wheelchair watching the daily movements. Every morning she asked the nurses to leave her there; it was her favorite spot. Mrs. Turner rarely stayed in her apartment, a necessity since she had dementia.

"Where are you off to today, my dear?" she asked Adelma.

"Well, I am flying into Honolulu, Hawaii, today, Mrs. Turner. Thanks for asking."

"Lucky you," said Mrs. Turner with a smile. She closed her eyes and imagined her friend in a younger, more able body, lying on a beach chair with the tropical winds dancing through her salt-and-pepper hair. That image would keep her happy until the next resident passed by.

Adelma and Mrs. Turner had made up a game where they imagined that the doors were actually portals to the wonderful places they had always wanted to visit. The two of them had started the game and tried to get others to join in, however, they found that many of the other residents either lacked imagination, or remembered very little of their long ago geography classes. In the beginning, their little game troubled the staff, but eventually they were cleared from the concern of senility after they shared their little hobby with the supervisors.

Adelma closed her door to the voice of Mrs.Turner still speaking.

"Aloha, dear!" She called.

Adelma guided her chair to the window, and pulled back the sheers to let some sunshine into her room. She placed the book on the table next to her easy chair, and moved her body cumbersomely into her chair.

Adelma read the request of the author again, "Hmm, a pass-along book, a secret mission of sorts," she smirked to herself, happy for a game to play.

She flipped the pages to the back to see how many signatures were written there. Only two: a stranger with horrible penmanship and her daughter Angel's autograph complete with her statement halo over the *g*.

"So happy you came my way," she said, tapping the book twice with her good hand before rifling to where she left off. The book was short and she was soon finished with the pages. Adelma's own memories started to bubble up inside her with the idea.

Her former life in Havana had been crazy, and raising a daughter in her line of work was difficult. Singing every night in the local clubs, Adelma's days were spent sleeping- there was little quality time with her child.

It wasn't the life she wanted for them, those long nights with Angel left alone in dingy apartments, always waking up to a spent mother. It was just the two of them. Adelma never talked about the man who fathered Angel, mostly because she didn't want to remember him.

Angel never asked either. Somehow through their mother-daughter bond, Angel must have intrinsically known it wasn't a topic to bring up. Her mother had been more than enough.

Adelma had asked to meet with the assistant manager of the bar as the ad for a singer stated. She sat waiting for hours before anyone spoke to her at all. Finally, a small, husky man with crooked teeth and one long bushy eyebrow splattered across his forehead, showed up and introduced himself as Fernando, claiming he was the manager. With the club getting ready for the night, he asked her to come and sing to him in his room upstairs.

Needing the job, Adelma followed, and once inside he slammed and locked the door. She was soon overtaken by him. She left bruised, abused, but with a job. And soon after, a child.

As her belly grew, Adelma was forced to see her rapist each night as she took to the stage. He lustfully bore his eyes into her from his regular table in the back. Dark eyes piercing through the crowd at her, her eyes sought the bright spotlights to avoid his gaze. After four months, her figure was starting to divulge her condition and she quit to keep it a secret, going to stay with her auntie in Jaruco until after the baby came.

Even with the violent start to life, Angel came into the world an easy baby. Adelma loved her endlessly from the very first moment she held her. The pain, the upheaval from her plan, none of it mattered. Angel was truly a gift from the heavens, and she named her so. Any resemblance of her father was divinely missing and Adelma was beyond grateful for that. She had never considered having a child before, but here she was- a mother.

When Angel was one, Adelma moved back to Havana and got a gig at a different club so she wouldn't have to see Fernando. She didn't want to explain to him who the baby was, and she especially didn't want Angel to be exposed to such a horrible man.

Adelma brought Angel to work with her, and the other dancers and singers would watch the baby when she was on stage. As she got older, Angel was left with random landladies wherever they were living at the time, or with Tita-like women during the day until she reached school age.

After that, Angel practically raised herself with Adelma still working nights and sleeping away the days. That child of hers had gotten herself to school every day from the age of six on, always kissing her sleeping mother goodbye before leaving the house. Adelma always felt her kisses.

The two of them moved a lot, and Adelma rented furnished apartments so there were few belongings between them. That became a happy accident when they left the country, not being able to bring much with them.

Adelma closed her eyes and remembered back to the evening she and Angel fled Cuba over twenty years ago when Angel was only thirteen. She remembered it as if it was yesterday: Handing the man on the dock all the money she had, and hearing him say that he would get them to the United States. Them along with countless others.

She had her reasons for leaving. Even with the protections in place and avoiding the streets where he was, Fernando had caught sight of the two of them shopping in the market. From across the street, his piercing eyes bore into her. His now gray bushy eyebrow lifted as if to demand if Angel was his. It was only a matter of time before he did something, or said something. She couldn't risk it.

It was pure providence that aligned her need to escape with the timing of the Cuban immigrants tidal wave into America. God might not have been able to save her from the initial scourge of that evil man, but *she* could save her daughter from being near him.

"Nosotros vamos a america," Adelma told her daughter when she arrived home from school that day in September, 1980.

"¿Porque?~ *Why?*"

"Porque dije, y nosotras nos vamos ahora. *~Because I said so, we are leaving now.*"

Angel didn't argue with her mother; there was no point. She was used to moving quickly and knew it was necessary each time. This would be the biggest move of them all.

Angel and Adelma packed small sacks with a few photos, clothing and some fruit to eat on the way. They got on the bus that would take them to Mariel Harbor. Many others stood as the bus was full of other people going to America. Angel sat on her mother's lap to make space. As the bus bumped along the road, Adelma took in the last views of her home country. Palm trees dotted the streets as yapping stray dogs chased the bus, running dangerously in and under the wheels. Sometimes they would feel a bump and lurch and the driver would curse.

"Mierda!"~ *Shit!*

She would remember her life here, but she was ready for herself and Angel to start anew.

With the water and sky as the backdrop, what looked like hundreds of different-sized boats scurried to scoop hopeful Cubans away. Adelma held tight to her daughter, slapping hands away as grabby men tried to fondle them in the chaos of the swarm.

Finally they were called to board. Strangers with a common mission pressed onto the boat, seeking a place to sit. More and more the boat was filled to capacity. It was night when the boat finally pulled away from Mariel Harbor. The dimmed street lights glinted lightly on the water, getting smaller and smaller as the engine chugged on. There was no going back.

Angel was tired. They hadn't managed to eat dinner with all the packing up. The fruit they brought had been eaten on the bus ride. She sat leaning into her mother, being lulled further by the rocking of the old boat. Some people nearby vomited with the waves.

Adelma softly sang to her daughter the song *"Drume Negrita,"* a Cuban lullaby she had sung to her as a baby. It was a tune that had been sung to her as a child as well.

Others around them inched closer to hear Adelma's beautiful rendition of the melody of long ago. She sang as much for comfort as to hide the retching sounds coming from the sick passengers.

Their time on the boat was loud and quiet at the same time: Loud with the engines and the people muttering troubles; but quiet as each dwelled in the uncertainty and aloneness that they felt. Adelma was in her head with fright not knowing what was to come, but she put on a brave face for her daughter to show that she knew what was best for them.

As the ocean swayed, the constant mumblings of worry from the fellow passengers kept Adelma awake the entire night. At daybreak, shouts of exhilaration started upon finally seeing the port at Key West. They had made it. Now they could start their brand new life.

The United States government was ready for the masses, and Adelma was beyond grateful for the door that had been opened to them and the others.

Upon landing in Key West, they stayed for a month in a tent crowded with others. Adelma kept a very close eye on her daughter so she wouldn't fall prey to some of the shady characters that were around. When they finally reached the mainland, Adelma was able to get a singing job right away in Miami- things looked promising.

Even with all of her efforts to protect Angel from the man who was her father, she found that she wasn't able to protect her from the boys or men who would come into her life once they arrived in America.

Angel became captivated by American culture, teased by the clothes, hairstyles and a freedom she had never known. Left alone during the day with her mother working, Angel fell into questionable circles trying to assimilate. She watched a lot of television, picking up a bit of the slang and romantic ideas that populated daytime soap operas. Angel dreamed of having a boyfriend, just like the girls on the TV shows.

Thinking back, Adelma wished she had taught her daughter the ways that men entice women, and what to do when their advances are unwanted. How to be more selective with her affections and interest. Adelma wished her own mother had taught her more of that as well.

Angel had fallen for the first boy who showed an interest in her. He was nice, and when he brought her flowers it had been the first time she felt special and wanted. Just having a man's interest was such a thrill that Angel had leapt into bed with him the first chance she saw. Adelma hadn't had all the conversations about all that could come with being with a man, and soon after Angel was pregnant with her Solana at just seventeen.

With the news, Chris's family urged them to get married. Angel saw what looked like her chance to have a typical American family, but the marriage had no chance. As her body changed, her temper ignited with the fear of raising a child at such a young age. Chris joined the military to escape the situation and the responsibilities he hadn't been ready for, and to get away from the strong-willed Angel who expected him to be much more of a man than he was. For her, it would be another generation of single, unpartnered mothers.

Adelma, Angel and baby Solana moved north to slow life down a little, to have a quieter life than one based in show business. Atlanta was smaller than Miami, and Adelma got a job singing nights, while Angel started cleaning hotel rooms during the day, leaving the baby with her mother. They were a team. With everything they had made a good life together, the three of them.

A tear fell down her cheek, it was joined with many more.

If only she could be with them now. If only she had done things differently. Lived differently, cared more about her health than those dumb cigarettes.

At fifty, her voice started to change, and she wasn't able to hit the high notes anymore. A trip to the doctor concluded that she had developed glottic cancer of the larynx and would need radiation. They were thankful to have caught it early, but it would mean big changes for their family. Radiation fought it back but took with it the beautiful voice that had fed them and nourished their physical and emotional hunger on their hardest days- it was forever gone.

Angel showed her mother how to clean hotel rooms. They worked together side by side for years, eventually starting their cleaning business together until Adelma's strokes changed that plan, too.

Adelma opened her eyes and wondered exactly how much of their familia's story had been shared with Solana. Angel was a protective, private mother who wanted so badly for her daughter to be able to live an ordinary American life. The life she craved.

Angel may have protected her daughter *too* much, as Solana had fallen into the same pattern with boys as her mother had. Having no men around, she also sought out any attention she could find.

The book had given her an idea. It needed to be passed around, and what a fun opportunity it would be to share with some of the other ladies on the floor.

Adelma signed her name in the back of the book as best she could. It wasn't the flowy signature she used to have, but she did her best. She had been writing and practicing her letters. She felt her writing was legible enough to share with others; maybe she could handle a fun invite to take part in a little mystery?

Finally, they'd have something else to talk about other than their aches and pains.

~

Mothering Me, 2002

*I*t didn't escape me that being home with my daughters was a gift. Many moms today do not have the luxury of it being an option. Since being a nanny before motherhood I have seen both sides: one as the helper to a mother who either chose or wanted to remain in the workforce; and then also as the mother.

Some parents used my services to run errands or to have a day to themselves. Others had part-time jobs away from home to keep their professional skills sharp so they could go back to full-time employment later on. I didn't judge; obviously, I was there to serve. If they did feel guilty leaving their kids, they weren't sharing that part of their life with me. All of the women I worked for saw me as a teammate in the raising of their child or children.

I learned so much from them. I remember being fairly new to childcare and I had asked the woman I worked for the most about how one deals with a kid throwing up. I was pretty nervous about it. She was nice and explained it very simply, "That as much as it's gross and you may want to throw up at the sight of it, you find yourself feeling so sorry for them that your care instinct takes over and you just do what you need to do."

Her advice hit home not one week later when a little boy who I watched a few times a month was especially needy and wanted me to just hold him instead of playing as per usual. He was about two years old and we sat in their big comfy rocker recliner and I rubbed his back as he sucked his thumb. He was quiet and still, a stark contrast to his usual self. He didn't say anything that would have led me to know he felt sick. He just lay his head on my shoulder.

Out of nowhere except probably to him, projectile vomit splashed all over the two of us and the chair. Poor little guy.

My boss had been absolutely right though. I went into comfort mode and cleaned him up, grabbing my jacket to cover the ick on me as I took care of him. His energy rebounded almost instantly and he went into the tub feeling much better having expelled whatever it was that was bothering him.

I was no longer a barf virgin. I'd been puked on, had to clean up puke, and

I was the grown up in charge at the time. Her explanation would be the one I would supply to anyone who asked me forever after- as it was perfect.

I can't say that this is true for everyone but when that kid needed me, I naturally knew what to do and could handle it. Many of those lessons helped me become the mother I worked to be.

So many children in my years as a nanny. So many personalities.

The time I saved one little boy's life when he started choking on a banana. His eyes terrified looking at me. I jumped up and started giving him the Heimlich, frantic. After the obstruction was gone, I worried that I had been too rough. He said he knew what I was doing and it was okay. That was during my two year stint as the caretaker for a group of five neighborhood boys each Wednesday after school, aged four through six. Those were some wild days. Lunch, playing, keeping them busy 'til their parents came. They got along for the most part.

My Thursdays were spent with one little girl and her older sister when she was home. In a house that felt so much like a palace, I was afraid to touch anything. Their mother, another mother to study, was a quintessential Southern belle. She was perfect in the care of her home, her personal style was always on point, her figure, a sinewy hourglass.

Fridays were a mix of whoever needed me that day: sometimes I was across town at the rich people's house on the lake; sometimes I cared for a little girl whose parents had tried for so long to get pregnant that they gave up and started the adoption process only to get pregnant with her on a vacation after finally giving up trying to conceive. That little girl was partly the namesake of my oldest daughter; she was dear to me. As they all were.

Oddly it was the boys that I found easier to manage and bond with back then. Then I go and birth two daughters, with zip sons. Daughters who like to be girly and play Barbies and have all of their little animals getting married in play ceremonies. They want to wear dresses and have tea time and I learned from them to lean into my more feminine side.

Mothers come in all shapes and sizes, with different goals and preferences, each making their way while caring for the people that they brought into the world in the best way they can.

Each mother, I feel, does their best to outperform their own mothers by attempting to fix something that didn't work in their childhood. They read books, they took classes, they promised not to be like her or act as she did when the kids left home.

My exposure to the many mothers and parenting models has been another gift. Every kid needs different mothering. Even in the same house and family what works for one kid will not always be successful for any other. All we can do is the best we can do while continuing to learn and change and tackle the challenges that come.

In the same way that I almost lost myself to motherhood early on, I have continued to struggle with finding the perfect balance of separating the mother in me and the woman in me. Often I let myself go to the bigger mission, believing that someday, after my children are grown, I will be able to pick up my personal development and dreams where I last left off and move onward in whatever it is that I choose.

We will see if it's true. The business is gone, I am fully back in the throes of being a stay- at-home-mom. I do hope I will remember to challenge myself to dream again someday.

~

P.H.

You were the mother of one of my earliest best friends. You had a happy and well kept home and I felt like you were the perfect Mom. You were always smiling. You always had cookies in the cookie jar and you stayed home, always being there when your kids got home from school. If I had to pick another Mom to be my Mom, it would have been you.

You wore Christmas sweaters and hosted great holiday parties. You were so warm and kind. You and your husband looked like perfect bookends in the library of the great American couple. Everything from my vantage point looked flawless.

As time went on and we moved away, I lost my exposure to you, only seeing you twice as an adult to go to your in-home holiday boutique with my Mom. You were dressed similarly to the way you did when I was younger and you had another dog who was exactly the same breed as the previous three.

Nothing changed in your home or at least that is what it felt like. You and your family were the same as before: static and content. The hinge-point in that scene seemed to be you. You were the stable, unwavering matriarch that had seen your children into adulthood; the beacon I strived to be, too.

As an adult looking on, I couldn't help but feel that you had given your whole life in service to others, leaving little for yourself. Or that is how it seemed.

No big changes had come as you stayed in place, seemingly satisfied with what was and is, having never bucked the system.

I wonder what aspirations you had when you were alone or asleep in the deepest slumber with no one else to worry about but you.

I wish you the time to chase those.

~

~2~

Adelma was excited for the little book club; the first meeting would showcase the little traveling book. She envisioned a special way to invite them. She would handwrite the invitations for each of them. Then they could read the book together and share experiences from their own lives just for fun.

She'd name their new group "The Bonita Butterflies." "Bonita" to signify beauty, and a butterfly to signify a lovely new beginning.

Adelma took her time writing out the handmade cards she had planned for her friends on the third floor. She was still getting used to writing with her left hand but she had made good progress, and her writing was legible. Fanciful butterfly stickers, one of Angel's gifts to inspire healing, were placed on the front of each of the cards after Adelma had written a small message inside.

She signed her first name on the bottom of each note. Her new signature had a new strength that showed what she had been through. She wrote the name of each person on the back of the card and used tape to hold it closed. No envelope. It would be fine. Easier to open for old, arthritic hands anyway.

The little book had brought up so many memories for her that she wanted to share, and it might inspire her friends as well.

She wheeled her chair down the hall after dinner service, knocking softly on each door belonging to a friend. She wanted to keep the group small so it was manageable, and picked the ones she knew read books.

The first door was Mrs. Nancy Shelcock's. 'Nanny' is what she liked to be called, and Adelma knew she would be taking her time to answer. Not only was she hard of hearing, she was rather slow and would often drift off after eating. She knocked again and was about to try to lean down to slide it under her door when she answered.

Nanny peeked out a sliver in the opening before opening it fully and offering a smile. "Well, Adelma, what a nice surprise. Would you like to come in?" She motioned into her unit.

"Not this time, my dear, but I have something for you; I hope you can come."

Nanny turned the card over to see a blue butterfly sticker on the front. She ran her finger over it and said, "Oh, I do love blue. I am sure I will be available," she smiled again. "Thanks for stopping by."

Nanny rarely had visitors at Sunny Day's as her family lived on the West Coast. One nephew from North Carolina would be coming at Christmas time, but it would be months again still for that. It was good for her to have something to look forward to.

Adelma rolled and knocked her way down the hallway. Sally Rubenstein in 3A got a green butterfly sticker; Mari Johnson in 3F received an orange one; and Jillian Halliwell got a purple one- each was delighted to have their favorite color remembered by their thoughtful friend. Saffron Jones got a yellow butterfly sticker and was especially touched to be invited as she had only just moved in.

All the women were delighted to have been visited by the mysterious Bonita Butterfly book club bandit that night, and all RSVP'd the next morning at breakfast, whispering into Adelma's ears that they would be attending.

Adelma had arranged with the kitchen staff to have some goodies and coffee available for the evening. Hazel was especially nice to help set up the library to have a circle where they could all visit and see each other to hear about the book. Adelma was one of Hazel's favorite residents.

Adelma's crooked smile hadn't dulled her luminous spirit.

"I can stay..." Hazel offered, explaining that she could help clean up afterwards, as she tried to hide her huge curiosity about the secret meeting. Hazel anticipated a lot of stories and giggles could come from these fabulous old women, and she had no one at home waiting for her.

"Well, if you're sure, that would be lovely." Adelma accepted. "You never know when one of us could laugh so hard, we could tumble out of a chair or something," Adelma laughed as her lip caught on her teeth.

"Wonderful, I can sit in the back and be on alert," Hazel reassured her.

Hazel didn't have anyone waiting for her at home, and this evening might give her some insight into activities that the residents would enjoy if she was chosen for the activities coordinator job she was applying for.

It was six-thirty and the women streamed into the facility library, gathering around the snack table set with cups of "Milo's" sweet tea and lemonade and plates of moon pies. Each woman tried to guess which book might be chosen to read.

Still holding their plates, they gathered in a circle and Adelma clapped as well as she could to get their attention.

"My Bonita Butterflies, I have brought you here today to share something special. It is something of a mission for us, as well as a great conversation starter. I hope some of the stories inside this book will help you reach into your own memory banks to remember many of the people that have meant something to you. Maybe people that you loved or cared about, both living and dead. My daughter brought me this book to share with you, and the author needs our help. She has a dream. Her request has landed in our laps and I would like us to work together to see if we can help her."

The women looked around at each other.

"Us?" said Saffron, "she needs *our* help?"

"Well, yes, she needs everyone who comes into contact with the book to read it and pass it along until someone recognizes themselves in her pages."

"My, my, my, how wonderful to be needed for something again," said Nanny Shelcock.

"How exciting!" said Jillian, clasping her hands together.

Hazel looked on as each woman smiled at the thought of a new purpose. Many had seen their families grow up and move on, and a few had ended their long professional careers many years ago. To see their eyes lit up and engaged- what a delight.

Adelma held up the book with her left hand. "Here it is. We *could* all go around the room reading the excerpts out loud; they are short memories written by the mysterious author."

There were some grimaces in the group as no one felt comfortable reading aloud. For some it had been more than fifty years since reading to their own children.

"I don't think I can," said Nanny, her eyes falling some, to stare at her swollen, sore hands lying in her lap. She lacked the strength to hold up a book or fuss with the pages.

"Me either," said Saffron, "My eyes just aren't what they used to be even with these thick corrective lenses."

Adelma was crestfallen, she hadn't planned for this, and she certainly didn't want to read the whole book out loud herself.

Hazel stood up, "I'll do it. I worked at a library for years and read to the little ones on Saturdays. I will do it if you want me to. It would be my pleasure."

Joyous sighs and smiles spread across the room.

"Oh, yes," said Nanny.

"Lovely," said Mari.

"Hazel that would be wonderful, a real la joya you are." Hazel nodded at Adelma with her understanding of the compliment: " jewel."

Hazel stepped forward and retrieved the book from Adelma, moving her chair into the circle where she could see everyone. She opened to the first page, and started to read the heartfelt request from the author.

Dear Reader,

This traveling book is my secret mission to live a more extraordinary life from within the confines of an ordinary one.

Only five copies of this book exist and this has made its way to you; you are now and forever a part of this story.

Inside you will find moments captured from one person's life. Each passage starts with the set of initials of the person with whom I share the connection.

We are all connected on some level; every person you meet leaves a mark on you whether good or bad. Often it is the worst people who *gift* us the best lessons.

It is my hope that this idea spurs you into living in a more extraordinary way; to think bigger and reach beyond what you currently see.

The memories inside may remind you of a time or a person in your own life; may you think of those people today for the good or the lessons you learned from them.

Please read this book then write your name and location in the back before giving it to someone else. Leave it on a bus, give it to a friend, it will only take a few minutes for you to participate and it is wonderful to think of the adventures it may have.

Let's see how small our world really is.

If you, by chance, recognize yourself in here, please bring the book and,

Find me...

The stunned women started nodding and murmuring in anticipation.

"Well, are you ready?" asked Hazel.

A resounding "yes" came from the group, and Hazel read on. The women quieted, and a few adjusted their hearing aids to hear her better.

After the book was done, they spent the rest of that evening taking turns telling stories about their own lives.

For some, it was the first time since moving to Sunny Days that they shared anything about themselves. There was talk of first loves, and family member drama or losses. A few had been widowed and each had been touched by the book in some way. A story inside made them remember something they hadn't thought of in years.

Stories of starting a family or building a business. Each shared where they were born, went to school and married. Nancy surprised the bunch by sharing that she had worked in an airplane factory in California during WWII to help the effort, before Saffron shared that she had once dreamed of playing baseball on an all female baseball team in the middle 1950s.

Emotions and memories that had been hidden inside them all for so long came out to play together. They felt as free as the little children running loose at the school grounds.

Laughter and happiness filled the room, and some tears stemming from both joy and sadness were shed. The room bubbled up with the effervescence of life itself.

Each one of them felt sorry for the author who might be sitting home waiting for life to happen to her. Each woman proclaimed that they believed they had fully lived every single day of their lives. A few shared small regrets, mostly of staying in one place for so much of their life, or of not going for a big job. Maybe they had listened to their parents about who they should love.

How wonderful it was to be together and have this moment and this book to bring them closer. Because of the book, there would be more topics to chat about and think about for the rest of their days. They agreed that the book club and sharing about their wild-ride lives was a much better way to spend their time instead of just complaining about the cafeteria food.

Each wanted to have some time with the book to absorb the pages themselves, then they could leave the book in the resident library for others to find it. Many others might like to read it and reflect as well.

After clearing the plates and putting the chairs where they belonged, Hazel hugged each of the women before leaving them for the day. She placed the book gently on Adelma's lap and waved once more as she went.

The new group, the Bonita Butterflies, stayed in the room, talking and laughing together for hours, until the evening staff came in to say it was time to lock up the library for the day.

Nancy Shelcock asked to have the first turn with the book, and Adelma handed it over. Nancy leaned down and gave her friend a squeeze.

A new, magnificent friendship had begun for all of them.

~

A Stroll with the Past, Me, 2004

*I*t had started so innocently, me perusing a website to see if an old crush was still alive and, if so, what he was up to. Pages full of classmates, old friends I had forgotten about. So many people-open to connecting or being found by old friends, flames or family. Before I knew it, he and I were in communication via the website's message center. We were two married people having secret discussions that only we saw. The rapport was building, and suddenly I was rushing home from the grocery store to see if he had written back like a love-struck teenager.

We shared bits of our lives: the good, along with some of the things we wished were different, and everything in between. That is where the complications started.

Sharing intimate information with someone other than your spouse, especially someone with whom you have a past with, can spark something dangerous. I thought I had things under control.

We were kids back then, dumb teenagers who didn't have any idea what the world was really about; but yet, there was this connection that we both still felt, one that caused us to hold each other in our minds even after so long.

How easily we fell into step with each other walking the streets of town close to where we grew up, it was all we planned to do. A simple stroll.

We flirted back then as teens, but never acted. It was fun and, at the same time, frustrating. He saw me as just a kid, with my being two years younger than him, and I guess at the time I was. We decided that friendship was the way to go, and we would walk home from school together sometimes. It was a long four-mile hike from where we attended to where we usually caught the bus together. We would talk about all kinds of stuff and laugh, and tease; I'd stifle my feelings. Over and over again.

I didn't realize that he had wondered about me over the years as well, that he had a crush on me back then, but was trying to be "good."

The walks stopped when he got a girlfriend; she didn't want him hanging out with me, and so it goes. I went on, and he went on, and that was that.

I didn't expect him to even recognize me, as I have what I would call a *pretty generic face. One that people often confuse with other people in the city where I live. Once I had a person I did not know come up and hug me as their friend, and I had to explain that I was not them. It was awkward for us both, but I wished later I would have asked who it was so I could know my Doppelganger's name for next time.*

As he walked towards me, he smirked. And I was transported back to being fifteen again, my crush heading my way. I smiled. His walk was exactly the same: a slight saunter, with a heaviness that grounded him as he stepped. People buzzed around us, weaving about to get to their destinations, and we were each other's destination in the blur.

He told me later, he almost bolted when he saw me, and I wonder where we'd be if he had.

He asked how I'd managed to become even more beautiful than I was back then, as kids.

I smiled, and said, "Well, I have managed to finally tame those big eyebrows I had back then; maybe that could be the difference."

He laughed, and I blushed I'm sure. I don't actually know what to do with compliments anyway. Deflect them into a self-deprecating statement apparently, I guess.

As we went to leave to get back to our lives I said, "Maybe I'll see you in another twenty years."

He rallied back almost immediately, "I don't think I want to wait that long."

Another compliment. It was amazing to feel that special, to be seen as unique in someone else's eyes. I should have known I was in for some trouble.

Before he left, he leaned towards me so close I could smell him. He wanted a kiss. I remember the signs from my dating years: the getting close, the breath, the parting of the lips, ready to latch on. I panicked and pulled away.

Then he covered it all up by saying, "Of course on the cheek."

I let him.

My whole life crumbled at the thought of his lips on mine. There would be no turning back. Love could only follow.

I watched him walk away and my heart hurt. A physical pain as a part of my soul was removed. It hardly seemed possible that so much feeling could come from eight hours of time. Eight hours and almost twenty years.

The fact that we held thoughts of each other in our minds, spoke to the fact that there was something there. Now faced with the reality that I will likely not see him for years, if ever, I am left empty in my pursuit of what it all means.

I would spend the next few days making amends for the betrayal I have caused my husband in my head, and the lack of myself I have given my children over the past two afternoons.

I am where I am supposed to be, where I am needed and loved. He is back with his family, too. Where he belongs. Where he should be.

As I hold my youngest in my lap, her arms and legs draped all over me, it becomes apparent that all at once, I am blessed beyond measure.

I need to remember that...

God, help me remember. Please.

~

~2~

Hazel

Hazel's ordinary day had made a surprising turn. On the drive home, an idea popped into her head from reading the little book and the subsequent chatting. It might be the perfect campaign to share with the director in her quest to win the activities coordinator job. She percolated on it some more as she poured hot water over her evening tea. The steam hit her glasses, fogging them for a second and she closed her eyes.

Hazel grinned remembering the women's faces light up from sharing something extraordinary about their lives. In that moment, it was as if all their wrinkles were smoothed soft and any pain they felt in their bodies had wafted away. Each beaming face spilled some of the marvels they had experienced. Looks of recognition came when one shared something they could relate to. A new energy fluttered in every one of them, all brought forth by the book and their shared contemplation about it.

So often the exchanges in the residence were about what meds people were taking and who had a doctor visit coming up. They'd whisper to each other about the ones who'd been taken away by an ambulance and ventured guesses on whether they'd be back.

It was magical to hear more about the richness and beauty of each of their lives, not just the harping on of the ailments or isolation many of them felt.

As the TV droned on in the background, Hazel stroked her dog Chauncy's wiry fur. She didn't mind the rougher texture as it reminded her of Jason's curly hair. He had been her love from high school, and they had found each other again, only a little too late. Chauncy had been her life raft for the last year. He had been Jason's dog.

It was all still fresh. The loss, the gap that left her house and heart empty enough to take on every extra shift that was available at the retirement center, no matter the role. She could cook, she could work in the rooms with the clients, she was willing to do anything. Anything to keep her mind away from losing Jason. She had just found him again. It was so, so sad.

High school sweethearts, the world could have been theirs, except for his meddlesome, dominating Mother. Hazel wasn't from the type of family that his Mother wanted for her only son. Her *"Golden Boy."*

Unable to stay away from each other, they hid their relationship from his mother and anyone else who might expose them. When Jason got a scholarship to college, they sent letters to each other to keep their relationship going. Soon with Jason taking extra classes, and her working two jobs to help out her family, they fell away from each other, eventually marrying others by the time they were twenty-five.

Hazel loved her husband and the family that they made together, but when he died in a tragic motorbike accident, she spent years working hard to keep her family together and safe on just her income.

She didn't have time for love. And so it went, with her children growing up and leaving home to build their own lives, suddenly she looked around and everyone was gone.

Right about that time was her high school class reunion, her thirtieth. She bought an off-the-shoulder red dress and pulled her salt-and-pepper hair up into a high bun. She rubbed some rouge on her cheeks and glossed her lips. She wasn't looking for anything other than a fun night out.

She saw him enter, and waited for a wife or date to join him. He was alone, as was she. He looked mostly the same: A little older, a little more pudge around his middle, but handsome nonetheless. He wandered the outskirts of the room, lost in the sea of slightly familiar faces.

Hazel stood with a couple of old girlfriends near the punch bowl. ABBA's *"Take A Chance On Me"* played over the speakers, a little too loud for her liking. He caught her glance and winked at her then nodded to the dance floor.

Hazel handed a friend her drink and floated over to meet him there. They spent every song after in each other's arms, and went back to her place that night. Every moment after was spent together. Along with the fun dates and weekend getaways, they managed to mix in some of the conversations about how they had ended up apart.

As it turns out his mother had interfered in his marriage, too. He hadn't realized all the ways she meddled until one Christmas his mother carpet-bombed his wife with insults causing her to leave her own house and take the kids to her parents. She filed for divorce just after New Years.

It hadn't been Hazel after all. His mother's dislike of her had nothing to do with Hazel, and everything to do with the woman's controlling behavior and thirst to always be number one in the heart of her son.

How that woman could sweet talk over the emotional knife blows remained a mystery to him, so much so that he sought out counseling after she finally died.

Thankfully, Jason's Mother couldn't obstruct their relationship this time. They were finally free to make a new life together, or so they thought.

When Jason fell on the job doing an inventory inspection at one of his warehouses, he was whisked to the hospital. A couple of broken ribs and more. On the MRI, they found a tumor. It was large and had already metastasized into his lungs, liver and brain. He didn't have long.

Hazel asked for a leave of absence to make whatever time he had left the best she could and Jason retired immediately and moved in with Hazel. They fell into a rhythm of good days and bad.

Hazel tried her best to make what life he had left better. And she had. They went on picnics and recreated some of their high school dates spending hours just talking, their arms around each other. Heck, they even made out in the back of her car while it was parked in the garage just for fun. Every day he voiced to her his appreciation of her, and she felt seen and loved for the first time in years. As he took his last breath in the hospice center nearby, she was there along with his three kids. He chose to die away from home to excuse that memory from her mind. The kids encouraged Hazel to keep Chauncy as he was used to her, and she was grateful to have the fuzzy guy to take up some of the space.

Life could be cruel. The time lost and the love of her life plucked away not once, but twice. Hazel had learned there was no time to waste. Not anymore.

She had worked at Sunny Days for six years before leaving for those three months for Jason. After his death, they were happy to have her back. She'd started out as one of the housekeepers, getting her hands dirty- *literally*. Incontinence and solid stool accidents were fairly common occurrences, although the staff was discreet with the incidents for the dignity of everyone. That hadn't been the fun stuff, for sure.

She'd moved onto the kitchen staff after two years and helped the main chef with the meal prep tasks and served up plates to the residents with a smile ever since. Her daily exchanges with them helped her to remember everyone and that she was loved by many.

Deciding to apply for the activities coordinator position at Sunny Days was about changing things up. It had been over a month since she'd applied, and she didn't know what the hold up was. Maybe they were waiting for more qualified candidates to come forward. Was it her lack of a college education or lack of relevant experience in the field that kept them from taking her seriously?

Whatever the answer was, she'd be inquiring about the position soon; she didn't want to waste any more time waiting.

~

What Have I Done?, Me 2004

My daughter follows me around the house as if she knows I am not actually here. My spirit is down today and I know he has gone back to his life and I am back in mine.

An airplane flies over the house. It seems noisier than usual. I cut an onion, thankful for the inconspicuous opportunity to cry.

A friend told me, "There, now you will never see him again." My heart sank, as I agreed. I need some space to feel, and to write.

More words have poured out of me lately as I have been very introspective about all of it.

My dog snores on the rug as if nothing has happened.

I gifted myself a rock carved with the words "Be still." It reminds me to do just that. Be still and know that I am; be still and listen to your heart- just be still. It will be my mantra today. The rock fits nicely in my hand and warms with the touch. I feel the strength in its hardness.

Summer is waning, and the girls will be back in school soon. My solitude is coming once again. It is in the quiet that I question everything. That I believe I am not good enough to be anything or do anything.

With him and in his messages, I felt seen, important, wanted. In the quiet, I am alone. Alone with my thoughts about my life, and what to do next, if anything.

Be still, the rock begs.

I am trying.

I write a letter to him in my head, one that I would never send- something that could have halted the chain of events to come.

The idea of running away together is inviting, but the truth is, I wouldn't want to run away together now. The things I want to share with him do not fit where we are in our lives. The day-to-day caretaking and expectations of living as husband and wife with children do not fit with how I saw a life with him.

I want to walk hand in hand in the park and talk about the Universe. Cook together in a kitchen, designed by us with no concern of picky eaters. Lay in bed all afternoon dreaming.

These visions do not fit with me running the kids to soccer practice, volunteering at their school, and speaking in front of city council meetings.

With him making the rounds and giving words of comfort to the sick and their families, and at home being a good steward to his sons' spiritual and emotional upbringing.

Maybe someday, we would be free together to explore the world and our big thoughts. If not in this life, then the next.

I continue the siege, the inescapable battle between head and heart- but will anyone win?

~

A.A.

I thought I was being helpful. I'd learned something that I hoped might comfort you in your recent loss. You and your husband had been excited, you'd wanted another child for a long time, and it was finally happening.

It was a little boy. You were showing and more than happy to have well wishers rub your belly at our monthly bunco meeting. We were all excited for you and your family.

Not long after, the news was beyond sad. You'd lost the baby, and no one knew why.

My curiosity has always been never ending. I need to know *why* things happen to help make life make sense, even a little bit. Sometimes I wish I didn't have this quality.

Anytime I had been in your presence, I'd noticed the red rash on your cheeks and wondered what it was from. You looked hot all the time, but never complained about the temperature. No one else seemed to wonder, or maybe they never noticed? Why did I have to notice *everything*?

After I heard you lost the baby, I went into overdrive to figure out why. No one asked me to, I just needed to. You were communicating to others that it must have been your fault somehow. I couldn't bear to have you think that. Maybe, if *I* found the answer, you would then know that it wasn't your fault, that it just happened.

It wasn't that hard really; a couple of words typed into the computer and voila.

"Lupus: an autoimmune condition that often represents itself with a butterfly- shaped rash on the face of its sufferers. *Miscarriages often happen to those afflicted with the illness.*"

It was so sad, but it made total sense. I thought the information would soothe. If you knew what it was, maybe your doctor could treat you differently and you could conceive again? Have your best chance to deliver a full term, healthy baby this time?

I wrote you a note of sympathy, and added in a couple of articles I thought might help with the explanation I had hoped would buffer your pain.

I would have wanted to hear it, for someone to tell me if they knew something about me that I didn't. *I'd* want to know if I were in the same place. As per my usual, I didn't aptly forecast the gamut of reactions that people might feel or how they might respond to such news.

I didn't expect gratitude, but I really did believe it would help ease your suffering.

As you know, it did not go well.

After I sent the letter, days went by with no response. Then suddenly you were standing outside my door, looking me dead in the face. You were rigid on the outside, your words were sharp and cold and I felt your rage underneath your script as you told me that I was never to mention anything about that illness to you *ever* again.

"Don't talk about my baby and don't speak to me about anything except the most surface topics at our neighborhood get-togethers."

I listened and cried and told her I was sorry. I was sorry for all of it. It didn't matter why I felt I needed to share that information. It didn't matter if it was helpful or not. The only thing I could do was listen and honor her wishes.

I never brought up the subject again. I rarely looked at her or said anything. When Bunco came around again, she had an announcement to share. I sat dead-still with my head looking at my lap, feeling red hot inside as you told our group that you were not going to try to conceive again. The topic was closed.

You were never again the warm friend that you used to be.

I had overstepped. I couldn't have imagined that you would feel as attacked as you must have or that you would respond like you had. I had no right to offer my theory; I was no doctor.

It didn't matter that I really thought that an answer might help with your pain, your sadness, your self blame.

I'd hoped it would free you from the guilt. Confirming that it wasn't your fault, it just was. There was nothing you could have done differently at the time.

Since we never spoke of anything personal again, I don't know if you ever sought a medical diagnosis, or if your doctors affirmed my suspicions. It never mattered to me to know if I was right; I only wanted some solace for you and your heart.

For me, it was just another reminder that not everyone thinks the same way as I do. A lesson I seem hell-bent to have to learn over and over again based on my continued assumptions and mistakes.

Despite my own need to know as much as I can about things that puzzle me, I guess for others ignorance *really is* bliss.

~

Yes, I Deserved It- But Ouch, Me -2005

She'd had enough. She was my oldest friend. The one that I had so much history with. She'd been my bridesmaid, had thrown me a surprise twenty-first birthday and, in exchange for all of our friendship together, I had listened to her obsess over her wanting to date a famous basketball star, purposefully staying single just in case he might notice her. She waited so long she blew right through her fertile years.

What I'd asked her to do was too much. Maybe I just wanted to tell someone about the magic I was feeling for the first time in a long while. It was to buy time and have an additional excuse for my second day in a row of seeing the man from my past. I was worried my husband would find out about the second meeting and asked her if she would cover for me if he called her.

I was going to use her as an excuse to go meet my old flame once more before he left town. Hubby wasn't even jealous of me seeing him, which might have been part of the problem. It didn't seem to matter to him what I did.

Hubby didn't even have her phone number, and I should never have asked her to cover for me. We hardly saw each other, but with my request she was suddenly entwined in my web of deceit and she gave me the what for.

Stupid, dumb, completely out-of-control, and asking way too much of any friend. And she blew up at me. Which I deserved.

She must have known it would be the start of an affair that would pull my family apart.

At first I was surprised at her reaction, she was supposed to be my best friend, not my husband's. She didn't even try to talk me out of seeing him, hold me back or even talk to me about it. What did she care what he thought? Why didn't she have my back? After all these years of knowing each other?

Well, she was mad that I asked and she told me to fuck off.

Talk about removing yourself from someone's life? I never felt such a rush of wind as I did with her exiting out that metaphorical door. No apologies would ever bring her back. After trying a few times, I finally gave up. Even years later, she was done with me forever. And only she and I would ever know why.

She must have known that I was plunging into a me that wasn't going to be a good person anymore. That things would get really messy from here on out and she couldn't bear to watch? Perhaps she had lost all respect for me? Or maybe, just maybe, it was the perfect excuse to leave my life forever and she had been looking for an out for awhile.

Whatever the reason was, somehow I didn't let her disapproval or upset stop me from going to meet Mr. Past for that second time.

I was just going to have one less person to be a witness in my life.

I was more on my own than I had ever felt before, and edging perilously closer to becoming someone I didn't even know.

~

~2~

Nancy

Nancy Shelcock opened the door of her apartment at Sunny Days and kicked it closed behind her. Setting her keys down on the entry side table, she took her new book to her favorite chair and put it down on the matching ottoman. She'd listened to the book, yes, but first she wanted to put her hands on some of her own memories.

She pulled open the bifold closet door and rummaged through the boxes on the floor. She wiped the packing peanuts away and pulled an aged scrapbook free, climbing back up gingerly from her squat.

Placing the scrapbook next to the other book she went into the kitchen to make a cup of strong, black coffee. As the whistle sounded, Nancy flipped off the stove. This was the hard part. It was getting harder to steady the kettle and not spill the water or burn herself.

She held the kettle with both hands and successfully poured the hot water over the heaping teaspoon of flaked coffee granules in her favorite mug.

The mug lifted her spirits every single day and gave her such a feeling of pride. Adorned with the well-recognized image of "Rosie the Riveter" plastered on the front of it with a backdrop of silver panels complete with painted on rivets, the cup was a gift from her granddaughter from the Christmas before last. Her only grandchild, Tammy, had been fascinated after hearing of Nancy's time working at the airplane factories in California during WWII.

Placing the steaming coffee on the table next to her, Nancy opened the scrapbook and slowly perused the pages of newspaper articles about what was one of the most rewarding times in her life. Some pages had photographs of her and others, each adhered carefully with gold photo wedges in the corners to keep them in place. The entire album was of her time contributing to the war effort before moving to the South later in her career. Photographs were dulled with time. Some black-and-white images and some in color. The colored ones were more grainy as they aged, but held stronger the act of being transported back in time significantly more than the black-and-white ones for her. Even with the color photos as they were, she remembered the world much more vivid in real life.

Southern California had been a beautiful place to grow up. The vast orange groves outside of town wafted the sweetest smells as she rode in her father's convertible as a kid. The palm trees stood sentinel on Windsor Boulevard beckoning everyone below them to the Hollywood sign. The bright sunny weather all the time meant days on the beach and dressing in soft flowy dresses any time of year. It was such a hoot to see movie stars around town. Nancy remembered writing of each sighting in her diaries as a teen; how she wished she would have held onto those silly little books.

She met and married Bob Shelcock in 1940 and their daughter Lainie came in 1941, right before the attack on Pearl Harbor. The strike was such a shock to them both, as Bob worked at the Lockheed plant in Burbank as an assemblyman in the electrical systems section of the plant; Nancy wondered what it would mean for her little family. When FDR declared that the U.S. was entering the war, Bob enlisted leaving Nancy and little Lainie behind to live with his mother.

Newly married and suddenly living with and spending all of her time with her mother-in- law Robina, Nancy sought out some sort of an escape. While Robina was a wonderfully caring woman with a happy heart, it was just too much time together for Nancy. Her own mother had been more of a no-nonsense, gruff type of woman who spoke her mind. Nancy couldn't get used to Robina's level of authentic sweetness every second of every day.

Scanning the newspaper for a part-time job, she found an ad trying to entice women into the workforce at her husband's beloved airplane plant.

They needed riveters and buckers to help assemble the planes as many of their employees had joined the war effort. The aerospace company was providing free training and gave a real opportunity to feel needed. For some it was a way to help out, but for others it was a necessary step towards being able to take care of their families if something should happen to their husbands while away.

Not all of the women had the support system that Nancy had. For her, it was a way to have some freedom and independence from home but it just happened to come with a huge new sense of pride and purpose.

Nancy went to the mass interview and came home with a position. Nancy, or "Nanny" as she preferred to be called, wasn't a tiny woman. Her large frame carried a strength that most men shied away from, but Bob had been able to see through her tougher exterior to her soft and beautiful heart inside. She was similar in physical stature to her mother-in-law; perhaps that had helped the cause.

Nanny asked, and indeed Robina said she would be happy to watch the baby for her so she could go to work. Robina was more than happy to have more of a purpose herself, and spending time with little Lainie was a gift. The new arrangement gave the two of them something else to think about and do besides having them both sitting at home worrying about Bob's safety.

She packed her lunch and drove to the factory. The first day was a whirlwind of activity but it wasn't just the factory floor that was all aflutter. The level of work on the outside of the buildings was matched with the intensity of output coming from the inside of the plant. She remembered it well, hearing the name of the operation finally, well into the war effort: *Operation Camouflage.* She flipped to the page in the scrapbook that showcased the goings on from the pages of the Burbank Chamber of Commerce's *"Community Book."* Each page of the article documented it so well, Nanny could remember each phase as if it were yesterday. It wasn't until much later that Nancy would see how well it had been pulled off from an aerial shot.

Trucks carrying artificial plants and trees were unloaded everywhere, and there were men and women painting large parking lot areas to look like rolling, grassy fields. Tall pillars were set up over the buildings to hold up massive camo netting and canvases that were painted to look like a rural expanse with farmhouses instead of the manufactory.

Artists and designers from the nearby movie studios were recruited to create this ultimate landscape of safety and deceit. The whir of productivity had been mind boggling, and as the "houses" and "farms" came together, a worker was tasked with dressing up to play a dutiful housewife who crossed the "field" twice a day to hang the washing and retrieve the "dry clothes" off of the fake clothing lines later on. All to accomplish the biggest, smartest cover-up Nanny had ever heard of.

It was a time of great uncertainty in the country. No one knew if the enemy would reach American soil. Everyone was on high alert. The planes needed to come off the assembly line on time and complete to be ready for combat.

Nanny was paired up with another woman. Together they would become a team and get used to each other growing more in tune every day. Their teamwork and learned camaraderie was a necessary step.

The riveter held the gun and placed the pop rivets into the panels, and the bucker held still the panels of aluminum, weightily pressing on the surface to ensure the rivets lay flat as they were punched through. Nanny was tasked with bucking. Nanny's partner, a smaller black woman named Albina Jackson, held the riveting role.

Albina had just moved to the area from Texas. She moved to be closer to her son, however as an enlisted man he had been sent away to the battlefields, too.

It was the first time Nanny had been in such close proximity to a black person. Her mother had hired a delightful older woman named Della when Nancy left home to marry Bob, but Nanny wasn't around to develop any kind of relationship with her. When her mother died suddenly, Nancy's brother sold the house and Della disappeared into the folds of another family. Most of her exposure had been in going to watch the local talented singers with Bob on weekends or seeing them on screen.

Nancy was instantly drawn in by Albina's great wide smile and welcoming heart. She was a little older than Nanny as her son was old enough to join the war effort already, but she explained later that she had been an early mother.

"I had my Levi at roundabout thirteen," she had shared.

Albina had worked hard since Levi came. She was no stranger to spilling blood, sweat and tears for a dollar.

Together they learned the job, and worked out their best rhythms. They'd often sit outside together and have lunch under the camo nets, watching all the people buzzing around to make the factory more safe and hidden from enemy view.

Nanny and Albina built a wonderful friendship despite her initial concern of others' judgments or assumptions. These extraordinary times called for everyone to set their opinions down for a spell. Purpose and patriotism trumped the long-outdated social constraints of the time, or at least they had with Nanny. She saw all of the people working together for the good of the country and the war effort but mostly for humanity. It's such a shame it didn't last. After the war, everything had gone back to the divided way it was before.

But not for the two of them. They had a sisterhood: One born out of a happenstance they had little control over, but it was fortuitous in that they both were gifted a lifetime of friendship from it. Nanny and Albina remained friends and had always stayed in touch.

With no other family in town and her son away, Albina would often be invited to the house on their days off. The three women would sit on the porch and talk about motherhood, life, love and the hardships that often turn out okay.

Albina was there to see Lainie take her first steps. Where societally there might not have been a social bond, a deep friendship developed between the senior mother Robina and the younger mother Albina with the two of them both having their sons away in the war. Robina shared that Albina had stayed in touch after the war was over; letters were dated until Robina's death. Those had been lost in the shuffle of moving around as well.

Nanny stared at the black-and-white photo of herself and Albina tucked up next to a fuselage of a plane in the factory in the back of the scrapbook. Nanny could still hear her voice, the way she would yell out, "Shoot!" when she was ready for Nancy to make the last stronghold on the metal sheets before pulling the trigger.

She ran her fingers over the exposed scalloped edges of the photo. Nanny misted up.

Nanny missed her friend so much. The women had worked together for about four years, but their connection was lifelong. Laughing on their best days and crying with each other when the worst ones hit. She felt honored for Albina's presence in her life.

When Albina moved back to Texas to take care of her mother, it was right about when Bob arrived home from the war. The two women kept in touch by letters for the most part and phone calls if it was a special occasion. Nanny kept most of her letters, and she wondered sometimes where her letters to Albina might have gone after she passed.

Albina was there as a sounding board, a safe person to complain to, after Bob came home maimed from the war. He had become a different man than the one she married, and more than just physically. Once patient and kind in his well thought out words, Bob became short- tempered and quiet. Sullen, even. He rarely even smiled in those first ten months at home, even while holding his precious daughter on his lap who was giddy for his attention.

He'd been injured while fighting in France and the doctors had amputated his left leg from the knee down to save him after a barrage of gunfire pitted his limb. Bob was more comfortable using a wheelchair than battling the crutches that were also sent home with him. In the wheelchair he could cover his lap with a blanket saying he was chilled. Without it he couldn't hide the void.

Nanny wasn't allowed to see his stump bare, and any time they lay together in their marital bed, the room had to be pitch black. Intimacy was off the table for years. And even when they started up again the closeness wasn't the same.

It didn't matter to Nanny that Bob had lost part of his leg; what mattered to her was that he shut her out of his grief about it. Holding it all inside, she saw the torture he allowed to fester. If he needed assistance with anything that required him to be bare in his true form, he'd asked his mother and she obliged. Nanny wasn't allowed to help her husband with bathing or other things until Robina passed six years later.

By then, Bob was more comfortable with his impairment and he had been fitted with a prosthetic. He had a limp and a cane but he grew to feel more whole. He had also gone back to work again. In the beginning he started with assembling parts as he could sit down and there was a nice group of other vets who worked together.

After the war ended, Nanny surprisingly found that she just couldn't go back to being a regular housewife. The thrill of her own paycheck and making things happen was too exciting to let go of. She stayed with Lockheed, taking college classes part-time at night to become an electrical engineer when Lainie was sixteen years old. By then Bob had found a new role in Union leadership helping to make sure all employees were given a fair wage and pension payouts upon their retirement.

Nanny crossed the room again and put her coffee in the small microwave of her kitchenette. She'd let her coffee get cold with her wander into the past. The microwave beeped and she retrieved the cup, setting the newly warmed coffee on the table next to her chair. She fumbled further into the box to find the family photo albums.

Her wedding pictures with Bob before his injury; Lainie's baby book and photos through high school. Nancy fumbled with the pages of Lainie's baby book. They were stiff and hard to grab with her often swollen hands. She looked at her fingers, turning her hands over and over to take them in. She rubbed each knuckle in angst.

It was when they lived in Texas that she started noticing her painful joints, mostly in her hands. It was especially bad at night, or upon waking early for the day. At first she passed it off as the downside of the non-stop calculations and the constant use of her hands. Many times a day, she would rub them with mentholatum and those around her became quite used to the smell. It seemed to help; at least in the beginning she thought it would be manageable. That is, until that one weekend just after her forty-fifth birthday, Nanny became very ill.

A fever of 102 for three straight days. Bob was about to take her to the hospital when the fever broke in the night, leaving a mysterious rash on her cheeks in its wake.

Nanny stayed home from work another week, thinking the redness would wane, but it persisted. She tried to cover it over with makeup, but somehow her red cheeks burned through and became a part of her appearance. Some weird virus; eventually it had to pass.

Years later a diagnosis of Lupus stung hard. There was no cure. She would need to take meds to help her with her joints, and be tested regularly to make sure her organs were functioning properly. There were some possible brain effects as well. She might not think as clearly. Heavy steroids were prescribed which added more pounds to her already sturdy stature. It was something she'd have to live with.

Nanny let her hands and the album fall into her lap. Her life wasn't the one she had originally planned when she married Bob, but it was a good one nonetheless. She had done so much more in her life than she ever dreamed.

With marrying at twenty-two, becoming a mother at twenty-three. She was supposed to be at home, ready with a stiff drink in hand for Bob after a hard day at work. She'd make pot roast on Sundays after church, and play canasta with the neighborhood women for a dally out of the stay-at-home monotony. Luckily for her, life made other plans and she had a long and full professional life to look back on.

Nancy closed her eyes. Her mind went to Lainie; she'd give her a call over the weekend. Not surprisingly, Lainie had been inspired by her adult student mother and loved school, finding her purpose professionally in the form of teaching at the highest level.

As a college professor, the role seemed to fit her very well as she was forever curious and able to speak to many different types of people. A later in-life mother, Lainie spent her summers being the great mom she was to her daughter.

Lainie was happily married and living in Chicago, and her daughter was in her last term of high school. A soon to be empty nest. Lainie was contemplating what would come next. Maybe some sort of academic adventure for her upcoming sabbatical. Lainie was toying with writing a book. Maybe some kind of a historical novel, last Nancy heard.

"I wonder," she murmured. A sudden thought. Lainie was probably closer in age to the woman who wrote the "Find Me" book. The references she made were more in line with Lainie's experiences.

Nanny hoped that the book wouldn't get stuck here in the retirement home. It needed to go beyond these walls.

If she thought about her own set of initials of the people who had helped her become who she was, all of them were long gone. Those people would never read any excerpts about them in her sharing what each had meant to her. But writing about those people might be a wonderful exercise in helping tell the story to her grandchildren one day. As well as revisit those great times herself.

Nanny drank the last few sips of her coffee, and ran her finger over the spiral coil of the little blue Find Me book next to her. She thanked it for coming into her life and reminding her of the *extraordinary* life she had lived.

A great big life that she had earned with her courage to go beyond the typical blueprint of what was expected at that time in history and of her gender as well. She'd never forget it again.

Nanny committed then and there to write her own memoir. She would dictate it into her tape recorder and have it transcribed by a service. Typing was too difficult now.

Her life had collided with some pretty epic parts of American history. She'd showcase her experience building planes for the U.S. for sure, but it was her friendship with Albina that had made the biggest mark on her life.

Their friendship was extraordinary. Honorary sisters.

Two women who might never have met if the world hadn't caught fire and needed them both.

~

I Needed that Feeling, Me 2005

My secretive, lovesick messages to Mr. Affair didn't stop; if anything there was more of a frenzy to figure out how to be together. Someone used the word "love" and it was embraced by us both.

As I foolishly continued to participate in the delusion of needing to find a lifetime of love with this man, I also wanted to ask him:

"As one who has pledged to supply spiritual nutrition for others, what would you say to a couple of people in our situation? Would you tell them to turn their backs on their marriages and families? Would you encourage them to linger outside their vows and lie to the people they say they care about?

I don't know his situation, but I know mine. My life ceased to be just my life when I had my daughters. I am now their mother, and they need me. My husband says he loves me and I believe he does as much as he is able to. Now I have him in my heart and everything is crazy.

Mr. Stability once joked that he would take the girls away from me if we split. That I would be very alone in my life after him. Without my girls I would die.

Where was Mr. Affair in all this? If his wife gave in and they were able to move, would that turn his relationship around? Would that fix it? He must love her some, or he would have left her already.

In my wait, I see nothing but problems.

I am not doing well. My fitful and sleepless nights filled with questions are wearing on me. We really have nothing to give each other, other than this mysterious mutual feeling. The words and promises that we shared which are not enough to actually make a life.

Today, I looked into my children's eyes and thought of all the lies I'd been telling, the hoops I was jumping through to keep the idea of this romance going. How can I do this to them? To my husband? I've never thought of chucking it all to be with anyone but him.

His babies are small, and they need him to love their mommy. His boys need him to teach them how to be good men. Being with me will not help.

Our notes are scripted, each one scrutinized by ourselves before hitting "send." We only show what we want to show.

I may love him, but do I really know him?

What are his favorite foods or what soap does he use? What does he watch on TV? Is he a baby when he's sick? What does he like to do?

Truth is, he can't take me into his arms and promise me forever. He can't offer me the moon. The feelings that we have are based on our past and the Romeo and Juliet notes of the now are all we really have.

He is bound to another, as am I. We are disrespecting our partners as much as ourselves.

Once we talked of morals in one of our moments and currently we are both stepping all over them, stomping them into the mud.

My heart hurts at the thought of letting him go, but I am not sleeping, giving or living to my potential.

It's like a merry-go-round going so fast, one can't get off. Up and down, around and around, it is ripping me to shreds.

This is not who I thought I was.

Or at least not who I want to be.

~

~2~

Hazel Jacobs knew better than to sit around waiting for something to happen.

It was lunch service a few days after the Bonita Butterfly book meeting, and Hazel was joyful to see each of them come through the line. Many of them winked at her with the little secret they all shared.

Hazel asked each of them to meet her after lunch in the library. She wanted to share her idea that had come to her the night before. She was counting on the idea to give her a leg up in her chances with the general manager at her interview for the position later that day. All of the Bonita Butterflies were happy to help.

Hazel finished up the dishes from lunch and went on a break, walking over to the facilities library. Each of the women were gathered as they had the day before, all in a circle, ready for Hazel, but they weren't sure why.

Hazel hugged each one, then sat to address the group.

"First, I want to thank you for letting me be a part of your group last night. I was beyond honored to read that book to you all and especially appreciative to hear the stories that you were inspired to share." The Butterflies all nodded and smiled at each other while Adelma squeezed Hazel's hand in response.

"I recently applied to be the Activities Coordinator here at Sunny Days and I would love to run an idea by you all to see if it might be something that you think the residents would like."

"Sure."

"Of course."

"We'd love that." All gave positive remarks.

"Anything for you, Hazel," Adelma said.

"If I get the job, I want to start a Sunny Days newspaper, one where every resident will be spotlighted. It will give us all a chance to hear more about each person's life and story. You have all had such marvelous lives, it's a shame not to know that about each other. I'm envisioning a monthly newspaper, and I will need some reporters." Hazel held up her fingers in quotation marks around the word *reporters*. She went on. "Each reporter will be given a voice recorder to interview a resident, and I will do the transcriptions and edit them down in order to fit each section. I have transcribing skills from my time as a court reporter."

"Wow, you've done that? So interesting! We will need a story about you too, Hazel," said Valerie.

"That's a great idea. We can highlight some of the employees in it, too. I think this will be a great way to connect people more, give us all some new things to talk about. Great!" Hazel clapped her hands in victory.

The Bonita Butterflies all volunteered to be reporters for the *Sunny Days Gazette* as they unanimously named it, once Hazel got it approved by management.

"I should be able to print the copies in the office and hand deliver them to each door when the time comes or hand them out at the cafeteria; I'll figure it out."

All were very excited to have a new project. The idea of sharing memories had been spurred on by the book.

Hazel hugged everyone again and left to go change her clothes for her interview. The Butterflies wished her luck. They all stayed and visited with each other some more.

"Girls," said Saffron, "We need to get this book around a little more to see if someone might recognize themselves in the story, you know, help the author with her mission after all. I say we leave it here in the library for more of the residents to find. Maybe Hazel can make a flier or something to highlight it for people who come in?"

"That's a great idea. Let's start a buzz," said Nanny.

"How very exciting! So many things to be inspired about right now. I wonder how they will pick the people to showcase in the newspaper?"

"Yeah, I was wondering the same thing. Maybe there will be a raffle or something. Hazel has probably figured it out already."

The women giggled and gasped as even more stories were shared.

Across the building on the top floor, Hazel readied herself for her interview.

The door opened and the director popped her head out, "Hazel, I am so glad you are here, let's talk about this position. Come in and have a seat."

Hazel came in and pulled her glasses off her face to clean them on her skirt before starting. She placed them back on her head and all was in focus.

"Thanks, Ms. Rhodes. I am excited to speak with you about this opportunity."

"I see you are well liked by all of the residents. I am sorry it took so long for us to get you in to talk about it. We were waiting on next year's budget numbers to determine if we could pay more than the previous coordinator and, as it turns out, we can."

Hazel felt warm with possibility.

"I feel like you would be an excellent coordinator: you have so much experience with the residents and I really can't think of anything that would keep me from hiring you right on the spot. Do you have anything you would like to share with me? Questions? Concerns?"

Hazel looked dumbfounded; this was the easiest interview she had ever been through. Ms. Rhodes hadn't asked her any questions at all. Her work and commitment to this place stood for itself.

"Wow, I am thrilled to take the position. In fact I have many ideas that I would love to implement. I'd love to share one idea that has been kicking around in my head the last couple of days."

"Let's hear it."

"I would like to start a newspaper where we highlight the lives of the residents and can help celebrate some of the marvelous people we have here at Sunny Days. How many stories are locked inside the walls of this building? We just need to know the right questions to ask to unlock the memories hidden inside. These people are so much more than just bygone beings and the medications they take. These people deserve more than just keeping up with the instructions to help them live another day. We need to celebrate them. In sharing their histories we might just build a bridge to togetherness and foster new friendships, especially with the ones that feel alone or left behind."

Ms. Rhodes put her hand out to shake Hazel's.

"Hazel, you have got the job. I am thrilled to help you in any way with this new project; just ask. This is exactly the kind of thinking our wonderful residents need. They deserve to be celebrated and loved and not feel like they were just put here out of convenience. I am beyond excited. Welcome to management."

Ms. Rhodes came around the desk and shook her hand again, placing a hand on her shoulder.

"I will make Sunny Days proud," said Hazel tearing up.

"You already do Hazel, you already do."

~

V.T.

You were my freshman high school gym teacher. I have to say here that I must have spent the majority of my life up until then completely oblivious as to other people's experience around me. Off in my own little world. Only being able to look out through those two holes placed in the middle of my face. I never wondered what it was like to be anyone else, or had a notion that everyone around me was different than I was.

I had no clue. I had managed to skip the majority of gym classes or at least hardly ever dressed down to do gym until this year. I always had my period or I was sick. I am not sure how I managed to dodge P.E. like I did in middle school.

High school was different. We had to wear our school t-shirts and shorts and were required to take a shower with everyone else sometimes. I hated that.

Anyway, you were super nice and smart and fit and I thought you might match my Dad's criteria for a cute girlfriend. I went up to you on the last day of school and asked if you might want to go out with him.

You smiled a little bit, and said no thank you in the most polite way. Later on I was told by someone else my own age that you were gay.

Everyone knew, she explained, *"You can tell. Duh."*

"What? You can?" I asked, stupefied. Well, I definitely couldn't.

I didn't really know what to look for in someone who was gay; they didn't dress any differently, they didn't act differently, or treat *me* any differently.

This gay thing was a total mystery. They didn't wear a button or have a secret handshake for me to notice in my people-watching. With that revelation came more unanswerable questions.

How do gay people know how to find other gay people to love and hang out with?

"Gaydar" was a word that I heard years and years later, and man I am happy they have that gift, so they can find each other and find love.

Otherwise they would spend more time having to push off the advances of dumb little kids trying to set them up with their divorced parents.

I really felt like such a dork around you after that. Dad was going to have to find his own dates from then on; I wouldn't risk having that kind of conversation again.

Hope it gave you a little bit of a chuckle that day, and thanks for not being weird about it.

~

Can't Keep Doing This, Me 2005

I've been keeping it all to myself, until now. So much has gone on. I saw the counselor today and he encouraged me- no, told me- to either stay in and work it out with my husband, or get out now. No more indecision, no more back and forth, no more straddling the fence.

Then to my shock, he walked me down to the lawyers office down the hall, plopped me in a chair with the legal man there in front of me and said, "Decide."

He knew me. He'd listened to me all these years. He had my back story. He knew my insecurities, my wishes, my wants. All the details of our marriage and my many complaints in this relationship. Maybe he knew me better than I knew myself, and if he thought that I should get out, it must be the right answer.

Or maybe he was just tired of listening to me go on and on about things that would never change, or maybe he was trying to get me to stop yanking around my husband. I will never know.

I brought home a business card and a plan.

It was up to me now.

I initially believed I would like to stay in the house. I hope to be able to keep it up if I cut down on my purchases. I have told my parents of my intent.

Queasiness hits and stays. I have nearly stopped eating. Today I ate a frozen burrito. I ate the whole thing which was probably the most I had eaten at one time in a week.

This was not something I was taking lightly. So many people would be affected. I never wanted to get a divorce!

I wanted to live with my husband for our whole lives and be happy, healthy, be able to travel, and go on adventures together. Keep intact this little family that we made.

But this man from my past made me feel things I've never felt. I see possibilities of a new life with him which could be much bigger, maybe, than my current one.

What if this is my chance? Maybe he is my soulmate? We have carried a flicker for each other all these years- what if he is it?

And it's complicated, and messy, and not the way it should be done. Not at all.

He is married, and so am I.

I am trying my best to untangle, but I am not sure if he has told his wife as he promised.

I was moving towards our future and had yet to see any movement from him towards our plan.

I am still pondering what to do as a profession, and with this break, I will be losing my runway of time to figure it out. I feel as though I am jumping off a bridge, hoping the bank is close enough to swim back to the shore.

I have confided to a few friends that I am leaving. One friend is on vacation and will be shocked at the news when she gets home.

My primary focus is the girls. They have friends over today, a day of playing with something else to keep them occupied. Youngest seems more questioning than Oldest. I don't think they really conceive of it all. Or what it will mean.

I want to make this as easy as I can. They will be the first of their friends to have divorced parents, just like I had. Am I destroying their lives in an attempt to live mine?

I sat with Youngest as she got ready to go to sleep. At six, she is my wise old soul, enlightened way beyond her years.

She said, "Why do you want a divorce, Mommy? Remember when Daddy took care of you when you broke your arm? He loves you, remember?"

"Yes, I remember." Tears welled in my eyes.

I remembered how he had taken care of me. Driving me to the hospital the night of the accident, sitting with me the next day as I panicked hysterically before surgery. Being there when I woke up. He had been there. He really had, for everything, every single time. But was being there in the hard spots enough to last a lifetime? Was being there for someone, and even loving them enough to live a whole life together, when you had stopped growing together, and settled into a humdrum pit of everyday life with no hope of it ever changing?

"So, Mommy, you and Daddy should just be together," she said, holding my face in her sweet little hands, looking at me deeply with her still bright, blue eyes.

By now, tears were streaming. I didn't want to let her down, I didn't want to break her little heart or upset her precious, innocent life. Inside, I wished I could go back. Take it all back, be what I used to be for her. I wish I hadn't met with Mr. Affair. Or spent any time with him. I wish I could have appreciated what I had before it was too late.

But now, we were all on a trajectory. I see no way to patch up this mess that I have made. To try may just prolong the inevitable, making it even harder or possibly uglier for all of us.

As my head spun with what to say, the words finally came.

I spoke to my wise little cherub in the best way I could, describing my feelings in a language she might understand.

"What if staying with Daddy meant that Mommy wouldn't be happy anymore?"

Her little eyes glistened as she looked up at me, and she said from the sages of the ages- I Swear to God, "Well, that wouldn't be good, Mommy; you need to be happy, too."

I didn't want to hurt my kids, I didn't want to upset everything that they knew and could count on, but I didn't know what else to do. This is the one and only life I get. I had to live the best life I could. To take a chance on being happy. This is it. There are no do-overs.

I laid with her until she fell asleep, then I kissed her goodnight and took all of my burdensome thoughts with me down the hall.

Her whole world was about to turn upside down, as was all of ours, but she was little and didn't deserve any of this. I will take the sadness of that moment to the grave no matter what else comes out of this. I never wanted it to be this way.

Hub seems willing to cooperate. His anger last night was short-lived. I was thankful that my neighbor had our daughters come spend the night. We needed to talk.

He has kept the news of our separation to himself, from what I can tell.

He doesn't have the support system that I do. My friends seem supportive and non-judgmental so far. My next door neighbor sat with me, and cried along with me, saying she really didn't know how unhappy I was.

"One never knows what is from behind others' closed doors," she said.

I feel surprisingly calm today after the emotional storm last night. I'm no longer hiding anything. Everything is out of the open on my side, things are moving.

Hubby says he hopes I know what I am doing.

So do I.

By God, so do I.

I had stood at the crossroads. A known and easier life to the left of me, total uncertainty to the right.

I knew all that my old life contained. Times when I wanted to scream.

Things I'd want to try and be told no. The boredom of the same places, foods and days. No promise or hope that it would ever expand.

But I had security and a roof over my head. Stability. Protection for my daughters-our daughters- a shielding to life's most bothersome issues. Money problems, being the weightiest one.

I knew what I had in that life, but over time, it still wasn't enough.

My dreams count. My soul needs space to soar. I need to be able to grow with my partner and work through our challenges and dream together. Working towards something, growing into our best selves with each other. Only that kind of love can last a lifetime, I imagine.

I look back sometimes at the fork in the road, and wonder if I might have been able to turn back.

What would've happened if I said, "I take it all back," and can I move back home?

Restart, renew, find a new arrangement together? Could I build back to the same place and trust that I used to have?

The counselor had convinced me not to sit on the fence anymore.

"I either want you in, or I want you out. No more complaining about the middle. You need to move off of this place."

I couldn't have both: a half husband at home and in my bed; and a half lover who I confided in and professed love to, over the internet lines. It wasn't fair to anyone. Least of all my husband.

The counselor had walked me down the hall to the divorce attorney in his building and sat me in a chair in front of him.

"Decide," he said with no understanding, no hand holding.

I am sure it was about the shock factor, to see what I would do when a step was there to take. If he gave me the easy option, would it scare the infidelity out of me? Or maybe he was just tired of listening to me. Maybe he wanted me to stop yanking around my husband? Each and every one, all valid reasons.

Whatever his plan, it gave me more of a nod of certainty to take that path. I deemed it almost his blessing; that it was, in his opinion, the right thing to do.

Into the unknown I go.

~

Heart Finder, Me 2005

R ight about the time that I was contemplating blowing up my life on a chance at a new love something else came into my world.

Something that would become my compass in life. Two leaves on my beautyberry plant were chewed by insects into a perfect heart shape. They sat on a single branch at the top of the bush, and teased me with what they meant. I snapped a photo and printed it out.

Was it a sign that I had all I needed at home already and that I just had to try harder? Or was it a sign that I needed to move on?

Hearts would become my guiding talisman from this time forward. If I am on track, I will see them constantly. If they are away from me for too long, I know I need to change course.

The heart: Symbol of love itself.

Think of the classic heart. Two perfect lobes coming together at the bottom forming a seamless union. It is the thing we all search for. Two coming together as one.

When one of the lobes is larger than the other, the effort is uneven. One is working harder, one is slacking. This happens so often in life and love.

People stay together, sometimes because you just do. It's hard to break the heart.

When one is holding more than their fair share of the love together, they eventually get tired. They wonder. They resent.

That lobe gets smaller and smaller, and the other fights by giving more. Trying to hold the shape.

But that is unsustainable. Destined to unfurl.

We search for the perfect other half. And for some it doesn't come. And for others, many come but still fail to fill the most important role: One of loving ourselves.

So we keep searching for our missing half. The one that completes us. Love itself needs another.

~

~2~

Saffron

S affron was excited to read the little blue book one more time before it moved on to the next Butterfly. She loved that their little group was named after a butterfly as all of these women had transformed themselves over and over in their lifetimes. She had a special bond with the insect including a quote she might share with the group someday.

Standing in her kitchen, she started the kettle for some tea. It boiled up and whistled and she doused her tea bag, leaving it to steep for the recommended four minutes. The aroma wafted into her nose and she was reminded of her mother. Orange spice. It was one of the only scents that she could still recall of her.

She pulled a vintage, amber-colored Blenko glass ashtray out of the dishwasher and carried it over to be used when she settled in. The decorative dish had never been tainted with ashes, at least not by her, but it was perfect to hold her spent tea bags. Saff's space was full of mementos from her antique collector mother, even though she had died more than thirty years ago.

She sat down in another one of her mother's treasured pieces: A wonderful cane-backed regency style chair. The chair had held a prominent place in her family's front living room. Back then it had the 1970s traditional look of a dark brown cane accented with a colorful velvet cushion. After inheriting the chair, she quickly painted the wood parts a coal black while keeping the burnt orange seat, a nod to her treasured Minneapolis Twins baseball team.

Baseball was a huge part of her childhood. The very first game she went to with her Dad was to watch the local professional women's team the Millerettes play against the Rockford, Illinois Peaches.

At seven years old, that game and seeing all of those women play together impressed upon her the power of women working at something together. As a youngster, she dreamed that she would have been able to play on that team when she got older, but sadly the Millerettes only lasted one season before moving to Indiana.

With them gone, she and Dad switched to watching the Twins baseball team anytime they had a home game. So many Saturdays spent sitting together in the same seats behind the fence on the first base line, eating Cracker Jacks until they felt sick. Afterwards they'd forget that crummy feeling, and overindulge all over again at the next game.

"The more you eat, the more you want," Bronwyn chuckled, "it's their slogan for a reason."

When her Mom died, she and her Dad grew even closer in their shared loss. The two of them liked the same things. Saff, a self-professed tomboy, would often follow her Dad into the garage when he was working on his old cars. They'd come back into the house so greasy and worn out, they'd go to the cafe in town for burgers and milkshakes. Any kind of tinkering Dad did, Saff was there to help him.

Hard work and using her hands came easily for her. She learned how to lay tile in her late thirties and had become quite the artisan. The general contractors loved to hire her as they knew she would do an incredible job for them. Seeking perfection, she saw every flaw in the work of others who didn't care quite as much.

As Dad got older she stayed close by, and together they built a smallish, A-frame house for Saffron to live in on the family's property.

Interested in recycling before it caught on, Saffron would take home the tile offcuts from her jobs to embellish and beautify her spaces. The house was homemade from stem to stern.

Together with her father they had poured the slab foundation over a weekend. Hustling from daybreak to dawn the two used two wheelbarrows to move the concrete into place. Each 2 x 6 was hammered into place as one struck the nail and the other held it.

Saff accented the floors and walls with her colorful broken tile mosaics and wood circles cut from the tree branches fallen from the clearing of the area. Old barn boards were used to wrap the lackluster 4 x 4 rafters. Stones from the property were also utilized to fully customize the space to her delight.

The antique wood stove from her grandparents' house was backed with a beautiful array of different shades of marble stone pieces which she painstakingly installed to look like the sun's rays coming up over a mountain ridge. It was the first home that Saffron ever really felt truly comfortable in as it was uniquely her.

She lived in the A-frame alone all through her forties and fifties, but after her father passed just after her sixtieth birthday, she moved into the main house and sought out a roommate or renter to break up the everyday quiet. After the three ads placed in the local paper expired, Saff had given up on the idea when fate stepped in with the pursuit.

Bronwyn appeared at just the right time. They literally bumped into each other in the women's studies section of the local bookstore. Saffron had always been interested in women's rights and had stayed single all of her life so she wouldn't be dependent on any man. Her mother had advised her to be selective because she shouldn't be stuck at home with the whole world teasing her to see.

The two struck up a conversation and Bronwyn just happened to be looking for a new place to live as her rented cabin was going up for sale. She was getting desperate but believed an answer would come.

Bronwyn had lived all over the world, and earned her wages as a travel writer before settling down in Minnesota full time in the late nineties.

"I've got a place," Saff offered as Bronwyn shared more.

Brought to Minnesota by the state's visitors bureau for a job, Bronwyn soon became enchanted by the state's beauty. It's unreal fall colors, the plethora of lakes to explore and its friendly people. She never regretted planting some roots in this place, even though she fondly remembered her vagabond days. Bronwyn beamed good energy at the bookstore; maybe that is why Saffron struck up the conversation.

Within the week Saffron had helped Bronwyn move into the artistic A-frame and both of them were happy to keep each other company out on the farm. Bronwyn was in her middle seventies when she moved onto Saffron's property; Saff was sixty-two.

An easy bond started developing between them, something that Saffron had never felt before. It wasn't long before they were sharing meals, talking and laughing together more often than not. They were just across the yard from each other after all.

Romantically, Saffron had always felt more on the neutral side, mostly disinterested in the traditional act of sex really, and she had never had a lover. Any rare zeal in her loins had been easily taken care of by herself, and the impetus of such urges hadn't shared a common thread. She was a bit of a loner and didn't let people get that close to her to avoid having difficult conversations about why things didn't progress.

In her younger years, her relationship avoidance was more out of the fear of losing her independence- a fear driven home by her mother- but as time went by, she realized she had a true ambivalence towards men as a species in general. Except for Dad- he had been different- but there weren't many like him.

In contrast, Bronywn had married in her twenties, and had birthed a daughter who stayed in France to live with her father. They had split when she was thirty.

Bronwyn moved back to the States then, leaving her daughter in the capable and responsible hands of her ex. She knew she would be on the move most of the time and wanted her daughter to have the stability of one home she could call her own. Mother and daughter spoke on the phone pretty regularly in her childhood but the phone visits had lessened to once a month by the time Saffron entered the scene.

Months went by and the women found themselves falling asleep together on the two sofas after staying up all night talking about the dreams they still held in their hearts despite their ages. Coffee together each morning, they took turns hosting.

They'd sit together on those cold, cold evenings, tucked under quilts and drinking hot cocoa to wile away the drawn-out winter days. Falling asleep where they were because the distance to the other's respective house was a little bit too far to trek in the dark and freezing cold night air. The many heartfelt discussions that led to the idea that would become the mission.

Bronny had summed it up perfectly, "Life has as many stormy days as it does sunny ones. What happens when they happen together? A rainbow. Let's make a rainbow to decorate the farm."

They spent most of that early spring planting tubers for their planned design. It was the hard labor after the dreamy hours spent ogling over flower catalogs that winter.

Saffron never knew who it was that initiated their first kiss, but she remembered the exact spot, date and time. How the sun felt on her skin and what scents were prominent in the air.

It was summer and the dahlias were finally in full bloom. Giant saucer-like plates of loveliness. All of the blooms seemed to pop at once, and the women deemed it time to see if their concept had worked. They would only look at the garden from above together. Saffron and Bronwyn opened up the blinds and closed their eyes. Holding hands, they stepped out onto the deck of the A-frame. They squealed with excitement and started a countdown to look together.

From there they could see their whole dahlia patch. Countless blooms showed back their brilliance. They could see the layers, the distinct arches of each color were as close as they could get to a rainbow bursting with life. Their plan had worked!

Smiles and joy took over their faces and they embraced. Upon letting go, their eyes met and they both leaned in closer, suddenly taken in by a passionate kiss. One that left them both happy but mildly confused at the same time.

Saff remembered back to the passionate hours after that first kiss. How they had wandered back into the A-frame bedroom to lie down and hold each other, clothes falling as they went. They lay exploring each other, the ceiling fan cooling every patch of exposed skin despite the summer heat. Somehow Bronwyn knew the right places to touch to make Saffron feel things she'd never felt before. She wondered how Bronny knew, how was she so adept in tantalizing a woman's body despite her countless years of being with men.

Their mutual contentment fell into a comfortable conversation about just that.

"I had a wonderful yet horrible teacher," Bronwyn said matter of factly.

She got up, tucked the dusty-blue sheet around her and pulled a book from her chock-full bookcase. Several old cloth-bound books fell to take up the gap. It was from Bronwyn's collection of George Sand books. She placed the stale but decorative book next to Saffron, and climbed in next to her under the sheet.

"A memento. It was when I was in France for the first time. I spent a summer as a grad student studying the multi-passionate author George Sand. "George Sand" was a pen name chosen by Amantine Lucile Aurore Dupin de Francueil. She was an outwardly colorful character completely unapologetic for who she was. She dressed in men's clothes and smoked in public which was damn near illegal back then. She married men and seduced women and lived as large as one could in her time. She advocated for women's rights through use of her pen. I always wondered if she chose the name of George Sand to make it easier to pass as a man in the publishing realm as they say she did, or because her name was so stinking long it wouldn't have fit on the spine of a book. Anyway, she was a 19th century French journalist, novelist, and activist. She felt like a good study subject for my Master's project. So that's why I was there originally."

They both stared up at the monarch butterfly that had flown serendipitously in through the open door. It danced over them and wafted out the way it came in.

Bronywn recited from memory: "'*Butterflies are but flowers that blew away one sunny day when Nature was feeling at her most inventive and fertile.' ~ George Sands*. This book is signed by the author," she cracked it open to show a firm yet flowy autograph.

"The book is super old and in French. It was a gift from a young teacher's assistant I met that summer. Mirabella was from the small village in France where the famous author grew up. She had spent one summer working at the author's museum. Mirabella was as beautiful as she was smart, and even though her French was flawless, she could break into a pretty decent and laughable American accent if she wanted to. She was friendly with us all and about the same age, just two years older than most of us. We'd hang out and she took us to all the hippest places in ol' Pah-ree." Bronnie swept the air with her hand as she flourished into the French pronunciation of the city.

"As the other students went back to school, I extended my visit. Mira had a fortnight before she had to be back in Paris and she wanted me to go home with her, to experience the museum and walk the dwellings of historic relevance to Sands. I stayed with her family and slept in her room, feeling our friendship was an added bonus to the trip. Each night she would fall into a deep but scarily restless sleep that had her thrashing wildly in the bed we shared. I would reach for her to calm her and she responded with violent wailing words heavy in old French, her eyes spellbound and fiery but she didn't seem present. In the morning, she had no recollection of the event and her parents kept extra quiet when I mentioned it to them out of concern. The third night with similar moments, I again tried to soothe her but this time she reached for me. She pulled me close and planted her lips on mine. At first I was shocked and tried to pull away but she clutched me closer. I found my stomach swirling with want. Something was there, something I knew I needed to explore."

"So what happened with you two? How come you married Pierre? What happened to Mirabella? It doesn't make sense."

"Each night was the same after that: more and more passionate sessions in the dark, with her treating me like any old friend when she awoke the next day. It was the strangest thing. Days before I was set to leave, I pressed her about our nightly romps. I begged to know where we stood, if I should stay, or what it all meant. She got angry- angry like those first few nights when she'd shouted crazed words at me. Again the words came so fast and garbled together I didn't have a chance to remember what each word was to look up later. She claimed the coitus never happened, that I was calling her *détraqué* (deranged) as she threw her hands in the air and stomped around yelling at me in front of everyone in the square."

"Geez, that's bizarre."

"Yes, she was amazing as a lover but it was so upsetting to have her forget everything about being with me. When she calmed some, she cursed at me and threatened that if I told anyone she would make sure I failed the class. The entire trip would be nothing but a stain on my higher education career. She was a stoic monster the rest of the night and told me to sleep on the couch downstairs. I left before she woke up. On the train, I grew hungry and dug into my backpack for my last candy bar and I felt this book. Inside was a note."

Bronwyn pulled an aged slip of paper from the front section of the book and read the French words to her lover, transcribing them as she read. She'd had plenty of practice at rehashing the words.

"Maybe the spirit of the great enigma George Sands took me over as I lay with you. If I did want you, it was hidden away from me in my waking hours. If what we did is true, I can only hope that you will forgive me. No matter what, we mustn't see each other again. I am promised to another. For your trouble, I offer this gift: I stole this book from the museum: perhaps the book is haunted, and the great Madame had possessed me? Her desires being met through me in revenge for stealing it. Keep it- most likely, it will never be missed.~ *dans la confusion* or in confusion, Mirabella"

"That is the strangest story of getting together I have ever heard. What happened to her?"

"She married later that year, a guy who worked at the college. Another student I stayed in touch with told me. She obviously never looked back.

I spent the next six months wondering who I was or what I was. Was I a lesbian? Bisexual? I guess I settled there for a while, in my head anyway. And that felt right, but since I was so rattled by the Mirabella experience, I fell for the first nice guy that came along. That was Pierre, and everything was easier for a while until it wasn't and I have remained mostly alone since, out of fear of being rejected. But you, you opened me up again, my dear Saff, and I am mighty glad you did."

As they lay next to each other, skin to skin, hair tangled together, they knew that this connection would require some more investigation, but they were both up for the task.

Hours passed and hunger pangs hit. They walked hand in hand down the stairs to chef-up a lovely dinner of fresh caught trout, green beans and rice. Something magical was afoot.

~

Looking For Direction, Me, 2005

Yesterday, I believed I had all the answers. Today I am not so sure. I still wonder sometimes if I could have just pushed along at the same rate and speed I had been going for the last twelve and a half years. Maybe there wasn't any more than that?

Maybe I had all that I am supposed to have and am already all that I am supposed to be. I have to know. Is free will really that big of a benefit?

It would be nice if life came with an instruction manual.

The best spouse for you is________.

Have this many children______.

This job is most suitable for you__________.

You will need to take this course of action at age________.

You will die at_______.

Make sure you spend at least one summer in ________ before then.

I sit looking at the picture of my family. Not the one I was born into but the one I helped make. That we made together.

I imagine a giant set of tongs reaching into the picture and plucking him away. I wait for my feelings about it.

I feel mostly sorry for my sweet girls.

I remember what it was like to be so mad at my Dad for leaving. Someday they might feel that way about me. Then five years later my Mom had told me she had asked him to go. It wasn't his idea. He didn't want to leave us but was given no other choice. Similar to what I am doing now.

I ask myself,

Could he change enough so that I can love him again? Do I even have the right to ask him to change or be different than he is? Could I learn to love him exactly as he is and not for who I think he could be?

Will we be able to live in the same house until I get situated elsewhere? A job, finding a place to stay? These questions, while expected, do not help with my confusion.

I am only in the beginning stages of this separation, and find it interesting that with all the talking about what my passion might be for a profession and how I should fight for it so he knows I am serious, the first thing I am passionate about is a divorce.

For a long time I didn't think I would be able to stand the label.

Divorcee.

I'm about to find out what it feels like.

~

$$\sim 2 \sim$$

A tear fell from Saffron's face and splashed into her tea. Her eyes were blurry with the remembrance of that day. All those amazing moments with her Bronny.

God, she missed her. They hadn't had enough time together. Not at all.

The summer of the kiss was the beginning of their romantic relationship. It was a whole new wonderful world for Saff. They leaned into being together and never looked back. They didn't try to explain it to anyone, and they didn't need to. Neither had felt this way before.

Over their ten wonderful years together on the farm, they invited more women to come and stay; setting up smaller RVs and mini cabins for anyone who might need a friend, a support system to escape abuse, or anyone wishing to leave the rat race.

They renamed the place "Rainbow Farm" and developed programs where young people could learn farming techniques and animal husbandry. The flower fields became a great income producer as well as a beautiful tourist attraction in the summers. Together they grew veggies, flowers, and Saffron built rainbow-shaped birdhouses which they sold in their barn store. The winters were about tucking in and working on the relationships and growth of whomever was living at the farm at the time. People came from all over to spend time with the amazing Rainbow Brood. Life couldn't have been more wonderful.

They knew the two of them couldn't keep the Rainbow farm up by themselves forever, so they had started the process of selling it to two of the current tenants. The sales agreement would give them enough money for her and Bronwyn to buy a large RV, and they would continue to be owners until the farm was fully paid for. The monthly installments of thirty percent of the gross sales would allow the tenants to build equity and have a living and the original "Rainbow Girls" could retire and travel the U.S. together. That had been the plan anyway.

~

Finally Moved Out, Me, 2005

I *haven't written for a while. So much has happened. I have been wandering and trying to find my path. I found an apartment for the girls and myself, and we have settled in with our personal taste all around us. Scouring online ads for furniture pieces and a set of bunk beds for the girls, I tried to make it feel like a home. We've named it the "Ladies' Lounge."*

I can feel myself growing. Granted, the divorce settlement has cushioned the blow and lessened my overall worry about everything financial, at least for the moment.

Even with the runway, I am on my own for the first time in my life, and I have to tell myself daily that everything will be okay. There are days when I feel powerful and hopeful for the future, then days where I am so painfully lonely I can hardly move.

*It is the quiet that is most unsettling. Even back then in my old life, if the girls were at school I would have a phone call or leave the TV on and hear in the background the washing machine whirring. There isn't the same amount of chores, living here by myself at least half of the time. The phone **never** rings. I have evaporated from the place I once belonged.*

I still can't believe how quiet the space is when the girls are away. They leave to go to their Dad's and the door would shut and I would stand still and just listen. Nothing. No sound at all.

I walk the rooms, and, unless I am talking to myself or if the TV is on, it is as quiet as a person sitting in a pitch black cave is dark.

It is in those moments where things really sink in for me.

"What have I done? What will I do?"

"What the hell was the point of any of this?"

I no longer have the husband, my garden or the beautiful house. I have less. Less time with my kids, less money, less security, less certainty, less people and less peace.

When I would try to venture back into my old life to spend time with friends, it felt wrong. And I didn't have any single friends. I tried to participate with the women from the old neighborhood. Going to birthday break-

fasts or playing Bunco with them, knowing my apartment wouldn't hold the group once my turn came around.

One birthday breakfast that I had dragged myself to in hopes of feeling a little bit more like the old me, a dear one locked into my eyes from across the table filled with many of the women I knew, mostly still stay-at-home moms.

I saw and felt the concern in her stare, the sadness, as she silently mouthed the words in my direction: "Come back," as if it was still possible.

My response was a smile before mouthing these words back to her: "I can't go back, I can only go forward."

Words, so perfectly stated, with no plan or forethought; words to this day I had never said before or since. She smiled, understanding, still with a sadness I felt from the other side of the table. I'll never forget it. She cared but I would be out of reach soon.

I just didn't fit in the land of stay-at-home mom's anymore.

I had a job. I had another residence, somewhere else that they would have to drive to. Our times together got less and less. Conversations grew even more awkward as I started to date.

Life seemed settled and then there was an upset. Change happens regardless of whether you are ready or not, or want it or not.

Expecting things to stay static is like expecting your face to stay flawless all through your life, or trying to keep your children small, or even fighting one's eventual slip into death.

It's how one deals with or embraces the changes that come up that carries the grit of our real success stories.

Once upon a time, a little girl's parents pulled her into the living room where they sat her down and told her they were getting a divorce. The little girl sat for a moment and started to cry, then screamed "NO!" and ran outside to find her bike. Jumping on, she raced around the circle where they lived, riding around and around until she was so tired, she finally fell off her mount.

That little girl vowed at that moment that she would <u>NEVER</u> get a divorce and break up <u>her</u> family when she grew up. A proclamation without any life experience at all.

Having broken the promise that I made to my little girl self all those years ago, I sit with the fallout. Self blame, loathing and inward anger have all become the strange companions that walk with me into this new chapter.

I know I could have done better by him.

Did I fall in love with him out of need, security and my huge yearning to be a mother?

I did love him.

Countless people share the same wish of having one partner for life. But to have that you must have two willing parties, working together. Sometimes that is not the case.

Sometimes the necessary growth comes from leaving the other person behind and venturing forward into the unknown by yourself. Seeking not only the new that is wanted, but seizing our own energy to build the new life to come.

I speak from experience. This is my story. I have written it down here. Others have lived it just the same or similar, I'm sure.

We are all on some sort of a quest, to live the best life we can live. And the definition of what a good life is as different as one person is to another. So it's really about finding your own definition.

As some believe we have only one life, and others believe we have many—once we have chosen to understand that life is bigger than the pieces and parts of everyday living, most want an experience that is worthy of the trials and tribulations of getting there.

Being there.

A simple haircut can symbolize change. A few strands cut here, others snipped there. Maybe a new color, or a new style and suddenly it's a new you. Don't like that person? Grow it out, dye it, add a new dress or new shoes.

As people, we can be amazingly adaptable. Pliable. Able to morph ourselves as need be. Some do it better than others. If we choose to. If we decide not to set all of our decisions in stone for a lifetime, especially with new information percolating in as we go, we can become who we need or want to be.

I am learning about how to live. This is not something I have a blueprint or a map for. Each self-help book that I read seems to point to one way or another, but each person needs to determine what works for themselves. Each person then extends themselves in different ways to achieve their defined enjoyable experiences.

For some, a simple camping trip to the Rockies constitutes heaven on earth. Others need to ascend Mt. Everest, risking their very lives for the thrill and the adventure to achieve the result.

Some people are content with spending the majority of their lives in a cubicle and going out drinking as their reward on the weekends. The beauty is we all get to pick our own experiences, and then if we want to change that experience we can change it.

That is the miracle of what can be. Too many stand back and watch. Wait. Life moves on without their input.

I am on my journey with the possible dead ends and hills before me. I stand looking back at the bends and curves I have left.

So many have said to me that I am lucky to be able to do what I want, as if they have a tether around their necks by society that is choking and holding them back from doing the same thing. It is not so much luck as a decision that one will not stand by and let life happen to them, that one must make their own way.

Every single one of us has the ability to take control of our lives if- and only if- we step into our power to do it. It might suck for a while, but if it is your path, your destiny will rise up alongside you and the two of you can stroll into the limitless together.

If one will just believe.

I believe that I am meant to do big things and see places that I have only heard about and have a love that will be legendary. It may take some time, but it will be so worth it. I am thankful that I am able to navigate the changes and invite even more into my life, knowing something better awaits me.

~

~2~

Saffron got up and brought a photo album back with her to her chair. She downed the last few drops of her tea and wiped the tears away from her eyes to see the images in the rainbow- adorned album.

Bronny had been eighty-four when she died. They were driving through Austin, Texas, when Bronwyn felt a pain in her neck. They stopped at a hospital to have her looked at, and while they were waiting, Bronwyn listed then fell forward towards Saffron. Luckily she caught her and eased her down slowly to the floor. By the time the doctor made it out to the waiting area, Bronwyn was gone.

Saffron melted onto the floor next to her love and held onto her, listening and begging for even the faintest of a heartbeat, a movement, anything.

"No! It can't be, I can't lose her, not like this."

Saffron was given a sedative as Bronwyn's body was lifted onto a gurney and taken away. When she finally caught her breath, she made the call to Bronwyn's daughter.

"Solange, it's Saffron. It's your mom, honey, she's gone."

There was audible weeping on the other end, and the two women held each other through the phone line from separate continents.

Finally Solange spoke.

"She loved you so much, Saff. You know that. Her years with you were the happiest I ever saw her. Mom was so damn happy."

"Your mom brought such beauty into my life," her voice cracked. "I'm not sure how I will be without her."

The vacuum of a life gone was thick in the silence that came and stayed. Sniffles and breathing took up some of the space. Even the lights seemed dimmer.

"I have to go now. I don't know what to do; I have to figure it out."

Saffron handed the phone to the nurse. Solange was told about who to call and what the next steps were. It wasn't up to Saff; she had no rights or say in this.

Saffron and Bronwyn had no legally binding agreements in place for each other in times of illness or death. They hadn't any papers to show they were married, not that they could have done so in the first place.

In reality Saffron had no authority or ability to ask to get Bronwyn buried back in Minnesota. Separated now by the gossamer veil of life itself and the legal system of the State of Texas. It would be misery and red tape from here on out.

They had been everything to each other for the last ten years. The trip was supposed to last a year after which they would find a small town and place they could live in together; a one story- something easy for their old bones to handle. They'd only seen some of the places they had planned.

Solange called Saffron on her cell.

"I am waiting for them to fax me the papers to have Mom cremated, and I will sign them so that you will be authorized to take her remains. Take her with you on your trip, Saff; take Mom- she always wanted to be with you. She told me all the time how you were her one true love. I'm sorry. I will do whatever I can to help. Call me anytime." The phone clicked.

She just had to wait: wait until Bronny's remains were ready to go and until all of the paperwork was done. Saffron had never felt so helpless. Paralyzed in place, so stuck and in insurmountable pain. She's lost her love, her best friend, the one who had ignited her heart.

All of those feelings again swirled around her from her chair in the Sunny Days home. She hadn't been back to Minnesota since it all happened. She drove to a couple of the places they had wanted to see, holding Bronny's hermetically sealed box up to the view, but as she did each time she felt more sad. It wasn't even close to the same. Nothing would ever be the same.

Saff drove towards Birmingham and north selling the RV on the way. She didn't want to think anymore; she couldn't. Seeing a billboard ad for Sunny Days senior residence on the side of the highway, the sign felt like a gift. A new place to call home. Most everything was taken care of in the monthly bill. It could work until she gained her strength, she told herself.

She wrote to the new owner's of Rainbow Gardens and asked them to send her a few of the things she had in storage. She shared with them how Bronny had died and how she would be staying here for the foreseeable future. Any checks could be sent directly to her bank account and she would be in touch.

That was two years ago. At times she would get a letter with photos of how the gardens were blooming, and how many visitors had come to the farm. She would write back little bits but she had been so sad for so long.

Solange called every month like clockwork to check in, and Saffron appreciated her loving kindness. She was as close to being a daughter as Saffron would ever have. Receiving photos of Solange with her daughter teased Saff as to what Bronny might have looked like when she was a young mother. So much time wasted. They'd found each other so late.

She picked up the little blue book and read the first passage again.

She dabbed at the tears in her eyes and got up to go to bed. She kissed the picture of Bronny that she kept next to her as she did each night, and took a lined notebook out of the drawer of her nightstand. She thought of the words in the anonymous author's plea.

The memories inside may remind you of a time or a person in your own life. May you think of those people today, for the good or the lessons you learned from them.

Yes, this was a way to remember her Bronny. To share the love that she had for her with others. To properly memorialize their life together. How she had found her and how they fell in love after more than a year of friendship just listening and being there for each other.

She hadn't told anyone at Sunny Days that she was a lesbian. She hadn't even known she was until that kiss. Being gay wasn't really something she felt she could be all the way open about even now with her new friends at this place. But maybe in this exercise, in the writing of their story, she would find her way into accepting everything about who she was, and she could let other people's opinions fall away. That beautiful woman whom she had loved with her whole heart deserved to be celebrated, and so did their love.

Maybe people would judge, but what if they did? Maybe if she shared her story, another person would have the opportunity to choose to understand because they would feel it, with her words, the beating of their soul-bound hearts.

Saffron closed her eyes and made a mental promise to pass the book on to Jillian Halliwell in 3D the very next day.

~

On My Own For Real, Me 2005

I sat at my desk in the window's niche of my new apartment. At an antique table that had been in my paternal grandmother's home. Carved legs with a veneered top, split in places, the surface held my notebooks perfectly. The piece was well worn but still had the potential for beauty and purpose if someone worked on it a little bit. Kind of like me, I hoped.

It was a sunny day outside, the sky was visible in the far-off distance but most of my view was of the multi-story buildings and massive parking lot filled with cars; it was a different kind of home than I was used to.

This is the first time in my life that I have lived alone. When the girls are with me, I'm not alone, but when they are with their Dad the silence thickens in my head. I leave the TV on, just to cope. I sit for hours slouching over in front of the gas-powered fireplace, the heat burning into my back escaping into magazines, or books begging myself to make sense out of my life.

I hadn't worked an outside job since we had our first daughter other than taking in another baby to bring in a little money and have some baby social time for our oldest. It didn't last long though.

I attempted a business a few years ago, when my youngest was a baby but that fell away, too, as the bills piled up for inventory and the sales never came in. All in all I didn't have a ton of expertise in anything, nor could I necessarily seem to get my brain to commit to anything long term enough to call it a career. But now I was getting a divorce so I needed a job, health insurance and a goddamn plan.

With Mom as a contractor, I had grown up on construction sites, and had spent MANY hours watching HGTV.

I walked into the giant orange box store for a job. I walked into the nearest one, found the HR manager and said directly to her, "I want to work here."

I walked out with a job, an orange apron hung on my hook at work with my name on it, and a different purpose. Employees there are not allowed to take their aprons home in case anyone is curious.

It was the start of a new story that I would write for myself. The end of my stay-mom life, and a new beginning where I counted solely on myself whether I liked it or not.

Working at the big orange box store was fun in the beginning, but as my wedding ring came off, the men swarmed around a bit. The days were long. With the miles I walked for my job, the extra weight fell off of me, extra pounds I'd been carrying for years. That mixed with my inability to eat much since my life was in such a tailspin.

The men that worked there seemed to like me, and I wasn't used to the attention. Especially from the married ones, they'd walk me through their departments and tell me all kinds of stories, and I learned that my being "nice" to them was a turn on, a glimmer of romantic interest. Geez. So now I had to be a bitch in order to be left alone. Lord, help me.

One guy said his wife wasn't really doing it for him anymore, and he thought maybe I could be his little side piece. He bragged about his Volkswagen camper bus and how maybe it could be a little love shack for us if I fancied him as much.

As if. No way was I going to be someone else's side piece. Again.

Days alone are spent mostly in front of that window, trying to figure out my next move. Trying to remember who it was that I wanted to be when I grew up. Reading over the stories and books I had started writing still compiled in boxes from the move. I had lots of time like this on my days off with the girls in school or with their Dad to sit and think about things. The mistakes that I had made along with the choices and questioning if I made the right decisions.

Hubby had been so stable. So routine. So safe.

I needed to stretch, see places, and experience new things. If this was the only life I was going to get, I wanted a great big juicy one. I continue to go into work and juggle my kid time according to each week's shitty schedule, trying to make the best of it. Nights, weekends, nights, weekends. This is getting to be a problem.

Even with countless hours to myself to do whatever it is that I want, I stay tucked inside my apartment. Even going to the grocery store is hard now. My eating is a challenge, nothing tastes good. Nothing inspires me; I am sustaining but not thriving. Not even close to being as happy as I thought I would be.

I only leave when I have to, when I have someplace to be. My responsibilities have technically been halved, but I feel more empty than ever before.

~

J.H.

My old best friend across the street. We were two peas in a pod, your mom even had t-shirts made for us claiming "Best Friends". We had a lot of fun together. I think I fawned over you a lot as you were the pretty one in our twosome. You were always so put together. Your parents were cool. Every year you had a big Christmas party that even Santa attended. I wanted the life I imagined you had, before finding out that everyone's family has challenges.

Early on, we could be goofy together, and me being a year younger I got to watch you for reference. When you got a retainer I wished for one, too. Why couldn't I have crooked teeth?

I would put plastic rings leftover from packaging into my mouth to mimic your experience. As you graduated to having to wear neck gear and headgear even during the day, I still thought you were the coolest. Why couldn't all these things happen to me? When braces finally came for you I put tin foil strips in my mouth to try to be just like you.

Our alignment throughout life was interrupted by my family's move out of the neighborhood. Before we moved, it was easy to be together, but the move made it hard and after a while we just didn't try anymore. I was nine, you were ten; it wasn't like we could drive.

Once we were both in middle school, we could've hung out at school at least, but we didn't. Things had changed, you had grown in one direction: the cooler, popular way; and I had become more awkward.

You were surrounded by all of the popular people.

Your hair was on-point. Somehow you had mastered Farrah Fawcett's feathered- back hairstyle while my hair was uncooperative.

You had the best clothes, too. Double or sometimes triple layers of Izod alligator shirts with Lawman jeans kitted out with your long-handled plastic comb, personalized with your name on it, visibly poking out of your back pocket.

By eighth grade, the braces were finally off and you were thin, and absolutely gorgeous. With a face and a tan, looking just like the actual Sunset Malibu Barbie we played with in years past. I wanted to be like you.

As I watched from afar, I saw your evolution. More effort, money and time was spent on your appearance, trying to become even more the beautiful beachy California style version of yourself.

As an adult, your hair got lighter and your men got richer. I wonder if that is the real you, and the one I knew in our early days was the imposter.

Did it get you the life that you wanted? Are you happy? Would you do life the same all over again? How will you cope when your skin starts to wrinkle from the years of both artificial and natural sun exposure?

What will happen when you no longer have the Barbie doll looks of your youth, will you still love the woman in the mirror?

~

Absentee Mom, Me? 2005

*W*ith *the divorce a strange thing happened in my life. One I would never have guessed would come to me since I had been a devoted mother since day one.*

When I went to work, the girls stayed with their Dad more since my hours were mostly evenings and weekends. It was so hard to be away from them. To not be able to volunteer and participate in their school lives as I had.

In that I realized that the majority of who I was as a person had been wrapped up in those two magical little beings. With them in school, and me away from them for days on end, I wasn't much of a person. I was lonely, sad, and for the first time in a long time I had too much time to think about who I wanted to be now.

Even though I think my temporary absenteeism was accidental, if I could see that I was becoming an absent mother to my girls I would have immediately changed course. It didn't work out that way. Working the hours that I did, I was forced to be away from them, and missing them more than I already did was so painful that I had to pivot my energy away from that sorrow and turn it into something else. Anything.

I had married so young, and without the separation of the college experience, I most likely missed out on a lot of exposure most people get to have. I hadn't dated much, hadn't traveled very far or done anything really on my own. In this time I soon discovered that what I needed was to have some fun. There was a whole lot I never tried in the world.

I hadn't had my first apartment alone, or gone on any grand vacations by myself. I hadn't tried very many foods as I had always been a notoriously picky eater. One who eventually married another picky eater. I wasn't daring, or adventuresome, and I used the word "no" way too often. By now, I had forgotten what I liked to do for fun, what lit me up.

I'd always decorated our houses, so when the time came for me and my daughters to have our own place, I jumped into my familiar role to make it a home. The Ladies' Lounge was whatever the three of us wanted it to be with no other adult to tell us no.

I was doing the best I could. Oddly the same thing I noticed when my Father had made a room for my brother and me in his new apartment after my parents' divorce was happening with me. I was overcompensating in the fun factor trying to cushion the inconvenience I knew my girls were suddenly dealing with. More games, more movies, it was a fun space on the top floor of an apartment building so it came with a loft where I put an air hockey table and a giant bean bag to read stories, watch movies or crash in.

Making up for what I'd done with buying things in hopes of making it better. Trying to make up for the hassle of all of it. Maybe trying to compensate for not being with them as much. Not being their Mom all the time anymore.

I had the girls as often as I could. Driving them across town to go to school every morning, their days with me started earlier than at their Dad's. Often my schedule meant scattered hours with me, and the majority with their father who had regular nine-to-five, Monday through Friday hours. I was forever asking him to keep them longer and longer. My heart was breaking. If I thought about it, I would just be sad all the time so instead I found myself sleeping a lot. Sleeping late because I worked late or staying up late watching TV to forget what I was dealing with. I'd sit with my back to the gas fireplace and read, or look at magazines, the heat burning into me, but I didn't care. I was a half person, I felt. Not knowing what was next.

Sometimes I would write, but every time I did they were sad, pathetic words that pointed me back to the whole thing being a massive mistake, a malignant but inoperable tumor on the rest of my life. If I had the predisposition to become an addict, this would have been the time to do it, but I rarely even drank having gotten that mostly out of my system in my twenties. I thought about taking it up again, that was for sure.

My youngest who was so young when we split started seeking out new mother figures that were there more. It was painful to watch her ask other mothers in the neighborhood to help her with things she knew I wouldn't be around for. Help with a project at school, stopping by for a snack after school, etc. It was painful to have her turn to other women in her life for some motherly stability and support but I understood and even acted as though I was okay with it, even though it was crushing. I was thankful to these wonderful women who stepped in when my kid needed a hand and would thank them for it. This stuff wasn't about me; it was about making sure my kid had the things she needed especially when I could not be there.

She developed a very close bond with her first grade teacher, one where she went in early to spend more time with her, one where she would go visit in the summers prior to school starting. One where she said to me more than once that she wished she was her actual mother instead of me. It was hard to hear all of these things, and I did the best I could to hide my hurt, but I knew it was just one of the consequences of my turning her life upside down, and her being so much like her Father in her desire and need for routine. The teacher was there every day, she listened and was loving- I was the one who had brought all the changes.

I had a decision to make: I could either own and accept my accountability in the situation and why my child had reached out to others for more support; or choose to make it all about me and my hurt feelings and take her away from them out of insecurity. As much as it hurt, I kept those feelings to myself and chose not to see those extraordinary women as my opponents, but to stand back in awe and appreciation of the sisterhood of another woman stepping into the place that I couldn't fill at the moment.

I chose to see it as Love instead of rivalry. Appreciation, allowing another woman to love my daughter extra at that moment in time because that was what she needed. Extra mothering, extra love to help her cope with the shit that had fallen on her with my decisions. It would be something that I made a promise to do for any other woman and her child should that be necessary.

With all of the fallout and my new rickety confidence in my motherhood came other things that pressed hard.

Depression. Maybe that is why I stayed away from my daughters more, initially. I wasn't coping very well despite the whole thing being my idea.

Throughout their childhood I had tried many different antidepressants, each working somewhat for a certain amount of time until I felt I wasn't myself and I would stop taking them.

I wasn't able to be there to help my daughters through anything that they were struggling with at the moment with my own life spinning in a blender. I did sign them up for divorce class at school- an extra support group that they could go to, to be with other kids in the same situation. They had another resource and new friends who were going through the same thing so maybe it helped; I wasn't in the right mind to ask all the time.

I continue to look for a reason, for my cutting out more, for avoiding taking them if I had something else to do. My only hope is that they didn't notice and feel my detachment as much as I did. With their father being so solid and so sturdy and anchored you could just look at him and know what he was- and that, I rationalized, was what they needed right then.

Someone to be able to trust in to take care of them; not someone who was all over the place and depressed. A Mom who would avoid going to the store, or who may forget to sign their field trip slip for school.

I am forever grateful that I had my children with #1 as he is a rock. A wonderful father.

The rock in him that I found impossible to grow with long term was the perfect rock for them to tether onto while I fell away on this little jaunt of whatever the hell this was.

His complete competence as a father had been displayed over and over throughout our marriage. Since hearing from one of our early marriage counselors that he needed to develop his own relationship with our daughter that was completely independent of me, and my support of that despite him not doing things the same way I did and letting him, he was perfectly capable of taking care of them and all their needs without me. In this moment I was glad that they had that relationship established already so it wouldn't be something that they all had to figure out in this already turbulent time.

There was a day when I was at work and my name came over the loud-speaker. That I needed to call home. I walked to the desk and called Mr. Stability, my children's father. Our youngest had taken a bad fall off of her bike and he had taken her to the neighbor's- a doctor and nurse household- to see if she might need stitches.

I asked to leave work and was told no, so I finished my shift and went to see her right after. She was bundled up in a blanket on the couch watching "Scooby Doo," one of the video tapes I often put on when the girls were sick or feeling down. She held a little ice pack against her black and blue little face, and my heart just broke.

She had fallen hard and, in the crash, one of her front teeth had pierced through her lip; it was split there, but by now it had stopped bleeding. She was a mess. My poor baby had crashed on her bike and I hadn't felt it inside, that there was something wrong with her. I hadn't been there to help cushion the impact of her catapulting onto the ground, I wasn't there to pick her up. In the bigger sense, I wasn't there for her. The amount of guilt I had for being away from them so much was now compounded by the helplessness I felt in trying to be there for my kids. What if I could never be there for them, what then?

I held her, and she said through her swollen lips, "I am never riding my bike again."

It was a statement I believed could stay true as she is my most stubborn and committed child. My little Taurus. When she makes a statement, she means it. She decides.

She decided to grow out her bangs one day, and she never waivered, putting them up into a headband for the six months it took. She had committed to *never eat a hot lunch at school for her entire elementary education; she had accomplished that, too. I didn't want her to never ride her bike again, to have that limitation on her life and childhood that way.*

If I would have been there at the crash, I would have had us sit for a while, and I would have made her ride the bike home, knowing she could carry that fear with her forever after if she didn't. Without me there they had ditched the bikes in the bushes and walked home, the three of them.

I had to accept that with my absence, decisions would be made for them without me and I would have to be okay and supportive of those decisions in the long run. I couldn't control everything anymore, especially when I felt I had very little control of anything at the moment.

I tried to spend more time with them, as much as I could. Each new day there was another excuse or outside reason I couldn't be there with them as much as I felt I needed to.

It wasn't enough though; it felt like it would never ever be enough again.

~

~2~

Jilly

Jillian Halliwell closed her door after thanking Saffron for the little blue book delivery. It was late in the evening. Her nightly routine hadn't changed in years.

Removing her wig, she placed it on the head-shaped wicker stand she kept on her dresser. Poking it a little with her artificial fingernails to put the curls back in place, she tugged lightly at her false lashes and placed them on the tea plate she kept by her wig for that purpose. Its black filaments showed well on the white and ivory detailed porcelain.

Pulling her silk nightie out of the bottom drawer, she tied the ribbon at the neck. Next was her nightly slathering of Pond's cold cream all over her face and neck before walking into the bathroom to wash off the rest of her makeup. She stared into the mirror. Each night, she saw herself change from one person to another. The current version, only seen by herself.

Jillian climbed under the covers, taking the book with her. Taking a sip of the water she kept at her bedside, she opened the front cover and started to read.

Visions of strangers blossomed in her head, but they inspired memory glints of other people she had known in her life. As her eyes tired for the night, she soon stumbled into a passage with whom she shared the same initials: it was about a woman similar to herself.

A woman obsessed with being beautiful, she changes her looks to appeal more to men than to others. The author wondered if her once best friend's looks would sustain her. It could have been her story, although she knew it wasn't. She read on.

It was well past twelve-thirty when she finished the last page of the book and set it down on the nightstand next to her. She flipped off the light and hunkered down into the covers. As she closed her eyes hoping to fall asleep, she smiled.

It was nice to have this little group of women to spend her time with.

They were much different than the women she had been in friendships with in her past life back in Atlanta.

As she watched the minutes tick by on her black box flip clock, her eyes fuzzed to who she might put in her own memory book if she attempted to write one of her own. To her dread, the list of people she would want to include was small.

Her deepest relationships had all been when she was young. As a child, free to be her wild and true self long before she started chasing the perfect appearance, money and status.

On Tybee Island, Georgia, in the 1940's, she and her family were among the small number of about a thousand-and-change people that stayed on the island year round. Her Father, a small grocery owner in town, worked a lot. He was always going into Savannah to get supplies, and often he'd buy extra of the non-perishable items to hold over til tourist season. Jillian or "Jilly" as she was known back then, would beg Papa to take her into town with him on his thrice-weekly trips.

Sometimes she could go along, but most of the time Papa needed to fill the truck with other things so there wasn't any room for her. It was her, her brother Gil and Mama that all stayed in the stilted house behind the store. It was a simple house, and Mama cooked basic meals often with whatever catch the fishermen brought in. She'd even cook up alligator if that was what was offered. It tasted like chicken.

Tybee Island was quiet most of the time and all of the year-round people knew each other, but in the summer months it was another story. That was when all the fancy rich tourists came to the island to *"get away from it all"*.

Back then she had wondered what they were all trying to get away from. It must have been so much more exciting than living in this little cranny all the time. Jilly craved the newness and chaos of a bigger city. She loved when the tourists came and the city exploded with people. She loved seeing their clothes, listening to the way they talked about all the money they had, and seeing the fancy cars that they all drove.

She'd walk past the Tybee Hotel and imagine staying there in the luxurious rooms or lingering on the patios out front, being served drinks under the palm trees.

"Jeeves, please get me another lemonade, I am just parched," she would imagine saying.

Truthfully, those moments back then before she eventually got what it was that she asked for- the money, the big house, and memberships in the elitist clubs- that was when life was more enjoyable. And freeing.

Gil and she would paddle the canoe over to Little Tybee Island and trudge through the marshes in their leg waders, listening to the woodstorks and trying to avoid the plentiful spider crabs as they went. The two of them would often take a knapsack with sleeping blankets and spend the night over there, especially if they hadn't double checked the tide log. They'd tie their blankets from the tree branches into a hammock and lie in them, chewing on hunks of beef jerky from the store and taking turns drinking out of the canteen of Coke poured from the soda fountain when Papa wasn't looking.

Jillian and her brother got along better than most siblings she knew. Maybe it was because they really only had each other most of the time. They'd stay up all night, talking and looking up at the starry sky. Sharing with each other all about the places they wanted to go to, the many adventures they each planned on having. Gil hadn't escaped Tybee as quickly as she had.

Jilly was sixteen when she was handed what felt like the winning lottery ticket of her life. It was May, right after Memorial day, when most of the wealthy families started their descent into Tybee. Many of the summer people owned homes there. The women and children came first, spending the first couple of days pulling the sheets off the furniture inside and scouring the house for Palmetto bugs. Dust and the extra noises flanked the nicer homes and made Jilly giddy with the frenzied feeling of busyness. Everybody was getting into that Tybee summer feeling.

It was no different for Jilly's family. While their family didn't have to reset their own home, they had plenty of extra work to do to get the store ready for the waves of people who would be coming in wanting to fill their summer coffers. Coffee, ice and canned goods at the very least, many made weekly orders for Papa to get for them in town. He'd be making more trips into the city to oblige.

Mama kept the store while Papa was away and did the books for the store deep into the dark each night. She planned for the ordering and always made sure they had enough ice cream to keep the floods of people happy as they came in off the beach after a long hot day.

The summer her life changed forever started just like any other. Jilly had risen early and got dressed. Doing her hair as best she could to replicate the women in some of the beauty magazines Papa had in the shop, she used up the last bit of hairspray left in her can. She made her way to the Tybrisa Pavilion to get a full snoop of the sights and smells of the tourists. She had contemplated getting a job at the ice cream shop inside, but decided to wait another year as Gil had been fully seventeen before he started working; it could be the last year of her life without responsibilities. She craved another summer to watch the tourists and see their latest fashions. One more summer to eavesdrop about the world outside Tybee.

Her plain dresses all in then-faded colors of gingham were far from fashionable; she didn't stand out. If anything she imagined her simple appearance allowed her to slide into spaces to listen in without much notice.

That was until she caught the eye of a certain gentleman named Apollo Balasi. He smiled as he walked towards her, his hand outstretched; was he looking at someone beyond her? He opened his mouth to say something and she quickly walked away, embarrassed to be noticed, especially by an older man. What would he want with a little island girl?

Maybe he thought she was a waitress? Someone to fetch him a soda?

Jilly sped quickly down the stairs to the beach access. There were many people in their bathing costumes dipping their toes in the water for the first time that year. Little children held onto Mummys' hands while some fathers stood shaking hands with the other men, saying how good it was to be back to the "Peach by the Beach."

She continued under the pier pilings and up the shore; hopefully she had escaped his interest. Jilly wasn't comfortable around men or boys really; she just liked to watch people and imagine herself having the confidence and money that they did.

Maybe someday.

June came, and the entire city was chock full to the gills with people. There were some teenagers that Jilly had played with as children from years past. People that she thought were her friends- ones she had hoped to connect with again- acted as if they didn't know her. The boys and girls in her age group seemed to cluster together into their financially-similar groups. They weren't interested in the local kids anymore.

Jilly found herself hovering near the pavilion and the beach access feigning looking for shells or the baby horseshoe crabs that were prevalent in the area. Really she was listening to them all brag about the places they had gone or how their businesses were doing. She longed to be one of them someday.

One evening in late August the latest jazz band was playing in the pavilion. Many people were cutting a rug on the dance floor, and the man that had smiled at Jilly early in the season walked up to her. He handed her a card and smiled down at her again.

"You are very pretty. You ever think of modeling or being a pageant girl?"

Jilly was shocked at the thought and felt flush with the compliment until another young girl came running up to them.

"Hey, are you thinking of working with Apollo, too? He got me all kinds of modeling jobs, and I am even going to be an extra in a film next month; you should totally do it." She hugged Jilly then bounded off to dance with some other young teens.

Jilly looked down at the card and read the dramatic type- just barely in the low light.

Apollo Balasi's School for Models. A talent agency. Atlanta, GA.

He turned it over in her hand, and in confidently strong cursive she read, "You've got something special!"

Tucking the card into her dress pocket, she dipped her eyes and thanked him before walking down Butler Avenue to get back home. She let her eyes adjust to the darker streets and pulled the card from her pocket to read the message on the back of the business card again. She strolled just smiling to herself.

'Some hotshot modeling agent thought she had something special.'

At dinner, Jilly broached the subject with Mama who snatched the card from her hands.

"Don't even think about it, young lady; he must be a shyster." Ma tucked the card into her apron front and set plates of catfish, potatoes and green beans in front of each of them at the table.

It seemed that Jilly saw her mother for the first time that night. Could Mama have been pretty if it wasn't for the hard life she had? What did she look like under the dirt and sweat of doing the laundry by hand, cooking and cleaning not only their house but also the store in the after hours each night?

She felt empathy for her Mother but it was mixed with a strong resolve to not end up like her. Mama was a strong woman, yes, but worn and aging by the second because of it all. Jilly couldn't remember the last time her Ma smiled, let alone laughed.

In the midnight hours, Jilly snuck back into the kitchen and plucked the card out of the pocket of her Ma's apron and tucked it under her pillow. That night she dreamed of beautiful dresses, getting compliments and hearing applause coming from an audience.

Apollo found her the next day. "I'll be leaving tomorrow. Did you talk to your folks? Will they let you come with me to my school? I don't charge anything up front but I get fifty percent of your pageant winnings and any earnings to make right on my investment."

He handed her a contract that included a line where he would act as her legal guardian up until the age of eighteen as long as she was in his care.

"Have your parents sign this. We will leave tomorrow. I have two other girls that are coming with. I am sure you will all become friends."

Jilly showed her brother the document and asked him what she should do.

"I can't tell you; it's a huge decision. Ma already said no, so you'll be going against her, not to mention it's basically running away to do it. I wouldn't want to be you." Gil backed up and held up his hands in surrender.

She spent the rest of the morning walking around town, imagining herself living here forever. Would she be happy? Or always wonder what she could have been?

In the end, little Jilly Finny forged her parents' signatures, wrote them a note and got in the car of a stranger who said he saw something in her.

She prayed she wouldn't regret it.

~

Trouble In Fantasyland, Me, 2005

After telling my husband that I wanted to split, and that I loved someone else, and the feeling was mutual, I thought things would progress. I believed that Mr. Affair and I were on a path, one that we would be walking on together. He had said that he was leaving his wife and that he'd tell her soon so we could start planning our new life together.

I did it. I did my part. I got everything rolling on my side: the divorce started; I'd moved out; I was working; I had a job, insurance, and an apartment. Things were moving forward. Right?

Mr. Affair and I would talk on the phone, and he would say yes, he was working on things but there was a delay or something else needed to happen before he would be free. He wanted to get his wife to move to my coast so he would have easy access to his kids, too. They were negotiating about the move but he hadn't told her about me and what that meant.

I tried to be patient and I waited to hear more news. Finally, I decided to go see him again, to confirm our feelings, and figure out how all this was going to go down. To see if the physical part of this relationship could start now. He agreed, and I booked my flight. Even though it would still be an affair for him, I was free in a sense having already left my marriage.

I flew out and got a hotel room, and he picked me up at the airport and we grabbed a bite to eat. He came back to the room with me where we stayed together until after midnight.

I'd brought a slinky teddy and climbed cat-like onto the bed. He watched me for a while then cuddled up alongside me. He pushed my legs open and I let him, then he laid his head on my lap gazing oddly into my lacy crotch. He looked but did not touch.

"Doesn't she wonder where you are right now?" I asked.

"She knows something is going on, but I haven't told her everything."

We talked for an hour back and forth in this position, with me getting more and more uncomfortable by the minute.

We still had a lot to figure out- him more than me.

I fumed inside, but didn't want to blow my temper.

Hello. I had just thrown myself into a fucking blender and he hasn't even told her yet? He hasn't done anything? It's been months.

Finally I reached for him, teasingly, a playful move to get the ball rolling. He recoiled.

It was as if when I got closer, an electrical shock zapped him or something. A force field sprung up around him. Maybe he thought I wouldn't come to see him or I wouldn't leave my marriage to be with him. He didn't count on me going through with it, or he hadn't considered the seriousness of what it was.

Or maybe in my being here and trying to be with him he was ultimately reminded that he was already a husband to someone and a father?

Whatever it was, he told me that things were still good between us, he just had some more work to do. We would be together soon, he promised.

He left, and I lay in the hotel bed, alone. We hadn't made love. We hadn't even kissed. I am far from home. Reliving the full awkwardness of the night-I felt the fool.

Here I was, having left my entire life behind for what I thought was my forever, only to have a chasm split us apart. A gap that neither of us was sure how to cross.

~

~2~

Jillian Halliwell awoke after a night of colorful dreams of Tybee Island. The wind in her hair, the sand in between her toes, remembering back to being there with her brother traipsing through the muddy marshes as a carefree young sprite.

She walked to the bathroom and looked in the mirror. The looks that had gotten Jilly out of her hometown were long since gone; her eyes narrowed into the creases hoping to see a glint of the beauty she once had.

Her movie star looks had catapulted her to runner up in the Miss Georgia pageant in 1945, and with the attention she started using the full version of her name, "Jillian" just prior to marrying hot shot lawyer Denby Halliwell.

Jillian pulled on a turquoise housecoat and zipped it up to her neck before pouring herself a cup of black coffee. As she sipped by the phone in the kitchen she dialed her brother's number.

Gil had settled in St. Louis after living in Tybee for many years and taking over Papa's store in 1950. He might have stayed forever if not for the Air Force jet mid-air collision right off the coast of Tybee Island in 1958. He had called Jilly in a state, telling her all about the accident. How a hydrogen bomb had been jettisoned away from one of the planes, falling dangerously into the waters off Tybee Island. The search parties hadn't found it, and it had scared Gil so badly that he up and sold the store and hadn't been back in all the years since.

"Hi Gil, how are you doing these days? It's been awhile since we've talked."

"Well, hi, Jilly. It's nice to hear from you. We are just fine, enjoying retirement, and we bought ourselves an RV, can you believe it? I've even been thinking of driving it down to Tybee Island, a nostalgia tour, you know. I'm sure if that bomb was going to go, it would have done it by now, right?" He chuckled. "And Lord knows, if it went off while we're there, then I guess it was meant to be."

"That's such a great idea. I am happy you and Mavis are going to travel a little bit. So happy you are still able to and feel adventurous enough to get down there. I dreamt of Tybee all night last night; I might try to meet you there. See what the place looks like now. I heard they rebuilt the pavilion; it's smaller but still a real nice way to bring people together. Such a shame about that fire and how the beach sat so long without it. So much has changed, I'm sure."

"Yeah, Lord, I'm sure. So many changes. Remember how the blacks weren't allowed to go on the beach when we were kids? Such garbage, and I was so shook up after learning all of the history of Tybee's part in the Middle Passage slave trade, too. Jim Crow laws affecting all of them, I never knew what the blacks there were dealing with. Everybody back when we were kids was so uppity, and Papa did nothing but cater to those rich folks' every whim." He grunted into the receiver.

"Yeah, I never knew about all the slave quarantining that happened out there, and all that was done to keep the black folks down. We were pretty oblivious I think. Yeah, there was a difference: different schools meant not much mixing of the whites and blacks, but as a kid, I didn't really know any of what it meant. So much has happened since. They are owning the history more; it's not hideable anymore. The many civil rights demonstrations, the wade-in protest there after we were both gone. I bet that was something else. Seriously, when I found out about all of those people who died and were buried out there, no headstones. No nothing. Good grief we were probably out there camping near dead bodies. I'm horrified with all that happened there." Jillian shuddered before taking another sip of coffee.

"Really hoping things are different there now. We've come a long way."

"Yeah, especially you. Rags to Riches, sis; look at all you have seen since running off."

"Yeah, hey, Gil, I never really asked how was it after I left? How was Mama, how did they take me leaving? Everything kind of fell on you. I'm real sorry."

"Water under the bridge, Jilly; it's okay. You had to do what you needed to do. You would have always wondered if you hadn't taken that chance. In one regard I was always proud of you for taking a risk like that, not knowing if it would pay off, or even if you would be okay. You must have known somehow."

"I guess I did, but it sure was crazy. Leaving and going to stay with that Apollo fellow in his big house full of young women; at least I had decent company. He never messed with us, which I'm grateful for- we could have easily all been victimized. And we had each other to talk to. We all had to go to high school and graduate and then there was the travel and the pageants, and dresses and hair appointments, and learning to do our nails; it was like beauty school mixed with charm school but concentrated. It was a whirlwind!"

"Mama loved getting your postcards, too, Jilly. She never said so at least to me, but I know she was proud of you for going big. I could see it on her face when she'd look through them. She always had them up in the store for the people who would ask about you. You were kind of a hometown celebrity back then. *Tybee Island girl makes it big.*"

"Thanks, Gil, thanks for sharing that about Ma. I'm happy you told me that. I read a book recently that made me wonder if I had any real friends since Tybee at all. Most of the people I called my friends in Atlanta seemed to be only friends with me because we had money. Fellow members of the country club, we'd all sit around and play bridge and brag about what we had bought or where we were going next. When Denby died and the money went away, they all disappeared too, and I never hear from them. I hardly hear from Violet anymore either. She's in her own little world too, I guess."

"I'm sorry, Jilly, that's too bad. But you said you've made some nice friends there at Sunny Days, right? Maybe that's how you can see the difference?"

"Yes, they are wonderful, and the thing of it is they don't care about how I look, or what clothes I wear, or how much money I have. We all have different backgrounds but each of us has something to share and learn from each other if you use it with a purpose and share it to help others for it to really make a difference. I guess I am learning now that looks fade and money is nice but it's important to be able to be yourself and to find the people that are your people. I may have missed that boat in my chase for vanity."

"Don't be hard on yourself, sis. We grew up watching all the fancy people have everything; it makes sense you wanted that, too. Good to finally know the difference between a superficial bond and true friendships. If those people left you, they really weren't worth you missin' them much."

"Thanks. Real happy I caught you this morning before you jet out on one of your adventures. Let me know when you set a date to go to Tybee; I may hitch a ride and go with you. You must have room for one more in that beast?"

"Indeed, sis, I will let you know of our plan. Might be fun to have you along. I love a good road trip because then you see and experience everything the world has in between. Happy to hear you are happy and making friends. Give Violet a call; she might like to hear your latest thoughts and about that book too. I know she was always more on the deeper side of being than in keeping up with the Joneses."

"Yes, I just might. I don't ever think I told her about all of our campouts in the marsh either. She would be shocked that I actually used to like to get dirty and catch snakes. Could be a bonding moment." Jillian chuckled and wished her brother a nice day before signing off.

"I love you," she said after she had hung up the line. It was dumb, but she and her brother had never said those words to each other, even though she knew they both did.

***

Jilly put a piece of bread into her toaster oven and placed her wig on her head before walking over to the mirror to straighten it, to frame her face just so. No one had seen her without her wig since she was in her forties, except Denby. It was her answer to the futile chase from the gray squirrelly hairs and had made her everyday beauty easier to manage.

But the wrinkles still came, and when all the money she might have spent on plastic surgery evaporated, she was left with what God gave her. Gravity could be such a cruel force, she determined. It was almost a blessing to be removed from that affluent environment as she had been after Denby died. She could stop comparing herself to all of the other women who were also fighting against time themselves.

Still, she'd had a few things done. With her nose job and chin lift she no longer looked anything like her own mother, daughter or brother. Her inherited mother's features had been the reason Apollo was pulled to her in the first place. There was nothing left of them now.

Jillian's face was now an almanac of lines- some natural, some surgical- she was fatigued with the constant fight for beauty. She pulled her wig off and tossed it on the chair, looking into the mirror at herself. This was her. The face and body that she had left.

She leaned closer to the mirror and searched her eyes for specks of her family. Her eyes had come from her father; Gil had the same: dark brown with tinges of green around the irises.

Jilly had kept with her daily routine of putting on the dramatic fake eyelashes, without them she begged for some natural contrast between her eyes and the skin around them.

Her once young face with the pinched out cheekbones hung heavy towards her neck. Her lips once pursed just so, perfect like a Kewpie doll, soured with lines radiating from every side.

Inside, she often felt as young and supple as she had back in the height of her pageant days when Denby was instantly taken with her and just had to have her as his wife.

He was such a good man, supportive and loving until the very end. The shattering realization that he was a lousy businessman as she had found out after his death had rocked her world and flung her into the trenches of her family's finances. It had been his inability to bring on new clients or other partners to shore up the business and when his father's clients died off one by one, their heirs took the money and walked away with their riches. They had no need of his services, and year by year the debts started to build.

Denby's final act as a lawyer was to add Jillian's name to a class action lawsuit for a potential settlement he'd heard about. One from the company that had manufactured the breast implants she had placed in the late seventies. His protective foresight had given her the ability to take care of herself. It had been enough to give her the ability to live here. Hopefully until the end of her days.

She'd been poorer than some in her early life, and richer and richer than most in her middle years. But somehow, after all of it, just having enough felt like enough. She put some softened margarine on her toast with one shake of cinnamon and sugar and took a bite before setting it down on the plate and climbing into the shower.

Today felt different. Today she would wash her hair and see what she could do with it herself. She might call down to get an appointment at the beauty parlor in the lobby in the next day or so. It was time for once in a long while to be who she really was.

Jillian called and left a message on her daughter Violet's answering machine.

"Vi, I'd love to catch up and see how you are doing. I was just sitting here thinking about my times catching snakes and horseshoe crabs in the marshes on Little Tybee. Uncle Gil and I would canoe over there and sometimes get stuck and have to camp out in our homemade hammocks and try to sleep with the cicadas buzzing all night. I hope this message finds you well. I love you, my sweet Violet."

She hung up the phone and got dressed, brushing her long but thinned hair into a nice high bun. She still put on her eyelashes but would pick up some mascara next time she was at the store. She would be working with what she had from now on.

Picking up the little blue book off her nightstand, she rummaged through the hall closet to find some tissue paper to wrap it up in on her way out of the apartment for breakfast.

She'd be handing it off to Sally next at the table they all shared. The book was making its rounds through the Bonita Butterflies, and Jilly did not want to hold up the show.

~

God Flies Coach?, Me 2005

I *had flown across the country to see Mr. Affair. We had decided to solidify our plan, but as it turned out, an answer did not materialize.*

I knew I would be in my head for the entire trip back. If anything, our time together brought more questions than answers.

My divorce process was moving along back home, yet I was still a secret at Mr. Affair's house; he hadn't had the gumption to broach it with his wife.

My trajectory is set. I was committed-with or without him- I was moving ahead.

A man I would soon know as Michael sat next to me on the plane. I was in the window seat. The other seat was empty. It should have been an ordinary flight back. But it became anything but.

I wrote about my exchange with the incidental stranger on the back pages of my itinerary paperwork after landing while waiting for my connecting flight, remembering as much as I could to process later as my brain continued spinning. I wish I would have had a recording of our conversation as it seemed to last for days. This talk with an oddly enough fatherly figure of my same age.

~Here is what I wrote~

On my trip back from Maine to Cincinnati, a man sat next to me.

As the plane took off, he started talking, questioning me.

"What's your story? Where were you?"

Somehow he was able to drag all of my information out of me. It was weird, but not scary, and he would just say, "You'll never see me again, so what does it matter what you share."

It was true, so I did.

He said he was supposed to sit next to me, and that he had all the answers. He managed to wrench out of me all of the details- about the affair and how me and Mr. Affair had just come together to make a plan for our future.

He asked why Mr. Affair wasn't there with me now, or why I hadn't stayed with him in Maine.

I said it was complicated.

"Nothing is complicated; kids are adjustable," he said as plainly as if it was undeniably true.

He asked me where Mr. Affair was from midnight to six a.m. on the nights I was there.

I said part with me, part with her.

Then he said, "You don't leave your life at three a.m."

I thought at first he said, "You don't leave your "wife" at three a.m."

Then he said no. "You don't leave your life at three a.m. You can leave your wife at three a.m., but you can't leave your <u>life</u> at three a.m. If you mean that much to him he wouldn't let you out of his sight."

It almost made me cry.

He asked, "Why the hell should he care about his wife being mad at him for being gone? He said he is leaving her anyway, right?"

He then wanted to make a wager with me that Mr. Affair wouldn't leave his wife in the next week. A week sounded too short, but I was hopeful and so I took the bet.

I would have no way to pay him if he won as he wouldn't give me his information or even tell me his last name.

He asked if I watched movies. "Yes."

He said how in the movies if the woman leaves, the man always comes with or follows after her.

"Do you think he is on the plane behind you?"

"No," I answered. Knowing full well that he wasn't.

The conversation with him that day made me doubt everything I thought I had with Mr. Affair, and now I am confused.

"Are you God?" I finally asked him.

His name was Michael, (which I found out later that the meaning of his name was just so.)

He smiled a great grin and his eyes twinkled at me. I believe with everything that I am that he was God, plunked there into that very seat to steer me away from more potential pain and suffering-rather a psychological prankster who messed with other people's lives on airplanes just for kicks.

He continued to download his wisdom to me.

"Just keep doing what you are doing. Keep going. My brother is leaving his wife for another woman. He's been doing it for three years. Don't waste your life waiting around."

"Human nature says that he won't do anything. People always pick the easiest option."

I sit writing furiously about our exchange while waiting for my next flight.

I focus on Michael's last words to me before we said goodbye.

"Someday, you will find an amazing love- the one great one- and together you are destined to go down in amorous history."

On my original walks with Mr. Affair, I thought that everything made sense, but moments after we parted I became uncertain. Fractured and feeling alone in this mission of what should have been togetherness.

I sat with internal questions for Mr. Affair: Why was it okay for me to fly out for the weekend, only to share you with your family and be given scraps in the night? Why does she get to have you when you claim to have me- and only me- in your heart? Why do you care more about her feelings than mine?

Nothing had changed for him; he had made no motion forward. Maybe that is how it was supposed to be. Maybe you should give it your all with your wife. I am not the one for you.

I imagine I will never tell Mr. Affair of the conversation with the traveling prophet Michael on the airplane, or how I felt afterwards.

On my last flight home I sat in between two unmarried women. The lady on the aisle watched "Casablanca" on her laptop. I couldn't hear the words, but I knew how the story ended: Two people in love but not ending up together.

I hate it.

But it is perfect.

I didn't realize it then, but I would never see Mr. Affair again. And I still owe that inquisitive stranger a dollar.

~

~2~

Sally

S ally Rubenstein sat with her Butterfly friends at breakfast, the group laughing and talking more than a typical Thursday. The busy buzz of their table soon becomes noticeable to the other tables and their inhabitants.

"What is with them; they are so animated this morning," said one.

"I don't get it," said another.

"They must have gotten into the happy juice early," said another, all speaking in their usual tones because the Butterflies were talking plenty loud over them.

The women did not care. They had shared secrets, and thought about people some hadn't reflected on for many years.

"I like your hair, Jillian; it is quite becoming," said Adelma.

"Thank you so much. It was a lot for me to let the wig go; I am sure it will take some time. All I could really do with it was put it up in a braided bun. I need to have it trimmed. Maybe I will find a new style?"

"I am sure they will do a good job. I like Trixie in the salon. She is really creative and fun. I was thinking of having my hair dyed back to my old red next time. Might as well have some fun," she smiled wide.

"Yes, Sally, I think you should. Here, I have the secret package; you are next on the list."

Jillian passed the tissue-covered book onto Sally's lap.

"Thank you, madam, it has been received." The two chuckled and squeezed each other's hands on top of the table.

The staff was clearing out the dishes and had started to push the chairs in at the empty tables so the Butterflies- or BB's for short- decided to dispel. Adelma led the way in her wheelchair and they all except one boarded the elevator to the third floor to go back to their apartments. Jillian stayed on the main floor and headed to the beauty salon; she had been told that Trixie had a cancellation and could fit her in at ten.

The women on the third floor all waved to each other as each entered their own apartments. Sally took the book with her into 3A and closed the door behind her. She needed to use the bathroom before diving into this new escape.

Sally checked her phone messages and called her daughter back. Rebecca's family was getting ready for her son's bar mitzvah in a couple of months, and Sally's attendance had been requested.

"I would love to come. I haven't been back to Philly in ages. Can you believe that little Joshua will be thirteen soon? How's he coming with his Dvar Torah?"

"Great! I can hardly believe it, Mom, the kids have grown up so fast."

"Tell me about it."

Sally thought back to when Rebecca was little. What a fun and curious person she was then and still was.

"Mom, I have to run. We are choosing the food we are going to serve at the party. Right now we are taking Josh to pick the flavor of the cake."

"Okay, honey. Send me the details and I will get my flight booked. It will be nice to be back home for a while. I'll stay for a week, okay?"

"We'd love that. Plan on it. Talk to you soon, Mom."

"Yep." The connection clicked off on the other end. Rebecca hardly ever said goodbye; she was too busy, Sally supposed.

Sally sat down on her sofa and swung her legs over for a mellow moment. She'd gotten into the habit of a quick cat nap after breakfast to let the food settle a bit.

After a lifetime of keeping Kashrut- or Kosher- lately, she'd been struggling not to taste the bacon that wafted all around the cafeteria. It teased her; the smell was divine. Her friends loved bacon and always asked for seconds. She had never tried it, nor would she, but the smell made her wish some things were different.

She settled back onto the needlepointed pillows that she had made as a young mother back in Philadelphia. She set the little blue book on her belly and opened to the first page. The introduction had been read to them all by Hazel, but only once, and each of her book friends had been somehow struck by the author's idea so Sally was happy to have some real time with the stories inside.

She got to the bottom of the request and lay the book flat down on her stomach. She shook her head. Only five copies sent all over the United States? Talk about a needle in a haystack! Sally wondered where the author was and what would happen if she moved around a bit. The experiment might take even longer if she had any chance at all to begin with.

The pursuit might have been easier if a man had written it, Sally surmised, as men typically don't change their last names. It was easier to disappear as a woman if one wanted to. Move, marry a few times and voila: she's harder to track.

Marriage. Sally and her husband were married for almost thirty years before he wandered off with a younger version of herself. Yarden and she had met in Jewish Academy back in the fifties. Things were stricter than they are now. With her father's insistence that she marry someone who was committed to the same degree in the faith, along with her mother's wishes that she stay close to home, her selection was small.

In the end, Sally picked the man with whom she thought she would have the most in common, who also just happened to be the one chosen by her grandmother.

Sally read on in the little blue book to another memory by the author. It so happened to be an excerpt where the author was in love with a young man of a different faith. She read the author's words aloud.

R.V.

Oh, if this wasn't the classic case of religion getting in the way of love.

I was not a churchgoer, and you attended religious high school. We met through a friend. You were artistic, creative and terribly torn about the bounds which were placed on you. You wanted to have fun, be like everyone else. Have certain freedoms.

How wonderful, kind and thoughtful you were. You were obsessed with Opus, the penguin from the "Bloom County" comics. You would draw them for fun and send me such cute love-filled notes.

Being pulled in so many directions, you coped the best way you could. Escaping into your music, writing songs that were pertinent, hoping to sing to the whole world.

You had a lot of womanly-type qualities making you easy to relate to. Attentive, yes. Romantic, yes. A good communicator.

Not wanting to leave your high school your senior year. A school where you had been for so long, your parents moved anyway and placed you with a friend's family 'til graduation. You had an old car which you fixed up and were so proud of.

You were your own man, yet still a boy. You grew and developed within those constraints and soon you felt the need to be with family again. Being on your own was too hard, especially sitting amongst someone else's family.

I loved you, but we were so young.

I found out later you married someone closer to your family's ideals. A church girl.

Much later, you and your wife had problems and I found myself knowing where you were. I went to see you. I was still unattached, you in the process of detaching. Your apartment was sparse, but you had enough to get by.

Posters of "Star Trek" and "Star Wars" characters as well as rock bands filled the walls.

There was a place to sit, and time to reminisce and catch up together. I picked up one of your action figures to keep my hands busy as we talked.

Still a boy in the body of a man. We talked and even cuddled as we watched "Star Trek." We did not kiss, knowing it would be too easy to fall in step with each other again, and we both knew we couldn't take that same walk as the exact same things would come up.

Everything had changed and nothing had changed. We sat and watched "Star Trek" and that was enough.

Sally's eyes diverted to the wall in her home that was filled with family photos. If Sally would have chosen her first love, those faces would have been different. There would be other children on that wall, and perchance she wouldn't be here in this place at all?

If only she would have been brave enough to push to be with Joseph, the boy next door. The sweet, kind Catholic boy from her childhood. His parents would have been against it, too, although she was not sure he ever broached the subject with them, and Sally was sure her Father would have threatened her with herem, the worst treatment she could think of. With him being a professor and on the Board of Governors at Gratz, the Jewish teaching College there in Melrose Park, PA, her going against the tradition would have been trouble for more than just her.

Life would have been more complicated- tumultuous even- but she might have ended up being happy.

~

Finding Mr. Fun, Me, 2005

*I*t was in an off-site work class where I sat in the back quietly listening, fretting the whole time about being back in a classroom again since school had always been pretty ghastly for me. I took impeccable notes.

One gentleman took a shine to me. He was this large being, dwarfing me in size. I hadn't noticed him, and was trying extra hard to pay attention to the information being taught. I needed to learn this stuff. While I wasn't being graded, I would have to act as an expert for any homeowners who might have questions. Even with my baseline interest because of my mother's business, it was hard to focus and get the info into my brain.

It was after one of the breaks that I found him there suddenly sitting next to me. Uninvited, unwelcome and frankly, too persistent in getting my attention. I kept my eye on the teacher, but soon found myself fielding notes just like in junior high.

While the teacher talked, he'd whisper softly, "what's your story," "isn't this boring," and "what do you like to do for fun?"

It was a three day class, and he spent every minute after that first break beside me, whispering, writing me notes and keeping me from the curriculum.

He wore me down and I loosened up allowing our interaction to become fun. We even got in trouble once for not listening, which would have horrified me as a youngster.

He wasn't even close to my "type" or so I thought, nor was I really interested in pursuing anything with anyone with my heart very much still attached to Mr. Affair. Even with the ambiguity of what we currently had or did not have, I had remained loyal.

In our exchanges that day, we discovered that we had once lived on the same street in the same town at the same time. We both had two daughters and he said he might actually remember selling me and my husband a television back then. All too many crazy coincidences to just ignore. It didn't feel like he *was making a pass- it felt like kismet.*

After the last class was over, we exchanged numbers and suddenly I had this person wanting to hang out and do stuff with me. All kinds of things I hadn't really done and I had tons of time to waste with my daughters in school during the day. Our schedules were similar, so it was easy. I told him that all I could handle was to be friends, and he seemed fine with that. Or so he said.

We started going out together, frequenting bars to shoot darts, play pool and even went to a few concerts together. All things I hadn't really explored much in my life before parenthood.

He was willing to try things, and he added a glint of possibility to my life. We started as friends, although he made it clear he was after me.

When Mr. Fun was around, we talked about "Seinfeld" and joked and laughed, and suddenly the dark clouds that I had been carrying around with me started to feel a little lighter.

His presence gave me someone to talk to about stuff, and a person to call when I was bored and my kids were with their dad. He filled the gap and made life a little more, well, fun.

We'd been pals for a couple of months- good friends I would say- when he suddenly raised the ante. I remember being in the car with him, driving home from sushi one day, sushi being another first for me.

It was a couple of months before his birthday. He asked if I would have sex with him for his birthday, saying that it would really make his day. He confessed that he had a hard-core crush on me, even if I was only lukewarm towards him as a romantic partner. He asked and told me to think about it.

My life was already damn complicated. Now this- geez.

I had some feelings there: his company had made me feel happier and brought my smile and some spark back to my life, but I knew if I did sleep with him, it would mean the complete severing off of any chance I had to be with Mr. Affair. I wasn't sure I wanted that, despite him continuing to drag his heels towards a life together for us in the seven months since I had seen him last.

I hadn't had sex in quite a while either so the idea of it was a little enticing. I agreed to think about it.

~

~S or R~

I remember you were pretty. Curly hair, glasses and a nice smile. How lucky I was to have sat next to you, a kind stranger who took an interest in a little kid at a hockey game. You were seated next to me in the stands and struck up a conversation with me, really out of nowhere. You must have been able to tell that my Dad and my brother were in their own little world, cheering and yelling as the players got rough and scored goals on each other. You noticed that I was feeling out of my element.

Bored.

Bored- or more like done- watching once the blood started flowing. Red splatters all over the window-like barriers surrounding the rink. People hurting each other. Whistles blew constantly, and the crowd went wild. I just couldn't watch.

Your name was Shae or Rae or something. I can hardly remember your features now, maybe curly hair, a soft brown. I think you had glasses. You kept me busy with stories and asked at the end of the game if I would like a pen pal.

It was back in the late seventies or early eighties. There wasn't the same fear associated with strangers as there is today. You seemed nice, and either worked for the Pop Shoppe soda company or just happened to carry coupons for the beverage in your purse.

I thanked you and was happy to go later with my Dad and brother to pick up an entire crate of mini-sodas the next weekend after we met.

You wrote to me a few times on nice, pretty stationery.

I am sure I was a lousy pen pal as I was only about ten or eleven years old. It's interesting to think now why a stranger would want to connect with a little kid at a hockey game and be friends? Why would my Dad go along with it? Maybe he wasn't paying attention. Or maybe there was something else going on that I was unaware of?

Maybe you wanted to date my Dad, or maybe the two of you were dating and I was totally clueless? Either way, thanks for the soda gift and for making me feel special in a packed stadium full of people.

Sometimes strangers- are put into our path to show us that we as a people can connect to each other in the most random of places. That if we share a smile and a little about ourselves, we may just find we are more alike than different after all.

~

Apartment Life And A New Friend, Me
2005

Today I am braless and profound. It is a day that I am oozing with creativity. With this new life certain freedoms have come to me, and I am feeling that the whole world is open to me. Unencumbered, satisfied. I am my own person. Soul-full and rich in spirit and mental wealth, today that is. The words are coming.

Today I have given names to my dreams, my future. There is a plan that I am happy to act on. I am learning and evolving right into myself. Should I say things are good?

I wear a hat that makes me feel as though I am sitting in a Paris cafe, watching the many people go by. Our new kitten chases the pen as I write longhand deep into the night.

The little thing came up to the girls and me while we were pulling grocery bags out of the car to carry up to our third-story, walk-up apartment. This perfect little creature meowed softly and our hearts melted as we looked around to see where she might belong. As a responsible parent I suggested we make up signs as she must belong to someone, the owner no doubt sitting at home broken-hearted. And we did and no one came forward so we named her Lucy and she was ours.

Lucy has been a godsend to me. Suddenly there was a break in the silence and stagnation of the apartment when I was there alone. I had someone to sit with me when I was afraid. She listened when I needed to talk. I had someone to sleep next to me when I was scared about the future. I had someone to need me again.

For the girls, it meant that we had something fun in the house. Lucy was cheeky, silly and loving and even when she would wake me up at five in the morning by jumping on my toes in bed for breakfast, I was grateful for the brain escape.

When she was around I wasn't in my head as much, I could focus on other things. Not the massive worry about what would come next, or if I would ever find my way. With her bounding around the house, I could circumvent the dread that I might have made the biggest mistake of my life.

She was an interruption from the feeling that I'd been selfish to think about making my life bigger when others- my daughters and my husband- had a pretty easy life with me in the picture full time before. My thoughts were pulled from the constant beating up of myself in my own mind, because things might not turn out like I planned.

I changed my life because I wanted to, as no other reason made sense.

As a young girl, I craved stability: a home with two parents who loved each other. When I achieved that as a grown up, it was good for a while but then I wanted more. Needed more. So I changed what I had. Now I don't have more of anything unless you count problems and things being harder and in actuality I have less.

Less stability and less routine, but more freedom, but less rules.

I remember when I decided I didn't care if I would have to pay for the wall in the apartment to be repainted, I needed something on my wall to inspire me every day. To keep me going when things got hard.

I took black paint and painted a saying that I needed to see and read every day.

"God, grant me the serenity to accept the things I cannot change, the courage to change the things I can, and the wisdom to know the difference."

I couldn't go back and change anything. I couldn't give up on the idea of leading an extraordinary life now, not when I must be closer to getting there. What is the point of giving your entire life over to the other people in your life and having nothing left for yourself?

To sit back as a martyr and say I did it all for you?

Would they have done it for me? Would they have given up their dreams for what I wanted?

So often people think they are doing the right thing by doing everything for their child or their family. Like they will get an award for putting all their own needs to the back of the line in their life until their kids grow up and leave to live their own lives.

When they've gone, you could be left with a husband or partner that you no longer know or even like. You could be stuck with the "you" who does not know who they are anymore or even what they like to do. And the years have passed and your body might not do all the things that you ask of it, or real disabilities can come, reframing the life you once imagined- quite different.

I think when one is unhappy and feeling out of control in looking for "The Happy," one can get sick from it. The constant weight of the what ifs on your psyche freezes you in place. Fear can jump in compounding with the hopelessness and then you are stuck trying to pull your way out of that hole.

I guess that's depression's definition if I ever heard one. Feeling trapped in a place of unhappiness or worry with no ability to see your way out.

Good days mix with bad, sometimes all on the same day.

Just keep going, I tell myself. Every day offers a new opportunity to feel better, be better, and find my happy.

~

~2~

S ally tucked her afghan tighter around herself. She thought back to the summer of 1938 when the rambunctious Lynch family moved into the old abandoned house next door. It was a five bedroom, two bathroom house and much bigger than the one Sally lived in.

And that house was filled to the brim with Lynches: Eight children in all, with four boys and four girls of varying ages. Joseph, the one that was Sally's age, was in the middle. He was sanctioned to the young boys' bedroom which he shared with his younger brother Matthew who was six. The two older brothers shared another room, and the other two children's bedrooms were filled with two younger and older sets of girls. Oddly, none of them were close to Sally's age. It didn't matter though; Sally was content to play with the boys as she was a bit of a tomboy back then.

With no fence between the houses, it had been easy to make friends with the new neighbors. Sally imagined the mother exhausting herself each morning with feeding her massive brood, afterward kicking the children outside to occupy themselves until dinner time. On most days, Mrs. Lynch would put sandwiches out on the porch around noon time, and none of those children missed out on a meal.

Often the boys in that family would relieve themselves in the bushes, as Sally had accidentally spied once, thinking they were starting a hide-and-seek game. She was careful not to go behind the houses at certain times of the day after that. They'd all play for hours out front, games such as "*Mother May I,*" "*Red Rover*" and "*Drop the Handkerchief.*" Even the older kids would play before leaving to practice their marbles and "*Box Ball.*"

With her older brother taking classes in the Hebrew Academy nearby, Sally was left to get herself to and from the elementary public school. She would often walk with the Lynch kids instead of alone.

From the start, Sally understood that the Lynch family was of a different religion from her family. The Lynches went to church instead of synagogue and didn't honor the Sabbath like they did. That family often had picnics with family and friends on Friday evenings, while Sally's family was recognizing Shabbat at the synagogue.

When Joseph's younger brother Matthew fell ill to Rubella and had to stay home from school, Joseph and Sally took their time getting back home each day. They'd discuss their different religions, and compare notes about what was most important in each. Her Judaism and his Catholicism were a curiosity for them both. Both born into a tradition, a set of rules that neither had questioned before and didn't dare try.

Their walk to and from school meant at least an hour of each day spent together. They'd wade through Tacony Creek, a tributary close to their neighborhood on the way home. Contentedly catching little green frogs and watching the water striders for hours, Sally made it a contest between the two of them to see who saw the most of each. Once Matthew was better, he was included in their adventures. Creek time soon became the best part of Sally's day.

In the spring they'd catch pollywogs in their lunch thermoses to bring home and watch grow. Most of the time they made sure to dump the critters out into the clay pots in the garden before bringing their lunch boxes into the house to keep from startling their mothers. Only once had she heard Mrs. Lynch scream and run from the house before Joseph decided it was best to double-check his thermos before heading in. Oddly, Sally's mother never asked her about the dirt in her thermos. Maybe she didn't want to know.

A close friendship blossomed between the two neighbors. As each started developing, the two became inseparable much to their parents' concern.

Sally thought back to the day when her father sat her down and told her she wouldn't be walking to school and home with Joseph anymore, that he'd signed her up for the Hebrew Academy and she would be with the other young girls in her own faith. She was fifteen.

"It's the way it is supposed to be. We need to be with our own people to be better able to teach our children to live our values. Marrying outside of the circle will mean that the marriage is not valid. It won't count in the eyes of God. Your children would not be seen as legitimate. Sally, I am well respected in the ranks of our synagogue, and I cannot have you falling in love with that Catholic boy."

"I didn't say I loved him, Father." Sally had said, even though in her heart she actually did.

"Let's not argue. I will be dropping you off at the Academy tomorrow. Move away from Joseph. You'll find a good Jewish boy someday." Her Father stood and walked away. Her Mother looked up from her sewing as

Sally made her way to her room.

Sally didn't come down for dinner. She slept restlessly that night, and the next day she dutifully dressed and readied herself to be driven to the Academy. As they drove off, Sally saw Joseph wave to her from his driveway. He'd still be going to public high school.

As the months went on, more and more of her time was taken up with events at the Academy or at the synagogue. Sally rarely saw him anymore. Mostly on weekends as his family walked to the Holy Trinity Church for services on Sundays.

Sally often sat outside on her front porch, rocking in the rocking chair, acting like she was reading as the large family embarked, hoping to steal a smile or glance at Joseph. This went on for months.

One day, Joseph lagged to the back of his family and dramatically motioned to her to look in the flower pot that was sitting on the table next to her.

Digging through the pansies, she found a small scroll of paper bundled with a beautiful red ribbon. As she pulled it free, Joseph waved one long wave and continued walking with his family into the distance. None had noticed his gesture to her.

She looked around before pulling the tether off to unroll the note.

'I miss you Sally. This has been so hard not to see you or be around you. I miss your smile, your laugh and how we used to adventure together. The way we used to walk and talk about all kinds of things. My mama has told me that you aren't allowed to be around me anymore, because we aren't in the same faith. Both our fathers talked about it. But it seems so wrong, for us to be away from each other because, I love you.

I've loved you from the moment you squealed after catching your first tadpole, with it wet and slimy in your fingers. The way your eyes lit up each time you caught a frog down by our creek. You are my best friend. I can't believe I won't have you in my life anymore. We are moving. It's only across town, but we won't have even the scattered chance of seeing each other. My Mama says you'll forget about me, and find a good Jewish boy, and I will find a good Catholic girl to love. I guess it is the way it is supposed to be,

I will always love you, ~Your Joseph.'

Sally read the last line out loud as tears streamed down her face. She loved him, too. What kind of a god would want to keep them away from each other?

The Lynches did indeed move away only two weeks later. The truck carrying all of their belongings filled and left in the space of a day. Sally stood at the window of her bedroom watching, sobbing. As the truck chunked off into the distance, her mother came into her room to fetch her for dinner.

Sally fell face-first on her blankets, a river of tears stained her cheeks.

"Don't you want to eat, honey?"

"No, I can't bear it. They were a good family. Joseph was a good boy. Why can't we be together if we love each other?"

Mother wrapped her in her arms and held on as her daughter wept. She smoothed her tousled curly hair and pulled it away from Sally's face.

"It would make everything harder, my darling. Which one of you would convert? Would you ask him to give up his religion for yours? Would you be willing to give up your faith and everything you believe to join his? What of the children that you might have together- they wouldn't be blessed the way they would be if you found someone from our faith. It's not the way."

Sally stayed in her room that night, a tray with a cup full of tomato soup was left untouched at her door. She came out to get ready for the Academy the following day. Before she walked out of the house, her aging grandmother took her by the hand and looked into her eyes a reflected wisdom hard won over the years.

"I know, my darling, that your heart is with that boy, but as the days go by, he will be less and less on your mind. Your heart will heal and you will allow someone else to take up that space. Believe me, you have a big wonderful heart- you will find love again."

Sally squeezed her grandmother's hand and walked out the door. Who was she to upset the system? To go against their faith. She couldn't ask Joseph to change his beliefs and he wouldn't ask that of her either. It was a stalemate.

As life went on and her marriage soured and then divorced, she often thought about Joseph and how if only they were born even twenty years later there might have been more accommodations made for their love. They could have done things differently. She'd long lost touch with the Lynch family, but knew from friends that they were still in the Melrose Park area.

As Sally drifted off, she wondered if Joseph would still remember her.

~

Out Of The Mouths Of Babes, Me 2006

My youngest daughter is a wise old soul. The other day I was getting ready and she came into my bathroom and said she needed a cold lunch today for a field trip. Then she asked where she was supposed to go after school. I told her that she needn't worry, that I've got this. I've got her. That I will always take care of her and her sister.

She looked up at me with her big, blue, telling eyes and asked, "Mommy, who takes care of you?"

I stopped cold. There wasn't anyone anymore. Her eyes begged me for an answer.

"Well, I guess, I take care of myself.

And suddenly it was true. Me and the girls are all I have.

~

~2~

Sally got up from the couch after her nap and walked straight to her dresser. On top was an old perfume decanter with a bulb spritzer. Removing the cap she tilted out the contents into her hand. It was a small scroll of paper. It had yellowed and was brittle with age.

She babied it, carefully unfurling the document to read. Tears filled her eyes, and she felt an impulse to do something crazy.

She walked to her phone and called directory assistance.

"Yes, please, I need the number for a Joseph Lynch, Philadelphia, Pennsylvania, please."

The operator spoke, "One moment. Would you like me to put you through?"

"Yes, please," Sally shrugged her shoulders, pacing around her living room as it rang.

It rang three times before a man picked up the line.

"Hello?"

Sally closed her eyes tight, "Hello Joe? It's Sally, your old next door neighbor; remember me?"

A gasp and then, "Oh, Sally, how could I forget?"

The two old friends talked for hours and Sally felt like a teenager again. Over seventy now, but her life wasn't over. Somehow, it felt like a new beginning.

The two arranged to see each other when she came into town for Jacob's bar mitzvah later that month. In fact, Joe offered to come as her date.

They talked every day, sometimes more than once, and all because she took a chance on reaching out again. She'd been given the push by the little blue book that had come so serendipitously into her life. Life still had plenty of surprises in store.

~

Suddenly Loaded, Me 2006

*W*ith the divorce came a settlement. My ex-husband and I split everything we had together, and he was always much better with money
than my family had ever learned or taught me to be. He was more than fair,
and he decided to keep the house, so he bought me out of my share.

There were some Roth IRA's, random stocks and some retirement dollars
from his company. I suddenly had more money than I knew what to do with.
A troublesome place to be with my familial legacy of lack all piled up in the
background and now money to burn.

Out of my windfall, I shared some money with my mother, father and
brother to help them out. Five K each. A gift for the loving support they had
given me over the years. I was happy to be able to give it. I didn't expect them
to pay it back; there was no talk of that.

My brother used his to start taking college courses, and my mom lumped
hers in with his as well to spur him on. My Dad bought a car but it needed
some work, so I added another few thousand more to cover that.

"I'll pay you back," he said. But I wasn't worried about it. Dad had bailed
me out plenty of times in my life.

I believed if I kept working and budgeted that I would be able to safely keep
my nest egg secure and navigate the world.

I soon found I was a spender. Especially with my newly trim figure due
to the many miles of walking the aisles at work, coupled with my difficulty
in eating due to the depression that had a tight grip on me. I had grown an
overall laissez faire feeling about food.

It was fun to dress this new body of mine, and it was easy to spend two
hundred dollars on a pair of big-name jeans. It looked so nice with the
high-priced belt with a fancy name and oh, my God: Italian shoes that felt
like butter on my feet. Need I say more?

With the divorce I no longer had an overseer of my spending. The three
hundred dollar rule was no longer in force. In my marriage neither of us

would spend three hundred without talking together about it first. Thankfully again, I wasn't interested in drugs or I could have blown through all of the money much quicker. I would need to watch myself to make sure we were okay. I kept working and tried to budget so the money would last a long time. But things were about to change.

Starting out I didn't mind the awful hours of late into the nights and weekends. But as the months poured on, my hours forever conflicted with my time to be with my daughters- that reality wore thin.

I remember walking out of the lunch room after picking up my schedule for the next two weeks. I had looked down and again saw nights and weekends. It meant that the girls would be with their dad exclusively for another two weeks. I wrote "QUIT" on the piece of paper I had written my schedule on, and started to bawl. Tears were streaming as I walked back the long open aisle to my desk. My boss saw me, and she pulled me aside.

"What's the matter?"

"I never see my kids because of working here; I can't do this anymore."

She grabbed my schedule from me, saw my note about quitting and said she would try to change things up a bit. But I knew that there was someone who had been there longer than me, and she always got the day shift. She had seniority. I would need to move on.

A new job came my way at a tile distributor. I would be in charge of redesigning the showroom and helping customers who walked in. My desk was up front, and I spent most of my time learning the incredibly asinine shapes of tile from bullnose left, to bullnose right, corner, etc.

There were so many that I can't remember them anymore. As it turned out, I wasn't there long enough to memorize them.

My boss, B, was initially impressed with me. He wanted me to start right away, so I gave notice at the orange box, and started the following week.

At first he was nice, taking the time to train me and talk about what the future would be. Then, I made a large mistake by sending out 300 square feet of tile instead of 300 pieces of tile ordered and delivered via truck to a customer on the coast. Whoops.

Oh well. I was new.

He started to be a real dick after that though, and everything hit a wall one morning. After dropping my youngest daughter off in tears at school, a touch later than usual because she was dragging and really needed her Mom, I was two minutes late to work.

Two minutes.

I sat at my desk, now placed closer to him so he could watch and listen over me. Make sure I didn't make any more mistakes. A co-worker sat nearby. I sat in my chair and told him I was sorry and started to check my computer for messages and orders.

He stood behind me- over me- as I sat with my back to him. My neck got hot, my face flushed- I prepared for an attack.

And it came, he started yelling in front of everyone.

"Don't you have any respect for yourself? How do you think you are ever going to get anywhere in life if you show up late and cannot be counted on?!"

There was no understanding. He didn't have children to know what I had going on at home. He didn't care. He was a full-fledged jerk that day, standing over me like an executioner waiting to pull the lever. Even my co-workers were afraid, they told me later.

*After minutes of this with scenarios running rampant in my head, I stood up, faced him and said, "**I quit.**"*

I grabbed my purse, left a pile of paperwork on my desk and walked out, with him yelling behind me, "Good, good riddance. You will never get anywhere. Good luck!"

Fuck off, B.

I was shaking. No plan, nowhere else to go, but I wasn't going to be abused where I was any longer.

I heard later he got fired.

Good.

Asshole.

~

~2~

Mariko

S ally Berenstein knocked on the door of Mari Johnson before leaving on her trip back home to Pennsylvania.

Mari had been traveling the week prior and had just returned home from visiting her son in Atlanta.

"Oh, good, you're back. I thought I missed you," said Sally, staring down at her shorter, younger neighbor.

"Yes, I am back. Is everything okay?"

"Oh, yes, it's very good. I am leaving to go out of town to see my daughter and attend my grandson's bar mitzvah in Philadelphia, but I wanted to get you the book before I left. I think you are the last one of the Butterflies to have it before it will go back to residing in the library."

"Oh, yes, thank you. I was looking forward to reading it. It was hard to remember all the stories inside from just hearing them that once when Hazel read it to us."

"Yes, I got so much more out of it having some time to read it myself. It made me do something rather daring!"

Mari looked up at her acquaintance friend, "Oh? What did you do?"

"I reached back into my own set of memories to a boy who stole my heart countless years ago. He still lives in Philly and is a widower. I am going to see him on this trip. It has been a lifetime since we've seen each other."

"That's remarkable. What a brave thing to do. I hope it works out for you."

Sally launched in with a hug that surprised Mari; she hadn't realized they were that close.

As Sally squeezed, she gushed, "Yes, me, too. I have such an incredible feeling about it. Thanks! I have been dying to tell someone; you are the first. I'm leaving for the airport right now. Enjoy the book."

Sally pulled away and reached down to grab her luggage handle to catch the elevator. She was literally leaving that moment and in a big rush.

Mariko stood at her doorway, four foot nine inches of dainty-yet-powerful Asian duality. She looked after her friend and smiled. She really did hope things worked out for her. Going into the past can lead to troublesome roads if one is not careful.

Mari closed the door and sat down on her couch, taking a sip of tea. It had grown cold. Walking to the kitchen, she poured it into the sink and refilled her cup with a fresh batch from her teapot. The cast iron teapot was one of the only family pieces she had left from her childhood back in San Diego before moving across the country to Alabama. It wasn't often that she took the time to think of the stops along the way.

She sat again and started to read, taking sips of green tea every few pages or so until it was gone.

~

A New Belief In Me, From An Unlikely Source, Me 2006

Finding our new normal. I had moved out into an apartment. After the move, transferring kids gave Mr. Stability and me some small windows to see each other in a different light. We weren't battling about projects or what to have for dinner, and he wasn't complaining about how I kept the house.

Stepping past the big conversations about what had happened to us and the circumstances that pushed me towards the affair, we would slowly build a new relationship in being friends enough to be good parents and cooperative stewards of our amazing daughters. The hard conversations would come sometimes, and we took the time to listen. We both owned some of what had gone wrong.

We'd known each other a long time, and sometimes one of us would call each other after a hard day of whatever. See, we didn't hate each other; it really was just a difference in what we wanted long term out of life that ultimately was our undoing.

I remember one short conversation we had, standing in the driveway after the girls had run inside to watch TV. We were well into the divorce process.

"I'm sad," he said, "because now I won't get to see all the things you are going to do."

I was thrown by his comment. "What do you mean?"

"I know you will do big things, is all. I always knew you could, but now I won't have a front seat to it all."

Tears came then for us both as I finally felt that he had believed in me after all. He knew I was capable of doing something bigger with my life and making a difference somehow, but he hadn't been able to communicate it to me in a way that I understood.

All those years.

We hugged and I cried all the way home.

The challenges that I felt he put in front of me that had beat me down back then, all those times he questioned my intentions or the path of what I wanted to do. Each felt like a hard no. That I couldn't do it.

His insistence for me to write a business plan for the house flipping business I wanted to start with him, his pushing me for a commitment to complete design school- it was all a part of what he wanted me to go through to help give myself the courage or confidence to reach for each goal.

I had taken it that he didn't think I could do it, that I couldn't follow through on anything for that matter.

If only we had known how to talk to each other, if only the counselor had pulled that out of him then, or I'd felt even a glimmer of his belief in me.

Or maybe it wasn't until I was gone- that he figured it out himself.

~

M.B.

I remember meeting you when our daughters were in kindergarten. Our daughters had become friends, and my daughter wanted to have yours over to the house to play. You were nervous and new to the area, so you wanted to come meet me and see our home before such a play date could happen.

You came over and brought your son who just happened to be the same age as my youngest daughter. All of the kids played together while we got to know each other. You were a stay-at-home mom, too, but had almost fallen into it. Once in engineering, you just couldn't bear to leave your kids, so you gave up your career for a time to raise them at home with you.

I usually get along with people fairly easily as I am able to key into aspects that we share as a bridge to find common ground. You were very different from any person I had spent time with before. You didn't seem to get my sense of humor. Any sarcasm or joking around I tried fell flat and often brought forth a pretty odd look. It was almost as if we were speaking different languages- not the usual ones, but of aliens and humanoids. I will claim the alien side because it's how out of place I felt. I found it difficult to communicate sometimes. I assumed we wouldn't be friends, but our girls were thick as thieves.

When I mentioned how I volunteered to teach art classes at our eldest's elementary school, you glommed onto the idea even though you claimed not one artistic bone in your body. It was out of your comfort zone, but soon we were partnering up each month to teach the kids all kinds of new things. The task was a wonderful one, especially since the arts were disappearing from our public school system circa 2000 on. I do pray that our society will come back to seeing the value of artistic expression someday.

In the interim the classes we taught were once a month. The hour we were given consisted of a short lesson on the specific artist which included some of their history, what type of art they did and an understanding of the mediums they used. The majority of the lesson was used to execute a project, one that let them explore their creativity while mimicking the artist some, while keeping in mind their age and motor skills. Each month we would get together to plan, figure out the project, and gather the materials from the art room closet at school to present to the students. Even in the challenges with our trouble communicating our thoughts to each other, we figured it out, doing this every year for our older children and following up with years more with our younger two if they were in the same class.

We were different but could still work together.

I had been around art for the predominance of my life with my mother, a creative in whatever it was that she chose. She designed t-shirts and wallpapers on her way to a full architecture degree. I had attended art camps in the summers with the nuns of a local teaching college as a child, and had loved drawing, painting and doodling forever.

I grew to understand and like you a lot, as meeting you was a growth experience for me, too. We shared in the commitment of fostering a creative space for our children among a school system that seemingly only cared about how well they did on tests.

Our partnership in the art program ended with my youngest child's last class together. The kids would be venturing into middle school. By then you were starting over again with a new little one, a son.

I was experimenting with something to do, too. A possible career. I helped you figure out a paint color for your house, and helped you choose some materials for your kitchen. In a horrible mistake the tile person installed one of your Italian made, hand-painted backsplash tiles sideways which ruined the look in my trained eyes. I was upset and said it should be changed, but you said you could live with it, it didn't bother you. Another difference between us for sure. Seeing that every day would have made me nuts.

You moved away and we lost touch, but I want you to know even though I might not have picked you initially to be my partner in those art lessons, you ended up being the perfect one to help teach me that anyone can get along with anyone if they choose to try.

I will always appreciate your friendship and how lucky I was that our paths crossed. I wish you well and hope that all three of those delightful kids of yours are flourishing.

You might not have meant to, but you being you taught me a lot about me. That our common goal made a bridge wide enough to take two people with few similarities and make us a team. Art can be a lifeline for some, making the most terrible situation more bearable or by building a community or friendship that wasn't there before.

~

Feeling It, Me, 2006

*T*oday was an emotional day. I allowed myself to cry and be accountable to the feelings I have carried around this last year. I am unsure of my future. Unsure how this story will turn out. I like to think that I am in control of myself and my journey, but I'm not sure.

Even though this is what I asked for, even though I wanted to not be married to him anymore, this was not part of the plan. The loneliness, the aloneness. I was not prepared to be on my own right out of the gate. Right now. I feel unstable, out of it, so far from what I thought would be my reality. I really thought Mr. Affair and I would end up together. That if I left and he left, we would figure out the details. I jumped and he didn't.

My angry eyebrows stare back at me in the mirror. I try to soften my face. So much has happened. I have created so much drama, so much hurt, and outright craziness all for the idea of a more romantic love and a bigger life.

These days, I flash anger at a moment's notice. I exhibit my sad eyes a lot, too. Am I manipulating myself? Are my tears even real? I sometimes feel as though I am going mad.

My new kitty lies on my notebook to the right of my computer as I type. I am sitting and looking out the window of my apartment. Lucy sniffs at the Buddha head on my desk. Om. If only I felt some peace.

I know that nothing in my life compares to the suffering that others have faced over the last few months in this country and throughout the world. Hurricanes and natural disasters have beaten our world. Not to mention the countless lives lost in this unending war. I know I shouldn't complain. I was not abused. Not thrown into the street, I was only unhappy.

I watch another sun go down and ask again if I made the right choice but the only answer that comes is the quiet.

This life was the more difficult choice. Change is harder than staying the same for some. Unless it's the sameness that is killing you. This road will be a bumpier one. At least for a while as I get my legs solidly underneath me.

I had the suburban dream: The big house, the minivan, and never a worry. Great and stable kids. Friends right next door to chat with.

Since I have nuclear bombed my life, things are more different than the same.

I spend most of my time alone.

I thought I saw the end result of what I believed I wanted back when I left: A much bigger life. One with more yeses than nos. A more three-dimensional existence rather than living in a straight line with the present and the future set with most of the decisions chosen for me. My ideal has gone out the window.

I was craving freedom from what felt like criticism and the constant feeling that I didn't measure up no matter what or how much I did. Now, as I face many evenings sitting alone with this mischievous cat, I find the solitude rather unsatisfying as well.

I should do this, and I should do that. Instead, I sit and do nothing. Tonight, I wrote a little and did some laundry. If it weren't for work in a few hours, I probably wouldn't leave the house today at all. Most of the time I feel I never want to leave.

A headache is coming on, most likely from the pure crap I ingested today and the stale, apartment air I have breathed in all day.

*My Mom says that when you are depressed you should just get really **into** that feeling. Put ridiculous curlers in your hair, get into your most unattractive or even dirty pajamas, and just really commit to that shitty feeling.*

She promises that pretty soon you will find yourself feeling so pathetic you can't help but smile because of the pitiful state of it. I am not there yet, but I am close.

Today, I am just really in my "shit". And tomorrow I may feel better, and then perhaps the day after that, better again- or at least I can hope.

"One day at a time." It's a saying for a reason.

We all have moments, days, years where we are only living one day at a time. Then suddenly you turn around and you are in a better place than you were. But I imagine you can find yourself in the same unsatisfied spot if you change nothing.

I sit making myself believe that someday if I keep going, I will feel whole again.

After all, I am on a new adventure with no one to hold me back; I am finally free. But it's all on me.

~

~2~

Mariko got up from the couch after reading the little traveling book in one session. She arranged some rice crackers on a plate to enjoy with her mid-afternoon sake. It was a daily tradition. She sat on the floor pillow by the window at a table low to the ground. Photos of family members long passed were arranged out in front of her. Each image was encased in an ornate gold frame. A large white candle sat in the background and she lit it with a long match.

On a bamboo tray in the center of the table sat a one-day-old cup of sake. She would sit in remembrance of her parents and grandparents who had also enjoyed a daily toast.

Each day Mariko would trade the cup she just poured with the one that was placed in front of her relatives. Her parents had taught her that it was rude to pour sake for oneself. Her system meant her cup came from her lost relatives while they were given the one she had just poured for them. It was the best way she could think of to honor and keep them all content.

"Kanpai," Mariko said as she raised it high to her relatives before tapping her cup against the other cup placed on the table. She closed her eyes and took a sip.

Out of all of her fellow residents at Sunny Days, *she* was the only one she knew of with Japanese heritage. She hadn't had anyone in her little apartment in the four years since she moved there. Mari's last name of Johnson was a far cry from her maiden name of Osaka, and Mari became the Americanized version of her real name Mariko. Named after her grandmother.

Starting out life in San Diego with a doctor father and nurse mother, Mariko believed everything was perfect in their life together. At age eight something happened that changed everything. Their little family had no idea what a turbulent few years they'd be in for once the Americans joined World War II because of the Pearl Harbor attack.

It was a time of great paranoia and uncertainty. Suddenly, as it seemed to Mariko, all suspicious eyes turned to focus on the people of Japanese descent. Although she would find out later, it was mostly those living on the west coast of America.

Both her father and mother had been born in the U.S., but because of a previous law they had not been allowed to become American citizens.

They went from being categorized as *Resident Aliens* to *Alien Enemies* with the signing of Executive order 9066 by Franklin Delano Roosevelt just after the Pearl Harbor bombing.

The family was given about two months to sell or lend out their property and belongings and would need to report to a War Relocation Station for transport to one of ten internment camps spotting the West Coast, Southwest, and one in the far South of the U.S.

Mariko remembered the frenzied chaos of her parents trying to find homes for their belongings so that they might get them back someday. The day her father signed over his stake in his medical practice to a friend, pleading with him to allow him to return once the war - or whatever this was - was over.

Mari overheard many of those conversations between her parents late at night when they thought she was sleeping. During the day they kept quiet with their fears and the building uncertainty acting as if everything would be fine. They packed up a few things and two changes of clothes. Mari was allowed to bring a doll that she had been given by her grandparents. She remembered her mother wrapping up her teapot in layers upon layers of clothes before handing the bag to her husband to carry.

Mari wore her school satchel and she and her brother both held onto their mother's hand as they boarded a bus bound for the dispersal center at the Santa Anita Race Track. So much change in such a short time period. Once safe and carefree in their family home, the Osaka's were corralled into lines along with hundreds of others to be sent to God knows where. They were there for two days before being transported by train into the depths of the U.S. Southwest.

Hours blurred by on the train, her familiar and comforting cityscapes fell away and the emptiness and muted tones of the desert replaced every color she had ever enjoyed. Dusty, dry, choked scenery muddied her terrified self as her life changed before her eyes. Stricken for the first time with the possibility of death, she looked at the faces of the others, people who were also captive under this political demand. All because of how they looked or where their families might have come from. Everyone was hopeless and helpless to do anything but sit, listen and do what they were told.

She'd always seen her father be the one in charge in tense situations- now he also sat with his eyes fallen, powerless because of a nationally documented opinion that his family and those of shared heritage were considered enemies of the very country they were all born in.

Arriving a day-plus later to the Poston Internment Camp in Arizona, this brazen and scorched piece of earth would be home to them all for the next two years. Mariko's family was *"lucky"* in that they had all gone there together. She had found out much later that often it was only the men who were pulled from the family and placed in the camps. She wondered which would have been worse: watching her father be stolen away not knowing where he'd gone and if she'd see him again; or spending the next two years behind that spiky barbed wire fence - together.

They stood for hours at the canteen waiting for their lodging assignments. Sweaty, hungry and tired, Mariko and her brother fell asleep on their parents' shoulders and awoke the next morning on tufts with light blankets laid over them. She didn't remember getting there.

Opening her eyes, she took in their new home. It was wooden and bare with two windows, one on each end of the building. A curtain was set up between her and her brother's space and her parents' bed- it was the only softness in the room. Bed was a bit of an exaggeration: they were hard canvas bags full of hay placed together in a pile, not even stitched to stay together. Nothing like the curtains on the windows or beautifully wallpapered walls back home.

Mariko was rushed by her mother to hurry and get dressed so they could go and get breakfast in the mess building. She wasn't sure she wanted to eat in a place called "mess."

Mother was adamant, pulling her out of bed, because if they missed the time there would be nothing at all for them until lunch.

Why had they been brought here? What was going on? were just some of the questions she sought answers for as they walked down a lane between large rectangular buildings. No one answered her. Maybe they couldn't explain it, or maybe they didn't know.

Mari looked at the photograph of her father and mother taken before the war. It was possibly their wedding day as both seemed very happy and in love. She nodded in respect and in awe of her parents and their strength back then. They never let on to Mariko or her brother Niko that they were in danger, and it would be many years before Mari would actually find out all that they had been through.

Mariko could still remember how hot it was, how nothing was the same, and how she tried to keep herself busy until meal times when she would go with her family to the mess.

It wasn't long until she found herself a shady spot behind the bathroom building to go to be cooler. There she drew in the sand with her fingers before taking one of Mama's dull pencils to use instead.

At first she would practice both writing her name in cursive and the alphabet, then she'd work on her arithmetic tables. Finally she started drawing simple animals. She sat in her dress on the ground getting dirtier by the day, but Mother was never hard on her. The area behind the bathroom building smelled terrible, so she had the space to herself except for the occasional scorpions and snakes she would always be on the lookout for. Only once had a snake come close, but she was walking at the time and was able to run away- luckily she was nimble. Mariko hadn't told her parents about the incident as she didn't want to risk them forbidding her from going to her secret place.

Doodling in the sand gave her something to do and somewhere to be. It was a place to escape where it was reasonably quiet, and away from the people crying or yelling. Mariko didn't like overhearing the worried conversations about what was going to happen next to the people there. Hundreds of people thrown into a wasteland, all stuck in limbo with no sight of freedom.

Each day her artwork in the sand was erased with the dust storms, the wind blowing them away. With that she felt safe but also invisible in this world.

There was a day when a guard was walking the grounds, and he came upon Mariko squatting in the shade. She was frightened and shy with his questions. He complimented her drawings and kneeled down to see them more clearly. The next day he brought her some pencils and paper to use instead of the sand. They were left over from his daughter from when she was young. She shyly accepted his generous gift and shared them with the other kids at school the next day. Mariko asked the guards for more art supplies for the children and maybe the adults, too. The request was granted.

As time went on, Mariko noticed that the adults that had been brought here were helping with the upkeep of the facility. Improving the buildings, digging out a swimming pool to help everyone cool down - they built a school. Her mother worked in the camp laundry facility and her father took a post at the on-site hospital. He even delivered babies. Some of the older women cared for the young children so their mothers could work as teachers or cooks.

After the school was built, Mariko and the other students had a more typical day of going to school and having a recess before going home to be with their families in the late afternoon. It was like a small city but there was little beauty and it just happened to be wrapped in barbed wire and no one could leave.

Mariko got up from her altar table and went into her bedroom to find some of her childhood memorabilia. It had been years since she looked through any of her artwork. Art had been how she kept her mind busy in those years stolen away at the internment camp. She used her imagination as a way to be somewhere else.

The family survived their stay, but after they were released instead of going back to California, they went southeast to Birmingham, the town her father's brother had ended up after his release from the camp in Jerome, Arkansas. They prayed for a new start for the family, and Mariko and her brother started back into public school.

In school, she grew a new hunger to understand what policies had forced her parents into incarceration. She learned all about the Constitution of the United States and what democracy was supposed to be. As she advanced in school, her interest in politics and justice continued.

By her senior year of high school she had long let go of her artistic endeavors. All of her focus was on getting into law school- she wanted to have a say in how people in this country were treated. After receiving her undergraduate degree in criminal justice at the University of Birmingham, she applied and got into the Birmingham School of Law.

Mariko flew through the program and passed the bar the first try. She soon found a public defender position in Huntsville where she met and married Buford Johnson, another lawyer in town specializing in criminal defense law. She fell in love with his Southern heritage, his great big smile and warm bear hugs. Mariko quickly changed her name to give herself more credibility and the added safety from ever having to be concerned about being seen as a potential enemy of the state again. Buford fell in love with her dedication and her spunky and powerful spirit all wrapped up in a tiny package. Together they had one son.

She'd spent ten years defending people who she believed were accused wrongly, getting one man off death row before advancing to her first judge position at age forty-five. It was there that she felt she would make her mark, being conscious of and protecting the constitutional rights of all who came before her.

Internment camps weren't going to happen again on her watch. She sat back, horrified, and for years not being able to understand how the president had gotten away with holding innocent people with no cause and with no due process for so long. When she would get hot under the collar about it, her parents begged her to try to understand.

"War is an uncertain time; the president must have believed that what he was doing was right," said her mother.

Her father had chimed in, "Look, they didn't keep us down forever. We came here and we built our lives again. You and Niko have become great Americans, living the American dream of success and freedom. We cannot complain about our lives and our community positions. The Osaka family has been fortunate."

His words stung as Mari knew others hadn't been as lucky. Many had died there, most had lost what they had. None of that could make up for the lifetime of shame that it caused for the many proud and gentle people who were only trying to make a life in a new country and prove themselves to be good patriotic citizens. That was all some of them wanted.

She leafed through her artwork and photographs from that time. In the bottom of the box lay a bamboo-handled horsetail brush - one that her mother had used to make signs for special celebrations with the family.

Mariko suddenly felt a strong urge to paint something. Make something.

She put her scrapbooks down and left, driving into town. Easily blowing three hundred dollars on art supplies, she skipped dinner to paint and paint to her heart's content.

Watercolor papers flew, canvases laden with oil paints were strewn, teetering on all of the surfaces of her home itching to dry. She painted her son from one of his baby pictures with his dark and shiny hair and toothless grin. Their old house on Stanton Street. She couldn't believe how easily the brushstrokes and color blending came back to her - *it felt like home.*

She stood looking over her apartment. It was a mess but a happy one. Her eyes glanced at the little blue book, and she opened it to the excerpt about the author and her friend teaching art to their children's classes.

In her profession, Mariko had made a difference for the better in people's lives; perhaps she could make as much of a difference for others in her retirement, too.

"Yes, I could do that. I will start an art class for the residents at Sunny Days. I will talk to Hazel tomorrow."

Exhausted from her whirlwind of creativity, Mariko fell asleep with her dreams in vivid technicolor. She imagined herself up on ladders painting mountains and waterfalls on gray cinder walls that had held little interest before. She signed her name at the bottom with her big horse hair paint brush.

Mariko awoke to a new and strongly felt purpose. The anonymous author's wish to do something big with her life had caused her own pulse to throttle up inside her, wishing for the same.

The book had sparked something in her, and suddenly she felt like creating something again. Something big.

~

What To Do, Me, 2006

*M*r. *Fun's birthday was coming up and I'd held off answering him about a birthday romp for months. In a last effort to see where I stood with Mr. Affair, I placed a call. Over the phone we decided I should fly out to see him again. We would really figure things out this time. Not like the last fruitless trip I made before. I needed to know where things were at.*

Obviously it was not in Mr. Fun's best interest for me to go, but he kept his friend-ly role true for the moment and was willing to drive me to the airport anyway. As my day to leave came closer, more anxiety and angst built up within me, and I told Mr. Fun that I didn't think I wanted to go.

*"Well, maybe you shouldn't then? What is it that **you** want?"*

The words hung in the air as a frantic thought. What do I want?

Do I want another night like the last one where I had to share his time with his wife, then go to sleep alone in a strange town on the other side of the country?

Hadn't I learned anything either with my serendipitous talk with God on the airplane? That mysterious man had won the wager, as Mr. Affair hadn't been on the plane after mine- not even close- or in the many months since.

I waited to phone Mr. Affair until after my flight had left so he wouldn't be able to convince me to come, and I decided to go goof off that day on the beach with Mr. Fun.

"I'm not coming," I said into the phone to Mr. Affair as I filled up the car with gas for our trip to the coast.

"What, why?"

"I just can't. I don't believe in us anymore, I don't believe in you anymore. There's someone else now. And I've slept with him." I said lying, as I hadn't yet, but was pretty sure I would.

An anger came from him then, a rage that burst through the tiny speaker on my phone. A voice I had never heard. He yelled, "How could you do that? What about us?"

"Yeah, what about us?! You sleep with your wife every damn night and have done nothing towards us being together. Nothing has changed for you."

"But, but."

I hung up the phone, and he called back, over and over, until I turned it off.

At the ocean, I was grateful to put my bare feet in the sand, and imagine the lifetimes of people that had walked this beach before me maybe suffering the same type of lovesickness. My time there always hits with the ocean making my problems seem small in comparison to its wise expanse. It is a soulful place for reflection, for feeling grace and being able to move on.

While there, Mr. Fun took a picture of me, one that would become one of my all-time favorites. I am wearing a brown turtleneck sweater and some lightly faded jeans rolled up to keep them dry from the surf. The wind blew my hair back a bit and the rays of the sun glinted off my sunglasses as Mr. Fun's shadow took up space in the foreground. In the picture, I look happy and more authentically me than I had felt in absolute years.

I think I took back a lot of my power that day. I wasn't waiting around to be someone's "maybe" anymore. I wasn't putting my life on hold or sitting around until somebody else got their shit together. This life was about what I wanted, who I wanted, and who I could become.

Mr. Fun and I got together that night, an early birthday present for him. It was awkward and not great as first times rarely are, but I hadn't had much time to think about what it could be, so it was fine.

After the deed, he shyly let me know that people (i.e.: women) don't really wear their nethers in that au naturel style anymore. I'd watched pornos with my ex-husband when we were working to spice things up but somehow the way those women coiffed their pubes into a vertical Hitler-mustache-like landing strip never seemed to translate into something I should do. I was grateful for the tip but still felt lesser in my power with the information handed to me the way it was. Oddly, I hadn't experienced men caring about the length of their hair down there- alas just another thing for women to contend with.

Even with all that, I continued hanging out with Mr. Fun. I was grateful for the distraction and the companionship for sure. Something to think about other than all the changes in my life and trying to navigate them.

Mr. Affair kept trying to reach me, sending me text messages to get back in touch. He knew he had pushed me away with his anger and lack of progress, but he said he still loved me.

I had grown used to screening his calls and not answering. I didn't know what to say to him anymore. I was done with excuses. Love had left the building.

Then one day about a month later I answered the phone and Mr. Affair likely wasn't expecting it. I am not sure where the words came from as I hadn't planned it or thought of it in the seconds before hitting the "talk" button.

Instead of answering "hello" as usual, I said, "I'm getting back together with my ex." It was as much of an experiment as anything else I had tried, but this time it was different.

It worked.

"I think that's a good idea," he said. "I know it is for the best, and now you will be okay."

I found it pure bullshit that he was so easily satiated by my lie. That no more questions came and his obsession with me and all of his feelings were suddenly and so conveniently gone.

His relief came through loud and clear as he said, "I'm sorry for everything. Be well."

Lucky him: now he didn't have to worry about my life being turned upside down by his broken promises and his very dally into my life. He was free to skip off into the sunset.

I was free, too, and I felt the full force of my choices and the gravity of what it all meant. I'd never been on my own, having gone from my Dad's house in my early twenties to my husband's house, all perfectly situated already. I hadn't done any of this before - could I even do it now?

I guess I will find out. I had Mr. Fun to listen to the hard stuff, to walk with me as I learned. To think of it, we were both pretty messed up and we kind of needed each other.

I could fake that I knew what I was doing when my parents asked how I was. My friends that I had back in the cul-de-sac fell away in droves. I hadn't anticipated that.

It's just me and Mr. Fun and whatever hijinks we got into together and my awesome kids every other week - onward!

~

G.G.

My paternal grandmother. I have only tiny wisps of memories of you which may have all melded into one. I was only six when you died.

I remember sitting in the front seat of a car. The dash was large with lots of buttons on it I wanted to push. Maybe it was large because I was very small with no hope of seeing over it. It was before child car seats, hell, before seat belts even.

You gave me a piece of Dentyne gum. I go back to that moment when I taste that artificial cinnamon flavor.

Mungo Jerry's song *"In the Summertime"* played on the radio. I was tiny and sat moving one of my fingers back and forth to the beat.

I remember your hazel green eyes that you passed on to my father, then he to me, or maybe I only remember your eyes because of the pictures.

Mostly what I have is remnants from you. An old secretary desk with a pull-down writing surface. Fluted hand-carved legs with most of the original hardware. Your gold lace-looking patterned China from Nippon. Your boxes of silver- two now incomplete sets.

An old book that you glued newspaper clippings onto the pages of to make your own journal. Inside filled with recipes, poems and little limericks that must have tickled your fancy.

What I love the most is your artwork that hangs in my home. Those pieces are irreplaceable. A portrait you did of a young Mexican girl in the foreground: her eyes closed, her hands tucked in prayer. There is a darkened doorway just beyond her, an invitation into a rustic but colorful Adobe structure. Dad once said that it must have been from a memory of your childhood back in Mexico.

As a seven-year-old, you and your mother and sister were living there while your stepfather was running his banana plantation venture. Suddenly the political atmosphere changed and you and your family had to flee for your lives from Pancho Villa. Your mother had left her husband behind and you, she, and your sister gained entrance on one of the British trains moving gringos out of the area to avoid being killed. I imagine you as a small girl clutching the only possession you were allowed to take with you as your family fled in fear.

It was a handmade doll built using wire with paper mâché flesh, its hand-painted face had a Hollywood starlet look with sharp red lips. Locks of your own curly red hair were glued to its head. I keep it dear.

I've heard stories of you but never had the time to get to know you. Seems like my Dad only tells stories about your husband, his father. I guess in order to really know you, I will have to ask him. Or maybe my aunt.

More snippets of you come to mind, things I heard about after you were gone.

You'd lost a child. I only speculated as to why after having my own daughter.

Our shared Rh negative blood. I had escaped a possible miscarriage having been blessed with a gift from science and one man whose blood was laden with rare and miraculous Rh antibodies.

I and millions of other women can give thanks to James Harrison nicknamed ("The Man With The Golden Arm"). If administered to a woman of Rh negative blood status it gives a barrier of protection between and to mother and fetus, helping thousands, then millions of mothers carry our children to term despite the incompatibility. I could have lost children as you did, but pure timing and modern medicine had spared me.

You were told not to conceive again. Your last chance at mothering came as a daughter offered in the middle of the night, a no witness, out-of-state adoption. Money played a part.

You weren't allowed any financial say in your home, and didn't have your name attached to anything of worth. Since you hadn't come from money, your husband assumed you couldn't be trusted with it. You were given an allowance for food and anything else he saw fit to provide. You didn't drive a car until he'd passed.

Even though to look at you, you appeared to have the best of everything at the time: furs, expensive jewelry, and a nice home. I don't believe you were able to truly be yourself. You were kept too busy keeping a spic-and-span house, and cooking meals from scratch three times a day. I imagine few moments to explore more for yourself.

Your duties as a wife and mother kept you small and in submission to your husband. His sudden death made it hard on you with no experience or rights over the family properties.

Era, or domineering husband or a bit of both? I wonder who you would have become if you had been allowed to bloom as colorfully as you could have?

***

Somehow- I have learned a lot from you without really knowing you at all.

~

Something To Believe In, Me 2006

I had called my mother and asked to come over. I was so full of pain and guilt and regret for leaving my marriage in the way I did. Feeling every bit of ownership of this suddenly shitty life I had made for me and my daughters. In my head for the full thirty-minute drive to get to her, I crumpled onto the floor upon seeing her. She helped me to the couch and gave me a glass of water to calm my pathetic sobbing some.

"I want you to watch something; I'm going to sit with you."

Mom had been forever telling me to read this book or that one, giving me the feeling that every book she ever mentioned just happened to have the answers in them that I needed at any given moment. Every single challenge: here's a book. I had long since tired of her handing me "life changing" books. In my rebellion in witnessing that her own life seemed far from great, I never did read them.

I was hesitant again as she said she wanted me to watch this movie with her because it had changed her. "Give it a chance; it might help. Please try to have an open mind."

She cued up the DVD player and I saw images of ancient people rushing around trying to keep something secret. The movie announced its title, and it was indeed "The Secret."

It was pretty bizarre as the people on screen relayed information they said had been around for ages, a "secret" that only a certain amount of people knew about. The most successful people in history.

Those who were not aware of "The Great Secret" were cast as the underlings of our society. Always believing that life is really just about what happens to them, rather than believing they had any control over anything themselves.

It felt like the people on the screen were talking directly to me. Talking heads telling me that I would be all right, and that my chances of living a happy fulfilled life was still possible. Alive, and attainable if only I chose to ask and believe and receive. It felt like a secret society or religion that people could be a part of, and I was more than nervous watching it.

Was this a cult? What had my mom gotten me into now? She had always *been a little woo-woo.*

I can't remember which scene it was when it happened, but I suddenly broke apart again. I bawled and bawled with the realization that I could change my life if I tried.

Mom cried along with me. The timing was perfect. I so needed something to believe in, something bigger than myself to try to make my life better than it was. I could not keep going this way. I sucked in all of the wisdom, and she let me take the DVD home to watch over and over again.

It was exactly what I needed and Mom knew. She always knew.

Maybe my life wasn't over yet. Maybe I hadn't wrecked everything forever? Maybe I could still build myself into someone that I liked- or even loved- if I tried hard and worked at it. Maybe I could grow into someone my daughters would be proud of.

I watched it again and again. It was the beginning of my working to believe in living again, in what was possible and what could still be. My choices and the aftereffects didn't have to be a life sentence.

Over time I began to grow dreams again. I wrote down the things that I wanted to have in my life. Wishing for a house for me and my daughters to live in someday. I saw a cute little bungalow with a garden window in the kitchen. A cozy place with real character, like my favorite home growing up. Something small that I could keep up with and paint fun colors and have as our own. A new "Ladies Lounge" but for keeps.

I kept that dream to myself and waited until I was stronger. I spent more time with my daughters and did the best I could. Living day by day, there for a while, soon I started to smile more and I could breathe a little bit better.

~

~2~

Mariko Johnson walked into Hazel's office the next day.

"Mari, how are you today? Look, I got the job!"

"Hi, Congratulations! So, I'd love to start going by my birth name 'Mariko'; do you think you could use that from now on with me? We are so happy for you and excited for all of the things you have planned."

"Wow, gosh, yes- what a beautiful name. I will help spread that around, too. So, what brings you by today?"

"Well, first, I wanted to give you the book that all of us have been reading, I figured you may want to peek at it before it goes back into the library."

"Oh, yes, thank you. I have been thinking about that."

"Terrific. Another thing, um, I have an idea."

"Great! Shoot!"

"Back when I was a youngster - actually when my family and I were held in an internment camp in Arizona - I discovered that I loved to make art. I have set it aside for many years with my role as defense lawyer and then judge, but actually this book made me think about picking it up again. I made these."

Mari spread numerous paintings across Hazel's desk to her astonishment.

"Wow, these are incredible. I had no idea you were so talented."

"You know, that book made us all feel like no one really knows what any of us are about or what we've been through. We just walk past each other in the hall, quiet, isolated. Some of us feel forgotten by our families, too. But really, we are *all* full of a lifetime of rich and inspiring stories. Every single one of us has fascinating histories of the challenges, hardships and triumphs we've been through. I think we might even have times and places in our lives that overlap each other, but we'd never know unless we shared. It goes with what you are trying to do with the newspaper and putting a spotlight on everyone, but my idea is of a class that gets people doing something. Rather than talking or sitting around, it will use their creative brain to make beauty. It may just give them a new purpose and way to relate to each other."

"Love this. Keep going," Hazel sat nodding at her.

"I want to do a program similar to the one outlined in one of the author's memories. She taught a monthly art class using a specific artist in mind, so, say Picasso. Our group will learn about the artist, then I will teach a project that will be easy enough for beginners, friendly enough for those with limited dexterity and using some of Picasso's favorite mediums. We can probably start out as once a month or once every couple of weeks depending on the reception. What do you think?"

"I think it's genius!" Hazel stood and held her hands up. "I love it. We can even have art shows to show off everyone's art, having a show as a quarterly thing."

"That would be amazing," said Mariko. "Do you think people will want to take my class?"

"One hundred percent. Could I share this idea with the head administrator? I would need to get her buy-in, but I think this could start other people here at Sunny Days to consider sharing their talents and gifts. I am loving this idea. Thank you for coming forward with it."

"Sounds perfect. Let me know when it is approved, and we can talk about costs of materials and things, figure out what to charge, or we may be able to get business sponsors to chip in?"

"Even better, perfect. I will see what I can get donated."

Mariko picked up her artwork and started to leave.

Hazel spoke, "Actually, can I keep these pieces for a few days for my meeting? It might help. Then I would love to hang them up in the lobby for everyone to see. An intro to the art class and their new teacher - would that be okay?"

Mariko thought for a minute: some of the pictures were of her memories from within the barbed wire of the camp. If it were on display, people might ask questions. They would know. Maybe they would judge her?

She flashed back to how her parents had hidden their time in the internment camps after they were released; they never talked about it with anyone except Mariko when she asked. Even then the conversations containing that time period were kept short.

Maybe it was time to stop hiding this part of her family's history. The country's history. Time to stop avoiding the bigger questions of whether it was right or not, or if the Japanese ancestral people deserved how they had been treated, and if the paltry reparations had made it okay. Mariko had spent her entire working life helping others break free from injustice;

maybe it was time to stop condoning it herself.

"Sure, why not?"

Mariko walked down the hall feeling taller than her actual height.

Let the questions come. Let the shame fall away.

It was damn time.

~

~2~

Hazel just loved the idea of the art classes. She turned the pages of the little blue book, finally finding the excerpt Mariko was talking about. She walked over to her copier and scanned the art class pages, then finding herself scanning some of the other pages so she would have easy access to them for the newspaper work as inspiration just in case.

She rethought how to get participation about the resident highlight stories. She could use the person's initials and a bit of their story the month before so some mystery could build of who the stories belonged to. Then the following month the whole story would be told with a sound bite for the next month and so on.

She thought about what Mariko said, about the timing of once a month to take the classes? The majority of the people who lived here were retired and had nothing but time on their hands. She grimaced. Then there were the ever-present sirens of the ambulances that came to take residents to the hospital or worse. With such a large number of residents, it felt like at least a once-a-week occurrence. These people didn't have unlimited time. Sad to say.

Hazel decided to shoot for newspapers every week. Each issue would be filled with great stories and the inspirational people who lived them. She smiled just imagining the friendships that might evolve once people knew some of their histories were similar. Maybe there were people here that went to the same school, or whose parents knew each other- one never knows.

Hazel walked with a spring in her step as she put the little blue book back into the residence library. It would sit there for the next few months, rarely getting looked at with the new newspaper and art classes being kept at the forefront of everyone's mind.

Find Me, Book Two, sat on a lower shelf. Its simple spiral binding hid any glimpse of the wonderful tales that were tucked inside. Sitting there, would it ever find its way to the owner again?

~

Seeing The Red Flags But Ignoring Them, Me, 2006

*A*fter the divorce, he was the first one in line. I didn't want to dive into the huge dating pool and start over. I wasn't supposed to be single this long, and wouldn't have been if everything I thought I'd planned had fallen into place.

But he was fun, and I needed fun. I didn't want to think all the time, worry about everything. He'd cook in the kitchen with me, not wait on the other side to be served. We went out, we stayed up late and watched foreign films reading the subtitles as we gobbled up popcorn with M&M's mixed in. We played lots of darts, went to bars, listened to hours of music in the car, and talked on and on about Seinfeld. We decided we'd name our son "Griffin" if we ever had one together. Thankfully, we never did.

As the months passed it was time for Mr. Fun to meet my daughters. I invited him to my eldest's soccer game. He showed up, and immediately started cheering for my kid, even though she didn't know him. She looked over at him with me and then he screamed, "If you make a goal, I'll give you a hundred bucks!"

Well, that kid of mine dribbled that ball straight into the goal net within minutes and she looked over in our direction with a great big grin. My ex-husband had overheard the promise as well.

I think maybe Mr. Fun was shocked, or maybe he hadn't figured out how good she was, but he was now on the hook for one "Benjamin" to a twelve-year-old.

She sauntered over to him after the game and held her hand out. Rightly so. He said he'd pay her later.

Well, Mr. Fun filched on that bet. Telling me later that no kid should get money like that. This should have given me more than an insight into who he was much earlier than it did.

I ended up paying my daughter and saying it was from him. It was just *the beginning of my making excuses for him. But he was fun and that is what I told myself I needed right now: someone to play with, to take my mind off the huge change I had just gone through. One still riddled with chaos, uncertainty and pain. I'd had Mr. Stability in marriage #1, and I wasn't happy. The opposite of Mr. Stability was Mr. Fun, right?*

Over the months my daughters grew to care about him. He had been trying to better himself, get his situation under control, pay on his student loans and the back payments of child support owed to his ex. He was trying, right? I had to give him the benefit of the doubt.

I insulated them some- from his shortcomings. Only showing them what I wanted to be seen, never sharing the hard stuff. I wanted him to be Mr. Fun for them. He didn't need to be Dad-like, too.

~

K.F.

We met using a dating service in the early nineties, both of us wishing to have some extra help to find love. A note came my way- you had picked me and I needed to come over to the office and respond.

My membership for the year was about up so I figured why not, one last chance for romance. I saw your kind and chiseled face with a dimple on your chin, and you reminded me of a younger Robert Redford.

Glasses, ginger hair, you looked smart. I'd never dated anyone like you. You were a bit older than me, but what did I have to lose?

I said yes and we went out to an outdoor art show close to where I lived. You looked geekily cute when you showed up, but your shoes were a ridiculous Elmer Fudd-type, something I would have to change if we were going to spend any real time together.

It was fun and you were nice. We decided to meet up again soon. You were older as I said, and the most together man I'd ever come across. You owned your own home and drove a nice car. The nicest car I had ever ridden in given I was in my early twenties.

You liked the sport of golf which just happened to be in my blood, with my great grandfather pro golfer and many hole-in-ones spreading across my family line. That impressed you and I had a hell of a swing that you'd see, however, I didn't care about keeping score and really didn't care which way the ball went as long as it was far. This irritated you which made me laugh. Eventually I would take it slightly more seriously with some lessons but that was later on.

We kind of just fell hard for each other, and I started staying with you out of town, mostly on the weekends at least in the beginning. You had a houseful: no kids but two dogs, and two-and-a-half cats, the "half" being a creature we very rarely saw who stayed outside.

Your house was a bachelor pad, and I remember the two art pieces hung on either side of your stereo cabinet: zebra portraits painted by one of your old girlfriends. It wasn't really my style but it would become our style soon enough as after only a couple of months together I had moved in and we were couch shopping and painting and wallpapering everything. Kitchens and baths we changed the look to a Southwest ambiance with rich hunter greens, reds and navy.

And the waterbed. Ha. Good times. Quite comical once we had married and were having our first baby and I was nine months pregnant and needed your help to get out of it.

You hadn't really been exposed to kids much despite your desire to have them. You and your ex couldn't conceive and you had almost given up on the idea by the time I came along.

You were the practical one and I was impulsive, the one who reacted often without thinking about the scenario much. Case in point: me leaving for the hospital without you when I was about to have our first child.

I'd gotten it into my head that I would have my babies really fast because my mother had. I was born after about five hours and my brother arrived while my mom lay on a gurney in the hospital hallway after an hour-and-a-half of labor. I figured that with each generation comes improvement in that realm; not sure where I came up with it but I did. I felt such an urgency having been induced the day before with zero results that the next morning my water broke and I just left you to go to the hospital while you were in the shower.

"Why didn't you wait for me?" you asked when you arrived and I just shrugged my shoulders from the hospital bed and reprimanded you for wearing a "Beavis and Butthead" t-shirt to meet our kid. So, I guess we were even.

Our daughter came *eighteen hours* later.

I was exhausted and had managed to scare the majority of the people on the delivery floor with my screaming before passing out from the blood loss, which was another story.

But you were there and you were *the Dad*, tirelessly walking the halls with our beautiful conehead daughter (it did go back to regular shape by the next day) as she screamed from the pain meds I had begged for while trying to climb out of my very skin during labor. I was told of that beautiful beginning of your and her relationship by my mom after I was awake again.

You learned and became the best father I could ever dream of for our two girls. Despite all of our hard times and challenges, I have never wished you away from being their Dad.

Once in awhile you meet someone who can teach you an awful lot without making you feel stupid for not already knowing things. That is you.

Maybe our age difference will be to our detriment someday, but I always felt that any time I might be without you at the end part of our lives would have been worth the time we shared together. No matter what comes or how life changes for us, I am very grateful I had my kids with you. You are the best father I could have ever picked for our girls.

~

~2~

Ned

Ned Coggins arrived at the Sunny Days Retirement Home today by taxicab. He would be spending the rest of his days here. It had looked like a nice place when he visited last month. The people seemed well cared for, happy and content even.

He hoped it would feel like home. His dog Chip sat up straight and put his nose out the window. The driver had helped Ned unpack his things on the curb until the manager came out to help.

"Welcome to Sunny Days," the greeter said with a genuine smile.

Ned had checked references very carefully on this place before signing up. He found not one flaw. The people who worked here seemed to enjoy the old folks. Ned had arranged for a large one-bedroom apartment for him and Chip. He could afford to splurge a little as he had been careful and successful with his money all his life. He had invested in the stock market and lived below his means.

His family, however, was not as prudent. He hadn't spoken to his brother or sister in over ten years. They would come to him and ask for money. At first he gave, but he realized early on that they would just come back for more when that was gone. He had decided tough love was the only way to get them to change.

He hoped that they would smarten up, but he wasn't banking on it.

About five years ago he reached out again but was met with animosity and attacks. He had decided enough was enough. Now it was just he and Chip and their new life together.

He'd spent a couple of days getting the lay of the land around Sunny Days walking the halls and the grounds.

One Friday, he bolted into the library to avoid that crazy Mrs. Turner. She seemed to think he was traveling to some foreign place and he thought she was losing it.

As he wandered the library, he found some old Louis L'Amour westerns that he remembered reading as a young soldier overseas. He would check those out once he was settled in more. Another find was a whole shelf of original "Hardy Boys" hardcover books lining another wall.

The space was very nice, comfortable and light. He'd be spending some time here. Ned sat down on one of the couches for a little rest. Next to him lay a little blue book: "Find Me" number two of five.

Strange, no picture on the cover, just simple letters in gold. He picked the book up and looked for an author. Nothing. Very strange.

He heard the ever-closer voice of Mrs. Turner getting louder. Spooked, Ned tucked the book under his cardigan and walked out the back door into the outdoor courtyard. He wasn't sure how to check out a book at the library but he knew he wasn't going to ask that loon Turner.

He made his way back to his apartment and locked the door behind him. He shot a look at Chip, let out a sigh and was glad to be home.

Dropping the book on the desk next to his purple heart and his stock journal, he walked straight to his private bath. Chip followed. He glanced back wishing he had brought the book with him for his sit.

No, he could read that later. Right now, he had to go.

~

Medicating With My Choices, Me 2006

*A*gain I decided to seek happiness from a bottle. A little pharmaceutical one - surely that would help me get there.

I started back on Prozac today. I hate taking stuff. Felt a little weird already, but I suppose it is working. I am tired. I will go to sleep as soon as my toenails are dry.

I have tried some other antidepressants in this journey as well. They work for a time to help lift the spirit, I would say, but they don't actually fix what is wrong with you, so the same shit comes up over and over again. Same shit, different day, often different year.

But hey, all my friends are on stuff, so there must be something to it. I guess people need to just medicate these days, in order to live their lives? Shrug.

~

It's Not You, It's Me, 2006

*I*t's not Mr. Fun, it's me. I am the one holding up the show. I start a new job in a week. Started a new life eight months ago leaving behind almost everything that I had and knew. I changed everyone's life just for me. So I could be happy. And yet?

Somehow, the wave of contentment that I thought would wash over me - the idea that life would be nothing but rosebuds and rainbows every day - had not materialized.

In actuality, this life is more difficult than I anticipated. Harder than I ever dreamed it could be. I have no idea what I am doing, and suddenly I am wholly in charge of myself for the first time in my life.

The promises of a great love vanished and caused me great pain and confusion. I sit now stung with my complete lack of confidence in myself in regards to love. The lies that I told cost me my marriage, my best friend, my security and my home.

As hard as it is sometimes, I will just get through each day, grappling with the guilt and trying to make sense of this path that I'm on. Believing that my purpose will reveal itself, or at least show me my next step.

On days when I am without my girls, I have him. Mr. Fun. He has stuck around and waited until I get my head on straight enough to decide that he is a good choice for me. He wears me down as we go.

He tells me that I need to work on myself. Build myself up, get going on my job, and settle into a new normal. Maybe go back to the counselor. My only known counselor at this point is to go back and see the guy who walked me into the lawyer's office in the first place.

Do I trust him? Maybe he was just sick of listening to me and used that shock factor tactic to get me off the fence in my marriage? Maybe he doesn't give a rat's ass about me? Maybe none of them do.

But in my trusting or downright lazy way, I do go back to him and sit and talk.

Today I didn't cry as much as I anticipated I would. Maybe the meds are working? Maybe their numbing or dulling of my feelings have begun?

Enough that I can climb out of my head and into the real work of taking care of myself and my daughters. That should be my real job now.

Mr. Fun feels right but also wrong. It might be the lack of trust in my own judgment that has me on the fence again, only a different one. Sometimes I am in, other times I am out.

His presence gives me a warm feeling as being alone means quiet where the words and deeds spin around contrarily in my head.

"Look what you've done."

"You don't deserve to find happiness, to feel whole or okay!"

Somehow I will have to force myself to forgive myself enough to keep going. Maybe try to love again.

We will see how long he sticks around...

~

R.L.

You were a friend of my boyfriend long ago. The biggest guy I knew.

Beyond sweet, you were always nice to me. After your friend and I had broken up, you stayed friendly, but not close enough to break the unwritten code of understanding between guy friends. I understood.

Later in my early twenties we saw each other randomly and got together when you were home from college for an evening out at a local bar. We were both unattached, yet not looking for anything. There was a nice back and forth- half tease, half friendship. He put a quarter down on the billiards table and we waited for our turn. Drinking our beers and catching up. Our giddy excitement when we finally got the table was hilarious.

As I arranged the balls in the triangle, you started to weave a fantastical tale. Each twist kept me captivated with your storytelling. I remember it had monkeys and bears and the story went on and on for hours. Through many games, your soft-spoken voice hypnotized me and placed me squarely into your new world. It was funny and imaginative and magical.

Maybe you were trying to distract me from the game? Enchant me into falling for you? Either way, just being around another person with seemingly no expectations; who wasn't trying to get to second base because he bought me a beer was refreshing. No icky feelings at all.

When you asked if I was captivated, the answer was a healthy "yes."

I asked you if you made it up.

A great grin took over your face, "Every single word."

I wonder if you became a storyteller, too?

~

Forever The Writer, Me, 2007

No matter where I was, I was always forming words together. My Plan B took up most of my time, then the kids, then any relationship I had going at the time, but my true purpose sat in the shadows all the while, waiting patiently for me to pay attention to it.

If my writing would have been a person, it would have given up on me long ago and moved onto someone else. Someone who cared for it more or was willing to fight for it.

When I have a gap, I reach for any pad of paper or notebook that is the closest. Scribbling the most recent unorganized thoughts onto the page. Topics are random as is life in general- I didn't have a plan.

Each story idea rose and swelled and fell away from me again with life's inconsistencies. But still the act hangs on. The need to reflect myself onto the pages. To document the now- this very minute. The notebooks stack up, begging to be sorted through. It doesn't happen and I buy more to fill with words. Scattered thoughts pulled from the years.

Pages from before high school into married and child-filled life up until now. Some thoughts are poignant and beautiful, but most are written with the very end of a pencil lead held with the tips of my fingernails. Sometimes that is all that is left.

If money and expectations were not an issue, I imagine myself to be a full-time storyteller. To weave tales for the masses for the rest of my life.

In my setting it aside as I do, I prove that I do not believe in myself, and turn my back on the possibility. There are more than enough people around me to tell me it's impossible. And I listen to them. Believing they know more or better than I do. I take it in as they say how hard it is, and that the odds of succeeding are not good, and only a chosen few will make it. Any regularly scheduled drive is not there so I must not be talented enough, smart enough or good enough.

It all weighs on me as I walk into my workplace wishing I was back at my desk, looking out the window, dreaming and filling in the words to my first novel. Wishing I could make up things up for a living. Celebrating my *imagination instead of stunting it.*

If only I was strong enough to ignore the naysayers and skip all the dribble in my life to pursue it. If only I believed in myself and the value of my words in the world. If only I believed what I say matters.

Another day, another dream crushing dollar. Maybe someday my stories will be read.

~

Ned came out of the bathroom and sat down in his only chair for a good read. Having left his glasses in the bathroom, he got up once more to get them.

Finally settled, he opened to the first page of the strange book he had found in the library.

Inside a request, there would be no repercussions if he didn't comply. Only the hope that reasonable people who came upon the book might play along. No guilt trip, no mean words, no curse. Simply, a plea. A mystery to be a part of.

"Why not? I have nothing to lose," he said to Chip. Chip looked at him with a sideways tilt of his head.

"I'll l-l-let you know how this book turns out." Ned said.

Ned read the pages carefully. While he read, some of the stories blurred into his own, making him think again of his love Mi Sun. He had asked her to marry him when he was stationed in Korea during the war reconstruction efforts. They had met when she was an interpreter and he was a building engineer working with his battalion on one of the bridges. She was in charge of making sure the soldiers had what they needed in materials on site. He had instantly fallen in love with her demure smile. The way she spoke English in a softer way sometimes as she was quite capable in it, but then other times if the delivery was delayed or didn't show up, oh, boy, were they in trouble.

Sometimes Ned and Mi Sun would sit and eat lunches along the Han River while the teams were resting for the lunchtime break. They would pick a nice spot under a Korean red pine tree and escape the heat of the day. Often Mi Sun would bring food and Ned would offer her money to help pay for the lunch items, but she mostly refused.

When the bridge was finished and it looked as though the two of them wouldn't be seeing each other anymore, he asked her if she would consider coming to America to be his bride.

She said she would need to think about it, and then the next day she said "yes."

It would be paperwork going back and forth as well as letters for the two of them for the next year. They wouldn't see each other again in person until she had been granted a fiancé visa to travel to America for their three month trial period.

Six months in, Ned was sent back to the states and he settled in Kansas. He had saved enough to put money down on a little farm there while he did government contracts as they came up.

Mi Sun kept herself busy with her role interpreting for the Army Corp of Engineers specializing in materials logistics.

With the necessary paperwork finally complete, she got on a boat to travel to Seattle, Washington, as a first stop in America before her train trip to Kansas. The boat trip was long and she continued to write to Ned, finally handing him all of those letters as she walked off the boat over two weeks later. Ned met her there with a stack from him as well.

Together they would ride the train in a sleeping car, with two bunks. Ned wanted to respect Mi Sun until their marriage and they hadn't discussed being romantic until then.

Ned closed his eyes and remembered how Mi Sun was fascinated with each part of the country they traveled through. It was like he was seeing each place for the first time too, using her new eyes to admire the beauty. The months of waiting, of paperwork and endless questions had been worth it. They were together again.

The Union Pacific Streamliner clacked through the great green and wooded areas of Washington and Oregon. The two enjoyed a lovely breakfast as the vessel kissed the river's edge making its way to the bustling city of Portland, Oregon. Heading East through Idaho, they lunched on small tuna sandwiches and chips. A dinner of chicken and potatoes was had as they breathed in the fresh air from the open windows of the diner car as it made its way held in by the Grand Tetons of Wyoming.

Barely able to look at Ned for the views outside, she only paid attention when the meals came. Ned let her be- after all she'd only known one place in her life and he wanted her to take it all in.

Mi Sun hardly slept, worried that she might miss something more beautiful than the last place she saw. As hard as she tried, she couldn't stay awake and missed all of Nebraska and nearly all of Kansas, too, before they finally pulled into the Union Station in Kansas City, Missouri.

Ned was excited to have his family meet Mi Sun. He had done well in his career and was in a stable spot- he wanted to share some of his bounty with them. His family had not done so well, but he had hoped with some encouragement and support, and maybe even a little investment in something they were passionate about that his family would come around to trying to have a better life. It was in that hopeful mindset that he extended an invitation to them to help welcome Mi Sun to America and into their family.

He had sent train tickets to his sister Dora, his brother Stan and his parents so they could all meet up in the city and watch a baseball game together. The Kansas City A's weren't the greatest, but it was a family outing and a way to show Mi Sun around a little bit. He thought it would be good to keep his family occupied so they didn't just jump in and grill her. There would be questions, he knew, but he prayed they would be on good behavior knowing how important this was to him.

Mi Sun loved watching the game, but between innings his family was cold to Mi Sun and to him. They assumed she didn't speak English and they didn't bother asking her any questions. Out of respect, Mi Sun watched the rest of them relate to each other while she took in the energy of each of them. When he and his brother went to the bathroom in between innings, Stan came after Ned in a sharp tone.

"What are you doing with her? We gotta keep those chinks out of this country. She will never fit in here."

"Stan, she's from Korea and that is ugly. What do you care anyway? I'm happy and I love her. I am sure you all will love her, too, if you give her a chance."

"Why did you bring us all here anyway, to witness your little romance? Throwing your money in our face to buy us all tickets and hotel rooms just to show off for your girl?"

Stan and Ned went back to the seats where he found his new fiancé's head in her hands choking back tears. His mother had accused her of marrying Ned for his money and she felt unable to defend herself in this new place- she didn't know the best words or how to convince them otherwise. Ned's family was already against her before she got here. Upon seeing Ned, she got up and ran to the ladies' room, and Dora walked speedily after her yelling. "Yeah, my mom is right, you shouldn't be here, I wonder how much he had to pay to get you here, huh? Did you ask?"

Ned followed, holding back his sister as Mi Sun went into the restroom.

"Why are you ruining this for me? What is your problem? I love her." His cheeks were red with anger. Ned had never spoken up for himself, never raised his voice towards his family.

"She can't love you - she barely knows you. And even if she did, she would learn that you are a selfish bastard who is always out to prove how much smarter you are than the rest of us. You are just like us: a family of scrambling rats looking to find our next nibble. You are nothing more- stop acting like you are."

"I have done better for myself, and you can, too, if you would try and believe you can. I will not have you all ruin this for me, dammit." He walked off and waited for Mi Sun to come out of the bathroom, then they left his family without saying goodbye.

Ned walked her to her hotel room down the street. He kissed her hand and embraced her before saying goodnight. "You won't have to see them ever again - their behavior was terrible. I thought they would be kinder and happy for us. I am so sorry."

He kissed her forehead as she closed her eyes which were still red from the day's trials.

Ned slept fitfully, wishing he could go back and erase all of the hurt, blame and ugliness he had exposed his love to by the presence of his family. Why had he believed that they would for once be happy for him? Or act like good, decent people for a change? He was ashamed. Between his career with the army, and after recently moving, he hadn't made many friends, his family was really all he had- them and Mi Sun.

The next morning when Ned went to pick up Mi Sun at her room for breakfast, her eyes were nearly swollen shut from crying. She asked him to come inside, then closed the door behind her, and held his hands.

"I cannot do this. I cannot live here, I cannot be with you. I'm afraid, and starting over in a new place, all alone. I would know forever that my being with you would keep you away from your family. Family is most important. You and I cannot be."

"No, that's not true. They are the ones who are troublesome, not you. Please, Mi Sun, please stay here and be with me. I love you. We can make it work."

Tears had filled her eyes again and it pained him. He didn't want to see her sad and feeling hopeless- he wanted her to be happy.

Mi Sun placed the sunglasses she had bought in the hotel shop over her eyes. They walked together to a nearby cafe and sat down at a table overlooking the river. Ned ordered a coffee and Mi Sun a black tea. Mi Sun kept her head down so she wouldn't catch Ned's eyes.

She stared sometimes at the beautiful ring he had given her. The flawless solitaire diamond glinted in the sun, so she hid it on her lap, reaching for her tea with the other hand.

She knew he was hurting, but she couldn't change her mind. She loved him enough to not wish harm to him with his family. He would find a more suitable wife, one that his family would accept.

They both nibbled on toast and he took a few bites of egg before they got up to walk along the river. They stopped short of the bank at the Chouteau Bridge and looked outwards together as some motorcars sped over.

Finally she spoke. Words he would never, ever forget if he lived a million lifetimes.

"Our love is like a bridge that isn't quite complete. There are no other bridges to cross. We are each standing on one side and cannot reach each other. We can only wave and walk back the way we came. "

Ned broke down. He didn't know how to convince her that things would be okay because he couldn't guarantee that it would. He couldn't promise her that his family would change because he hadn't seen them ever try. He was asking her to move to a new country and start a new life. It was too much to ask. He knew it now. His heart was crushed, but he tried to act strong on the outside.

"My mother gave me a one-way ticket back home before I left; it has no date or expiration. She knew how hard this would be for us to make a life and for me to be away from home with no one to help me. I can't marry you Ned. I am going back home."

He pulled her into his arms, and she put the ring back into his hands when he let go. They stood knowing this was the end.

He hugged her once more, whispering into her ear that he wished her a happy life and asking that she please write him a letter when she arrived safely back home.

He put her on a train back to Seattle and gave her some spending money and a note as to why she was in the United States. Anyone with any questions could reach him through the Army Corp of Engineers, Kansas City district.

She waved to him from the window as the train pulled away. It was the last time he would see or hear from her, as no letter ever came.

Luckily he was pulled into a large project at work: a new dam and lake was finally approved and the project might take twenty years of his time and energy. He was thankful for the intense work and purpose. When the project finally concluded to great fanfare, Ned sat on the banks of the newly built Harry S. Truman Reservoir and enjoyed a picnic by himself.

He hadn't found love again because he never got over Mi Sun. He spent his last few years prior to retirement traveling the states, inspecting and seeing many of the country's great bridges. It turned out to be his lifelong passion. He hadn't meant to stay alone that whole time, but it just happened that way.

He had blinked and most of his life was over. No more projects came needing his undivided attention. Now it was just him and Chip whiling away in their last act of his life at Sunny Days.

He patted Chip on the head and ran his hand down his back as the pup had jumped up into his lap. He wondered if the author was closer to finding one of her books. If anyone had found themselves in the pages and tried to find her.

It made him wish he had a way to connect to Mi Sun- most likely she had married and changed her name. Or she could be dead by now. He grew sad at the thought. His uncaring family never reached out to him, and he often found himself being the better person and calling to see how everyone was. Over the years he had tried to reconcile with his family and build some kind of relationship, and each time he was shocked and hurt by their hostile attitude. But they were family, the only one he had. Maybe he should try again? Just one more time.

He signed his name in the back of the book, and picked up the phone at his side. He'd make one last call to his brother before he'd give up on him forever. The number was disconnected. He dialed his sister's number, and her craggy voice came on the line. Still a heavy smoker, he assumed.

"Eh, h-h-hello?"she said before starting a coughing fit to clear her throat. "Hello?"

"D-d-d-dora, how are you?" Ned forgot his stutter was amplified when he spoke to his family.

"Huh, who is this?"

"It's your brother Ned-d-d, how are you doing?"

"Like you care."

"I d-d-do. How is the fam-m-mily?"

"Well, Shari's daughter is having another kid soon, and the car is broken down again. Wait a minute: why are you calling? What's happening? Is Brother Stan all right? He was always my favorite, ya know."

"No, Stan-n-n is fine I th-th-think, I'm j-j-just checking on you all. I g-g-guess it was just nice to hear your v-v-voice. Have a nice life."

Ned hung up the phone, "Oh, well, n-n-now I know. I am really d-d-done."

All of the unfairness and abominable ways his family had treated his love bubbled to the surface. A shit family is what he had- he'd be making no excuses for them to himself or others again.

Ned grabbed a pen and the nearest envelope he could find; amongst the many of his bank statements. Viciously he started penning a note, one he knew he would have to make legal later on, after finding a charity to give his riches to. He unleashed his anger onto the paper he jaggedly scribbled.~

Last Will and Testament of Ned Coggins

I, Ned Coggins, of sound mind and memory leave all of my worldly assets to Sunny Days Residence home.

Ned Coggins.

Ned sat in his chair staring at the empty walls of his new home. It was missing the typical homey touches he'd always longed for. No family portraits, no artwork purchased on an exotic trip somewhere, not a single photograph of him or anyone else for that matter.

Not everyone was born into a family that felt like home. Some people- the unlucky ones like him- were born into families laden with the tortuous legacy of many generations of messed up people. One set of already selfish people bore a few more, each layer being taught all they knew about looking out for number one and so on, and so on.

He had fallen into one of those families: people so lacking in awareness and empathy that they never even tried to be a better person. Ned had moved up in the world *despite* them.

They could all sit on a tack with their own choices from now on.

~

Alone But Not, Me 2007

The unmarried life is not all it's made out to be. I am farther away from some things, but hopefully closer to my truth. It is strange how I feel sometimes, as if I am walking around like only half of a person. A ghost. Not fully here or there. Anywhere. Hours pass in my days quickly with not much accomplished.

Nothing to show. I am in my head often, without resolution.

This is my time, people have told me. It's time to grow and become.

I am bound to individuals, my children, my ex-husband, my family. I've had Mr. Fun in my life now for almost a year. Friends, then dating, now finally together as boyfriend and girlfriend.

It is good for me to have some people around. Before he was there, I rarely left the house except out of responsibility. But sometimes I feel like I take care of him, and it exhausts me.

Didn't have relationship bliss the first time; may not get it this time either. Is bliss even possible?

I have so much work to do on myself that I don't need to be thinking about taking on anything else like a real commitment again.

But he wants to be my man, as I make the changes and fill the voids within myself.

Yesterday, a five-mile walk with a friend. Today, a coffee date with another friend who I hadn't seen in too long.

I have friends if I seek them out, although it seems rare that they call me. I try to understand the phenomenon of how life can be busy without major things going on. I remember back to my role running a home, caring for children, living my old life.

I wish I had more single friends and other people to do stuff with. When you are divorced, you carry a bit of a social curse with you that your married friends don't want to catch. In my choice I am no longer the old me but may be someone who might come after their husbands. Good God.

Side tangent: I wonder how often this actually happens, I mean you have totally bitched to me all about him- why would I want him? Oh well~ onward.

I would remember this time in my life: the isolation and the friends leaving in waves because I wasn't front and center, of close reach in their lives anymore. I hereby commit to always step forward and be there if any of my friends ever get a divorce. To be the support that I wish I had in this transition.

Tell them the truth of it. That people they once thought of as stable and forever friends would slink away when their marital circumstances change.

It's hard not to take it personally- 'it' is very personal, and that separation further feeds the not-good-enough track that continues to play in my subconscious as always.

I beg to know the 'why' for the divide.

Maybe those friends forget about you because they are busy, or because you are growing differently and they are still in the same place. Maybe they don't know what to say to you, like when someone dies? As the days of not staying in touch add up, it's even harder to pick up the phone. All I know is that it rarely rings.

Maybe they are actually a bit jealous of your newly found freedom, and being close to you is a reminder that they don't have everything they really want either?

Maybe in seeing you learn to thrive again, they wonder about their own lackluster, on the edge marriages themselves. Maybe they are afraid to face that truth and what it might mean to themselves?

Some may be sitting back in judgment, holding tight to their own beliefs that no matter what, people who marry should stay together. Till death do us part.

Whatever it was, if I was going to make it, I was going to have to develop a new crop of friends. People who had similar interests and goals.

I want to get back to my writing. Maybe I'll take some classes, find another writing group like the one I was in, in my twenties.

If this world is finally my oyster like people and the books I read seem to say, let's shuck this baby open!

~

~2~

Dora, Ned's sister, checked the caller ID screen on her phone. "Sunny Days Home" is all it said along with a phone number. She wrote the name as well as most of the phone number on the back of a bill and put it into a junk drawer.

Dora had a lot of junk drawers.

Her daughter Shari showed up for her weekly pedicure and was told of the call by her visibly upset mother.

"My money-hogging bastard of a brother called today just to say hi- he should have sent a check!"

Shari told her mother, "Blow it off, Mom. After all, Uncle Ned is all alone in this world and you have me, Lloyd, and all the kids, too."

Dora snithered in agreement before slapping her thigh and nodding so hard she cricked her neck.

Jokes about poor ol' Ned are brought back from the dead and shared around the family dinner table. About the time he sent everyone tickets to come meet his fiancé, and how she got wise and dumped him and went home. Teasing- even in mixed company- that he must have been lousy in bed. Together they made fun of his stutter, and his miserly ways.

While listening to her mother and Uncle Stan go on and on, Shari silently thought about reaching out to her Uncle Ned. To get on his good side. Surely there would be some inheritance or something. She could pretend to be the wholesome little niece to see if she can get anything out of him.

She hadn't the time, now, with working at the dental office sterilizing instruments of torture and working part-time at the salon to learn nails.

Shari put the whole idea aside. He wasn't that old yet. Right?

She had some time to come up with a plan and a way to hide the whole thing from her mother.

~

Adventures At The Weenie Warehouse, Me, 2007

*A*fter *I left the tile showroom job, I had to decide what it was that was important to me. Ideally, I would have a schedule more in tune with my daughters'. Weekends to goof off together.*

A friend had a thriving business in a realm I hadn't really known about: adult toys. As a self-professed prude, this opportunity was an eyebrow raising one that I took a few days to consider. But after hearing that a few of my friends were also employed there and the dollars per hour was beyond what I had made previously, I was in.

One rather conservative friend of mine asked if this new role would lead to a new job for me of becoming a stripper. She was quite happy to know that no, that role was not in my future.

That space became a comfortable place to be in the company of other women who were also trying to live their best lives. A gaggle of women, packing adult party goods together.

We spent our days in a large warehouse full of penis-shaped-this-and-that and we packed up orders that had been submitted online. It was easy work, and I was with friends- ones who understood when your kid was sick or was having a hard time and needed you to leave early. My God, I don't think I had smiled or laughed that much in years.

Each day we would arrive, and we would commiserate about life while packing boxes. There were questions about how each had spent the weekends, and the sometimes bitching about the husband not doing his fair share. The single ladies had to fill the others in about their dates the previous weekend. Always someone to care and talk to.

I can't really remember any drama or arguing amongst the women in my time there. We mostly made fun of the UPS man who thought he was hot stuff, and his thought that the penis paraphernalia strewn about was an actual lustful nod to him. He smelled like patchouli and weed and all of us saw right through him, even though we teased back as much as he did. Every time he was around, it reminded me of the scene in "High Fidelity" when John Cusack is kicking Tim Robbins' butt in his mind and yelling, "Now get your patchouli stink out of my store!" Classic.

I had a huge crush on John Cusack by then. Cusack had been my arranged "exception" with my husband years before, but alas our paths never crossed.

There were the hormonal hungry days when we all binged on Cool Ranch Doritos only to find that they were loaded with MSG. And moments admiring the three chihuahuas in all different shades that spent their days napping all over the office.

Take your daughter to work day came, and I took my youngest to work with me. I kept her away from the most risqué stuff, but gave her the little project of counting the little "rocket ships" to put into plastic sleeves for the bachelorette goody bags.

One woman successfully hid her job from her husband for many years. But that is her story to tell, not mine.

~

Buying My First House, Me 2007

I might have bitten off a little more than I could chew at the Shari's down the street from my apartment. I just bought a house on my own. One of my first steps to actually being the grown up my age tells me I am.

It's so funny, this no document loan thing. You just say a number of what you make per month and you can get a house. They don't even check.

While I anticipate making what I said I'm making on the paperwork, I am not right now.

We are going over the inspection today. All of the things that need to be fixed. Honey do's. With no honey. I check my barometer on the freak out scale. Will this matter in a year?

It might.

I love the house. I totally see us there. The girls weren't with me for this showing, but they went with me to the other ones. I think they will be okay with it, as long as they never have to go down into the basement. My youngest thinks basements are creepy. This house reminds me of my favorite house growing up. With its textured plaster walls and wood floors, I just love it.

Enough of a fixer to keep me occupied for a while. I'm ecstatic to move in. The girls are also excited. It is so far away from my suburban cookie-cutter home life I once had, but I am not comparing this small house to the larger ones back then. It is just the right size for us.

Even us having one bathroom will be workable for now because the girls are small and still take their showers at night. We won't be fighting over who needs the bathroom in the morning and, when it does come to that, I guess we will figure it out.

We can walk everywhere we need to. The store is up the street, and restaurants are close by. It is in a growing area and I am sure it will be a good investment. I am full of fear and excitement. I push on knowing this is the best thing for all of us. It is for the best to invest some of that settlement money before it all goes to bills and other things. Good times are coming- I feel it.

I dreamed of a house with a garden window in the kitchen and I wrote it on my dream house list that I wrote after watching "The Secret" with Mom, and this house has that.

I instantly felt at home there, as it was the home of an artist. Creativity lives here. It really is the perfect house. This stuff really does work. I will manifest some more!

~

$$\sim 2 \sim$$

Now a successful pet project, *The Sunny Days Gazette* newspaper put an ad in for other residents to offer classes of their expertise to the other residents. Any and all types were welcomed.

Ned had settled in nicely and jumped at the chance to teach a money class about stock market trading for beginners. His class even came with a fifty dollar starter fund courtesy of Ned.

Soon all of his "Wall Street Wizards" were making extra money, and he had many friends. Ned was enjoying his life and the company of others for the first time in many years. He hadn't been there that long, but he was already making a difference.

Ned had done extremely well for himself. No family, no children, a great job that paid him very well. Sometimes he even earned hazard pay for the places and situations the government put him in. With no family at home to worry about or plan for, he was more reckless in accepting his assignments.

People would have been shocked if they'd known all he'd seen, especially with his calm and subdued exterior. He thought about writing down some of his adventures someday. For now he would continue to focus on helping those around him, many who desperately needed his knowledge.

In his effort to become a great teacher, Ned signed up for multiple subscriptions of all of the financial newspapers and magazines that were available. He reasoned that once his students were up to snuff on the basics, he would share the periodicals like *The Wall Street Journal* and *Kiplinger's* with them en masse. The periodicals came in and filled his apartment as many of the students didn't want them. Space in the apartments was at a premium for most of the other residents although Ned had few belongings. He hadn't counted on that.

His students wanted tips, not to do the deep dive that he had done to learn all about the stock market, bonds and CD's.

As the weeks and months passed, Ned's apartment filled up more and more with the papers. He hadn't brought much furniture with him during the move since he rarely entertained and didn't need a place to be completely outfitted. He had planned on buying furniture but hardly left the residence except for catching the bus to go to the grocery store once a week with the others.

With his engineering mind, Ned initially conceptualized and then built his stacks of newspapers into functioning pieces of furniture: A couch, a chair, a coffee table. Rolling tubes of newspapers, he glued the ends closed to build the framework to hold each stack together, mastering the skeletal systems for each piece. Sometimes he used staples. He braced the back of his "couch" against the wall and was amazed that if he staggered the layers of his newspapers he was able to build a more supported structure.

He was captivated with the challenge of it all. Building things made time in his apartment fun and gave him a little hidden hobby to work on if he wasn't preparing for his class.

Chip didn't mind the newspaper habit either, as he would often sneak off to a spot and lift his leg in relief when it had been too long since the pair went outside.

His favorite piece that he made was the bedside nightstand with a thrice-folded square and sturdy drawer that he was able to pull out at his whim. A knob fashioned by a rolled up magazine cover added a splash of color to the black-and-white newsprint fixture.

Inside that drawer is where he kept the little traveling book. It was an everyday reminder that life was about taking chances and he should try to trust others to help *him* sometimes, too. He'd take it out of the drawer and read a little more each night- it helped become drowsy. The woman who wrote it was doing a big thing. She had known many people who had loved her, each changing her in some way.

He couldn't relate to that.

In living his entire adult life alone, Ned had more than enough socializing with his class once a week and trips to the grocery store; he didn't want to spend extra time with the other residents in between. His place became a haven of his passions of engineering and financial education.

When a newspaper or magazine would come in, he spent time leafing through to see what money matters he could share with the group before adding it to the pile that was slowly limiting his space inside. The piles of periodicals had the benefit of adding an insulating factor of the floor-to-ceiling paper which dulled the sounds of the outside, to his relief.

Ned had even become adept at opening and closing his door after listening at the door to make sure the coast was clear so no one would be able to peek inside in the transition. He found that he was becoming more of a hermit, and would sometimes miss teaching his classes to stay home and read over the latest news.

A knock on the door one day changed his trajectory. It was Hazel. She was concerned about him missing the classes he had and wanted to check on his well being.

"Can I come in?"

"No, this isn't a good time. I can meet you in the library at three o'clock for a quick chat. I am embarrassed of my place; I need to do some neatening up."

"We have some staff that would be happy to help with that if you need help, just let us know. We can offer weekly, monthly, whatever you need."

"I will think about it," Ned answered and started to close the door but Hazel nudged it open a smidge.

"I'll see you in the library at three," she said with a smile.

"Yes, okay." Ned closed the door and locked it, then stood leaning against it.

That was a close one, he thought, looking back into his ramshackle home. Ned suddenly felt like one of the very eccentric millionaire types he'd read about in the scandal pages. The people that are pitied for losing their minds even when they are seen as having everything someone might wish for.

Surely his money could help him avert his potential path to madness. He thought of the only woman he had ever loved. He had never reached out to her in their later years. Maybe if she was still alive she would be receptive to a reunion of sorts, even one built of friendship.

He'd seen something about a private investigator rooting out some lost person in order to get them the inheritance they deserved. Where was that article? Which newspaper was it?

Ned scoured the top layers of his furniture pieces, then started peeling into the lower sections. His "couch" was in shreds before he found it.

"Private investigator Garrick McDonald out of Washington, D.C., has decoded the case of the century. Millionaire heiress Dahlia Audhild, last remaining member of the Audhild family of the Schnell rubber tire empire, had left a big mystery in the wake of her death. Her will leaving all of her money, houses and the business itself has been bequeathed to a long lost child, one Benjamin Ryan Lancaster. Initial searches for the young man proved fruitless. That is until Garrick McDonald thought outside the box deciding that her original note did not specify that the child was male. Diving deeper into the Lancaster region of England, he found a family with a daughter named Benjamina O'Rian-MacDougal. Having grown up as the daughter

of one of the castle caretakers, a bachelor black man named John O' Rien, Benjamina was born and lived her life alongside the nuns who kept care of the parish. Upon her marriage to Kendall MacDougal, she moved south to Stodday where she was questioned by Garrick about her family and mother. With no answers, they together drove to see her father and it was revealed that indeed she had been born to Dahlia Audhild and her father had promised to be silent about their relationship until she passed. The search for Dahlia's heir was over."

Ned wrote Garrick's name on a piece of paper to take to the library with him later. There he could look him up on the computer to see if he might be able to find Mi Sun.

The little blue book had helped him to think bigger about life and had brought so many new people into his life, he wondered if there was room for one more. One that would change everything.

He showered, put on a clean shirt and headed over to the library to meet with Hazel.

~

~2~

Ned walked the hallway to the residence library. Luckily it was empty except for Hazel. He was glad there wouldn't be more people there to ask him where he'd been, and what stock they should look at next.

"Hey, stranger," said Hazel, patting the table before him. "Let's talk."

Ned stiffened, "Hello, how are you doing?"

"I'm great, maybe a little tuckered out from the job. So much is going on, I feel like I am a juggler in a circus but I'm excited too."

"I bet. So many classes and making sure to get the newspaper out each week. I've kept every single issue so far," he averted his eyes away from hers. *He could fill up an entire recycle truck himself by now, but he wasn't telling her that.*

"But how are you? I noticed you have missed a few classes; are you feeling like it's too much? We can always scale back on things or you could take a break. I am sure I could get some local business owners to come in and do some talks about things, give you a rest?"

"Yes, I think that would be nice. I have a little bit of a project I want to work on, and it will take a bit more of my time."

"Oh, how exciting! Anything you want to share?" she asked curiously.

"Not yet, but I will let you know if I need any help or advice. I think everyone is pretty set in the class, and getting some guest speakers is a great idea- maybe someone who can discuss taxes or how to navigate family inheritances. Some of those folks have done well for themselves with my tutelage. I am pleased with my brilliant students."

Ned started to rise and Hazel placed her hand on his.

"Are you sure I can't help you with anything? Do you need someone to talk to? I am so thankful that you came here and shared your great knowledge and experience with all of us- what a gift."

Ned patted her hand with his and pulled up out of his chair. He nodded goodbye and walked into the men's bathroom on that floor, waiting just long enough until he thought she had gone.

Exiting the restroom, he spied her entering the elevator before making his way back to the library to sit down at one of the computers.

He pulled up a screen and typed in "Yahoo" to search for the great detective Garrick McDonald.

Garrick McDonald, Private Investigator popped up. "Found him!"

Ned scribbled down the phone number on one of the yellow pads placed on the workstation. Noticing that he had scribbled hard, he pulled off seven more sheets of paper to make sure that no one could see what he was after.

"Not that anyone cares what I do," he thought to himself. His family didn't care. Hazel says she does but it's her job to care, right? Now Mi Sun, she might care at least a little. Ned hoped and prayed that he would find her; it had been too long thinking of her and he needed to know that she was okay.

Ned tucked the pages into his shirt pocket and snuck off to his room. A smile crept across his face in the elevator and got wider as he pulled his key from his pants pocket. The hallway was empty, he was alone. He could call the man right now if he wanted. The time difference was only an hour; surely someone would still be at the office.

Ned lightly shut his door and sat down in his chair by the phone, placing it on his lap. He pulled the note out of his shirt pocket and stared at it.

What if he really found her, what then? What if he had waited too long and she was gone? Ned frowned at the thought. Could he really bear losing her again?

Ned placed the phone receiver at his ear and dialed the number. No more waiting, no more wondering about her. He'd pay anything he just needed to know.

It rang once.

"Hello," a man's gruff voice came on the line.

"Um, yes, hello, my name is Ned Coggins and I'm l-l-l-looking for someone. Can you help?"

"Tell me more Ned Coggins. I will help if I can."

"Back in '54 I met and fell in love with a woman in Seoul Korea. I asked her to marry me and she came to the U.S. on a fiancé visa. She didn't stay. I don't know what happened to her. What do you think are my chances of finding her again?"

"Well, it's possible for sure, but I will need as many details as you can think of. Do you have any photos of her? Do you think you could fax me a copy? My rate is five thousand to start the investigation with updates and further deposits every week until we have found out what you need to know."

"What is the weekly fee, if I might ask."

"Certainly. It's fifteen hundred a week until either you decide to stop or we have an answer."

"Oh, yes, that will be fine. So I fax you everything I have. I may have the paperwork that got her over here to start with that may have her parents' name on it, too; I will look."

"Yes, all of that will be great. I need you to send me a cashier's check to start and then we can make arrangements for the weekly payments."

"I don't want to mess with that. I will just send you enough to get going and stay busy for a while. And I don't want the weekly updates; just tell me when you've found her. Dead or alive."

Well, yes sir. As soon as I get the cashier's check and information I will get started. What's her name?"

"It was Mi Sun Geun, G. U. E. N. was her family name. Mi is spelled M. I."

"Got it. Well, I will get working on this as soon as the deposit gets here. Just curious, what are you hoping to have as a resolution here? Do you still love her? Did she do you wrong?"

"Do I love her?" Ned sat quiet for a second, "Well, I guess yes, yes I do. She never did anything wrong other than break my heart when she left, but I can forgive that; I came to understand."

Ned wrote the business address down on the piece of paper with the phone number and pulled his memory box out off the top shelf of the closet. He didn't have much when it came to personal things. Mostly what he had was his financial papers and the makeshift furniture he had made.

Shuffling around he found his birth certificate and his social security card, then finally a photo of the two of them on the bridge-build where they met. It was grainy and in black- and-white, it was taken from pretty far away. One of the other engineers had accidentally gotten them in the shot as he tried to shoot the progress on one of the spans. It was the only photo he still had of the two of them. He had hoped to take more when they were in Kansas City at the baseball game in one of the photo booths, but with all of his stupid family drama, they never did.

Ned looked at the photo and tears welled in his eyes. Two people still just getting to know each other then, their whole lives held such possibility before them. He knew it would be a harder road with her leaving her home country to come and live in his, saying goodbye to everything she knew. But he hadn't taken into account how terrible his family would treat her. If anyone was going to mess things up with Mi Sun it should have been him.

Seeing her off at the Union Station, ticket in hand to trek back to Seattle and onto a ship back to Korea, he flushed with shame. How many times he regretted that he should have gone with her. At least seen her to her destination, or maybe they could have stopped somewhere along the line and started a new life together in whatever town looked hospitable. So many other options than how things ended.

Ned had seen his family only a handful of times in the forty-plus years that had passed since, he knew he had chosen wrongly. He could have made it up to her somehow if only he had prioritized her rather than continuing to be manipulated by his family into thinking he didn't deserve his own life, family and happiness.

Truth be told, none of it mattered as nothing that had happened already could be changed. Lord knows he had thought back to that moment at the train station a million times in his life, wondering if he should have done it differently. When she actually let go of him and stepped onto the train, he froze. Time stood still. He waited for someone to intercede, say something or stop her. But nothing happened. It didn't escape his notice that she didn't turn and look at him one last time. He couldn't see her eyes but saw her hand reach across her face to wipe her tears away.

She sat quickly, and looked down at him through the window. Tear-stained face, she was trying to be brave. So alone. She'd been through so much already: A war torn country, international travel, weeks on a boat, countless hours being tossed in the sea. Through it all she seemed most affected by her experience with Ned's family. It must have been the final straw. Maybe she knew she would never be accepted, that no matter what she did nothing would matter because *they* would never change. Accepting that reality and removing herself from it was the only way to keep any peace in her life.

Mi Sun had been the brave one. It was he who was a coward. Never coming for her or putting himself out there again to find love. Keeping his life tight and busy so he wouldn't hurt like that again or hurt anyone else. And here is where it got him: Alone for his entire life, unloved, even by his own family.

No more, not one more day of wondering about what could have been and wishing things were different. It was time for action. Ned called a cab and made his way to the bank. He asked the cab to wait outside as he wanted to send out the check today, too.

Ned stood in line looking at all the other people in the bank line. Regular business he supposed. But not him. He was doing a great big thing, one that could change everything. He closed his eyes and prayed to a god he hadn't talked to since he was ducking bombs back in Korea. He placed his hands on his heart and opened his eyes upon hearing the teller say, "Next."

"I need a cashier's check for one hundred thousand dollars."

She looked stunned at first then pulled in her shock. "Yes, sir. I will need your bank account number and I.D."

Ned handed over the necessary information and was sent to wait at the bank manager's desk.

"Mr. Coggins, I see you have been a loyal customer of Bank of America for the last twenty-five years. Do you have any concerns that would be contributing to you making such a large withdrawal today?"

Ned looked him square in the eyes and said, "No one has anyone for ransom if that is what you are getting at; I'm just spending a little of my hard earned cash- is that alright with you?" Ned's blue green eyes glistened.

"Oh, yes, sir. I didn't mean to be intrusive; we just like to keep extra care of our senior clients as there are a lot of people out to take advantage. My apologies."

"That makes sense." Ned softened. "Thanks for asking. I have no qualms about spending this money; in fact, I wish I would have taken this chance many years ago."

"Hope everything works for your best outcome, Mr. Coggins." He was handed an envelope and extended it to Ned before reaching to shake his hand to end the transaction and send him on his way. The bank manager would have to find another way to ask about such things, not that this kind of money was asked for very often. He sat shuffling papers around on his desk, trying to forget the exchange.

Ned climbed into the back of the cab and told the driver to take him to the FedEx location in Huntsville. He wanted this money to get to Garrick as soon as was utterly possible.

Ned sat back and watched the scenery between Gurley and Huntsville. A decent four-lane highway. Ned was glad that the driver wasn't particularly talkative, he just gave Ned his quiet and didn't drive erratically either. Ned could relax and just watch the world go by.

The last time he had been into town, he was making the drive from Huntsville out to Gurley, to the residence he had found after doing his research. He liked Gurley because it was quiet, a town of yesteryear, almost one that time itself had forgotten.

Trees stood on either side of the highway, a large strip of green nothing sat between the divided road. He wondered who it was that mowed that never ending patch of grass. Did they ever finish or just start over from the beginning? The blue sky had scant clouds and was as bright as he'd ever seen it. It suddenly reminded him of the "Big Sky" over Butte, Montana he had admired on his stopover to connect with Mi Sun in Seattle before they made their way by train to Kansas City. That was a beautiful part of America, God. Why hadn't they settled there?

The miles ticked by. Houses stood back away from the road and were built in different styles: brick used on some, old wood falling into tatters on the others. Not many fences that he could see, except some who must have fancied a white picket separation out of sentiment. Maybe people were friendly and they were fine with visitors coming by with no notice or barriers, or maybe people just knew just to keep to their own.

Ned gripped the envelope; sweating a line across where he held on. He didn't want to set it down on the seat or risk having it blow out of the window that hung low to let in some air.

Who were the people who sat in the houses that they blew past on their way into the city? Were they satisfied with their lives as they sat?

Old churches were cared for more delicately and kept up. People continued to go, serve and be a part of that community trying hard to maintain those places probably more than their own homes. They were an extra home and family to go to. One that often invited strangers in, in hopes of having an addition to the flock. To save them, to add to the tithe each week.

But that part of culture and society hadn't appealed to Ned. He didn't like the idea that something other than himself was making the rules. Free will they touted, yet many he'd known felt rigidly stuck within the canons of the place, knowing or believing that if they didn't behave, the afterlife would be punishing. That fear kept them in place, often in terrible marriages, too.

Ned had seen some of his co-workers struggle in their relationships: sometimes they'd break up and sometimes they would get help to patch up their marriages. Probably in equal amounts. But the biggest difference between those people and him was that the other people were actually *trying* to love. To be open to a relationship, even one that hurt for a while and didn't work out.

He hadn't tried at all. He had just given up.

In his job if a design didn't work out he could revise the drawings, try another material. He didn't chuck the project. Why had he given up on love?

The cab pulled into the shipping store and Ned unhooked his seatbelt.

"I'll just be a few minutes." he said to the driver who nodded then quickly pulled his cap down over his eyes and placed his feet up on the dash.

Maybe Ned could take his time and give the old guy a siesta.

"I need to get this to this address just as soon as possible."

"Okay, we can have it there on Thursday. Do you have anything else that goes with it? We will put it into a hard envelope to send that's a bit bigger than that so as to keep better track of it en route."

"Oh, I hadn't thought of a note. Yes, I suppose I need to have something. Give me a minute."

Ned stepped out of line and over to the postcards near the window. He looked out at the cab; the driver hadn't moved. He perused then spotted a postcard with a man and a woman riding a rocket into space. *"Rocket City"* was Huntsville's moniker since NASA had built their massive field station there to work on the research and development of the rockets that eventually got U.S. astronauts to the moon. It was perfect!

Ned pulled the postcard off of the rack and walked over to an address station to use one of the pens on a chain. He scribbled in his best hand-writing through his excitement.

Garrick-
Find her. Good news only, and keep the change.
Ned Coggins

Ned included the original photograph that he had of the two of them after keeping a copy for himself. He wanted Garrick to have the best version. He also included their original application for the fiancé visa drafted back in 1956. He stuffed everything into the cardboard envelope with the cashiers check and got back into the line to pay.

Everything that meant anything to him was in that parcel- this was the biggest gamble he had ever taken. Even when he played the stock market working massive deals on margin, he hadn't felt the thrill that he felt right now.

It would be the waiting that would be the hardest. But he'd waited forty-eight years, what was another few weeks or months?

Ned paid and put his credit card back into his wallet. He had some cash for the driver and he'd throw in a big tip. After all, the man had helped him pull off this "much at stake" caper; without him there would have been clumsy trips on multiple buses and hours of sitting around with a hundred thousand dollars burning a hole in his pocket.

The cab pulled into the parking lot back at Sunny Days. Ned felt lighter and more accomplished than he had in years. He was doing something-something big- and he allowed himself to feel the thrill and be excited for a possible reunion.

"Mi Sun, I hope you are out there somewhere. Hold tight, Mr. McDonald is on his way."

Quite a day it had been. The dinner bell rang as he entered the lobby and Ned walked directly to the cafeteria. He was famished, and thoroughly excited for whatever might come next.

~

Thinking about Gifts, Me 2007

Not gifts that are material gifts you shop for or ones you gift from a talent that you have.

Gifts in a different way. *Relationship gifts.* A long time ago, someone wise told me about such a thing.

When in a relationship and one of you has a preference or a concern, and the other one doesn't care as much about the thing, you decide to make it a gift to that person.

My example. Years ago, after the divorce, my ex wanted to take the girls skiing. I worried about their safety and not being there if they needed me or if something happened. I had no control about where they were and what they did in his care. Mr. Stability gave me a gift that I am so grateful for. He requires the girls to wear a helmet on the mountain when they ski. They still do to this day. Just that little thing, bending on his part, meant the world to me. He could have made a stink about it, caused a lot of drama. Made me worry and suffer with them being away from me, but he chose differently. He gave me a gift.

Sometimes, when we compromise, we can feel resentment.

"Fine, I will do it your way."

And you feel like you are giving up something or being man handled into it. It's a negative.

Gifting is a way to feel positive about that compromise. It's a positive.

If something is very important and worth fighting for- ok. Do it. We all have to pick our battles daily with life, work and family.

But, maybe ask yourself, is this an opportunity to give a gift to this person? If yes, then say it.

"I'm going to give you this one as a gift."

It is an incredible feeling.

~

Complicated Mr. Fun, Me 2007

I wasn't into him, until I was, and then he wasn't into me and was into someone else, then he came back to me after she rejected him.

Mostly we were friends, and I couldn't fault him for falling for another younger girl when I couldn't seem to make up my mind about him.

We'd leaned on each other and taken up space in each other's life. There was love there, and dependence. We took trips together and the girls had someone else to look out for them. It wasn't all bad, and it wasn't all good either.

Remembering how I felt when he told me about the girl on "MySpace" that he had found. He said they had a huge connection, and he needed to go investigate those feelings. At the time, I was all in with him, and was surprised that he had feelings for someone else. But in a bigger way I deserved it: a taste of my own medicine.

I wasn't going to be able to compete with a younger woman, one without children or all of the strings attached.

She was a free spirit, and together they talked about having children of their own. I knew he wanted more children, and I didn't see that in my future.

When he arrived on her doorstep unannounced, she rejected him on the spot. He came back broken from the effort and didn't go into the details with me, and I didn't push.

Maybe in seeing him, she realized he had a few more miles on him than he seemed to from behind the paltry resolution of a computer screen.

Whatever it was, it made him want to try again with me, and I didn't really fight it.

We'd been friends, then lovers, then friends again. It seemed to be our pattern somehow, and neither of us knew how to get off the roller coaster that was us.

I didn't have the power or confidence to go it alone in this world- maybe I never would.

I let him back in, to all of it, to my heart and my body, my daughters' lives and my home, as if nothing had ever happened. I wish I would have grown the belief that somehow I deserved better than this. That I could have stood on my own for a time and gotten stronger.

Still more lessons to learn.

~

~2~

N ed had fallen asleep in bed after reading the little blue book again.

Suddenly he was jarred awake upon hearing a commotion in his room. Looking around the barely lit space, his eyes landed on some frantic movement on the floor. Chip appeared to be having a violent seizure.

Quickly, he tried to get out of bed to help Chip, but his foot became tangled in the sheets and he tumbled hard into a pile on the floor.

Ned shouted for help over and over. Pleading, not only for himself but for Chip who lay still on the rug. Watching, waiting for help, he felt his little buddy leave. His best friend was gone.

His neighbors heard his urgent cries for help and the nurses came running in. They had a hard time navigating their way to him because of the stacks of newspapers piled all over his place.

He was rushed to the hospital, and an x-ray showed a broken hip. He would need surgery in the morning to repair it, and he lay waiting overnight, quietly crying in the agony of losing Chip.

The surgery should have been routine, but Ned suffered cardiac arrest on the table and was gone. Wafted away to walk his old dog home.

~

I guess he asked? Me 2007

*T*here must have been a question or a discussion because one day we went by the jewelry store to look at rings. We went to the most famous one in our area, the one with the annoying jingle you can always sing no matter how drunk you might get.

There we spoke to the sales associate and a certain topic came up.

"Do you have anything you would want to show us in trade to bring down the price of the one you are looking at?"

It was like "Big Ben" itself had struck in his brain. Suddenly he was rummaging through my jewelry box in his head, my old wedding ring, my ten-year anniversary band. He started his campaign on the way home as we left empty-handed.

"When are you ever going to wear any of those pieces again? You won't."

"Well, I could give the diamonds to my daughters later on or have them made into something else."

"I guess, but will you? This is a great way to get you into that beautiful ring we saw; imagine what everyone will say!" he mansplained to me over that weekend. I couldn't deny that they would sit, but I didn't have to do what I did either. Another dumb decision to go into my portfolio of stupidity. Suddenly I was polishing up my ten-year wedding anniversary band, the one with the three diamonds signifying the past, the present and the future and we were on our way back to that store.

It ended up being an approximate trade plus maybe six hundred dollars which I spotted him of course, because that is what I did. I came away with a princess cut that sat up on a prong surrounded by tiny diamonds. It was shiny and beautiful and I held my hand out for all to see.

We were engaged. He was especially proud and showed it off to everyone, "Look what I bought for her." I didn't say anything to the contrary; I was used to keeping up the ruse.

I can't remember why we never got around to getting married, and I can't remember how it was that days, then months, then years went by with the ring coming off and on with no date talked about. The only thing I can say *is that it worked out exactly as it should have: it was good we didn't actually marry, and it was one more lesson to learn in this life of mine.*

I pass no judgment on any woman who wants to contribute towards their wedding or engagement ring. It was just the way it went down that I found gross. And now I don't have those diamonds to give my daughters. I had to pawn the ring later to cover bills as things got harder and harder, netting me the extra six hundred dollars I'd put in and the rest- over two thousand dollars- becoming a wash with my old ring.

Pretty fucking embarrassing if I'm being honest. Thank God I didn't marry him. Thank God I didn't have a child with him or we'd have been tethered together forever.

***

*There must have been some screaming banshee inside me that didn't let me
go through with that part.*
Even though I'd been ignoring her for the most part for years.
~

~2~

S unny Days had lost one of their own. Ned Coggins wouldn't be coming back. In the all day cleaning before giving his apartment to a new tenant, his *final straw* handwritten will of sorts was found. It was brought to the residence manager.

"We aren't sure what to do with this, but it seems legit. From the state of his apartment and his handmade furniture made out of newspapers, he might have been a bit of a whack job. This is all way above my pay grade," said Clay, one of the night maintenance men. "We've got a lot of work to get his suite ready for the next person on the list."

"I'll take care of it," Ms. Rhodes replied. "Don't worry yourself a bit about it."

"Thanks, I'll send you a note when the room is ready for occupancy." Clay went back to work.

Ms. Rhodes sashayed over to her occupant file cabinet. She had the skinny on everyone who lived there. She had pegged Ned Coggins as a millionaire long ago.

She pulled his file and laid it on her desk, placing the note within reach and drumming across it with her magenta fingernails. She knew Alabama law when it came to things like this. First money would go to a spouse, then children, then any family who should come forward. She couldn't see any relations in his file so he must have been that lone wolf type, never settling down and just hoarding all the cash he could throughout his life.

The "Will and Testament" was a reach for sure. Scribbled on the back of a bank statement envelope, it wouldn't hold water as it was. But she knew how to make it good. A couple of signatures of witnesses to the drafting of the document and it'd be legal and legit. She knew where to buy signatures. A grin sliced open her face as she planned her next move.

She pulled her cell phone out of her desk drawer and flipped her contacts to Reggie. Reginald Banks. He owed her a favor, had no trouble screwing the government either, and once he knew that if no one was found to collect his money that it would go to the state, he'd do anything to stop it.

"Hey, Reggie, what are you doing right now?"

"Geez, Ruby, it's kinda late, unless this is a booty call."

"You wish. No, I need another kind of favor. There's some money in it for you."

"Oh, yeah! How much?"

"Ten K, but only if you show up in twenty minutes at the Piggly Wiggly. You do this for me and I will pay ya later."

"When later?"

"Not sure, it depends."

"Well I guess I can help. I didn't have the opportunity to make ten grand ten minutes ago. So I'll be there."

"Great! See you soon."

One more call to make. Maybe she should stagger the signers a bit, no use giving them any more access to each other. She needed to keep this quiet.

Jimmy Hankins, he'd do anything for a buck. She scrolled to his number.

"Jimmy, boy, I need you, baby."

"I *know* you do, Honey lamb. He drawled. "What's shakin' bacon?"

"I need your autograph on something, with you being famous and all. Can you bring that cute little notary stamp of your daughter's over too? Every little bit helps."

Jimmy thought for a second. "I don't want my daughter to get into trouble for anything. What do you need that for?"

"Okay, never mind about that, too big of an ask, but can you still help me? I need a witness."

Jimmy was using every brain cell he'd been born with. "A witness for what?"

"Jesus, never mind. I'll find someone else."

She pressed "end" on her phone and scrolled to who else she might be able to recruit.

They couldn't be attached to the residence in any way. Suddenly a name popped into her head.

"Velda- she had some pretty big bills come in after the accident." She pressed send and Velda came onto the line within a few rings.

"Ruby, God, it's late. What do you want?"

"You know how you are always talking about going to Vegas but you couldn't ever afford it? Well, I thought of a way to help get you there."

"Oh, lordy, lordy. How? I'm dying to see all those lights and the shows. Wayne Newton, *Hubba Hubba*."

"I need your autograph on something. I won't tell you what it is, but

I've got a nice paycheck for you that you can use to go see Mr. Las Vegas himself. Might even be able to buy you a personal visit from him to your table if you can get your clothes on and meet me at the Piggly Wiggly in ten minutes."

There was a squeal and a scurry and the line went dead.

"I guess that was a yes."

Ruby pulled on her coat and tucked the envelope and a stack of post-its into her pocket. She'd cover up what they were actually signing, helping her accomplices avoid being charged if anything did go down. She knew that this was not the proper thing to do, but who was she to go against the wishes of *that sweet old man*. It was her *duty* to help him see through his financial intentions, even though he hadn't gone to the trouble of making it all legal-like.

Pulling onto Hwy 72 E, she drove as fast as she could without bringing any attention to herself. Her town's "Sheriff Coltrane and Cletus" were not going to ticket away any of her hard-earned money anytime soon.

Velda arrived with curlers in her hair, and a ratty old bathrobe tucked over her rose- covered mumu. One slipper made it out of the car with her as she leapt from it.

"Did I make it in time?"

"You surely did, Ma'am. Please sign right here."

"What? No never mind, I don't even want to know." She scribbled her name in the space not covered by post-its and shook Ruby's hand when it was offered.

"Thanks, Velda, I'll be in touch soon. Don't you worry your pretty little head about anything."

Velda climbed back into her car and sped off as if driving a getaway car. Ruby hoped that she wouldn't get a ticket on her way home but if she did, she'd happily pay it. It was well worth the investment if she could pull this all off.

Not two minutes later, Reginald Baron Banks slipped his silver Mercedes Benz-E Class into the parking spot at the end of the Piggly Wiggly lot. Reggie rarely did anything fast but Ruby was impressed that he was actually earlier than the time she'd set given that he had to drive down from Harrison Cove Road.

"How did you do.. what?"

Anticipating her questioning his ability to rocket to the meetup spot given where he lived, he shared, "Well, I was actually over at the widow Peterson's house in town when you called, but I am sure I can count on your discretion about that, right my dear Ruby?" He tipped his glasses down to meet her brown eyes with his rather bloodshot blue ones.

"Of course." she meeked. Ruby staggered the post-its around to make space for Reginald to sign. He had quite the elaborate signature she knew from experience.

Reginald pulled his Mont Blanc Meisterstuck gold-coated pen out of his suit chest pocket and put the shiny cap gently in his mouth as he cued up for his "John Hancock." Ruby set the document on the hood of her car to give him a stable surface for his masterpiece. She wanted to rush him but thought better of it; she only had this one copy with Ned's and Velda's signature, and she wouldn't get another chance.

He placed the cap on his pen and blew softly over his wet signature. It tightened in view and he was satisfied.

"There. Remember you owe me some money, my dear. I will be in touch weekly until I have it in my hot little hands. Count on that. I promised to take the widow Peterson to New Orleans for leaving her in the nude like I did. Sweaty, spread eagle and everything- down right humiliating to up and leave her like that.

Ruby did not want to know this information but she thanked him and hoped he didn't notice she did not extend her hand in the traditional exchange of a service. No need to muddy further the waters or fluids of the evening.

She drove back to her office and planted the document in a high kitchen cupboard to be found by the professional cleaning crew that came after the first run of her guys. She'd buy herself and maybe the whole building something nice when this was all over, she was certain of that.

The next few days came off like a dream: the wild discovery of a note, having Ned's signature verified by his bank, and all of his assets were sold to the benefit of the Sunny Days retirement home.

Ned's clothing and what real furniture pieces he had were graciously dispersed to those at Sunny Days who were in need. His kitchen pots, pans and silverware and his bathroom items were shared out amongst the residents as well. His apartment sat empty for a meager three days before a new couple moved into it. Cleaned, painted, everything cleared as if he had never been there at all. The need for space was constant. His few belongings including the little blue book were kept together and boxed up in case anyone came forward.

"Find Me" two of five with all of Ned's personal effects would sit in a document box, piled on top of others in a metal framed warehouse in Gurley, Alabama, for who knows how long.

~

Entrepreneurial Again Me, 2008

*M*r. Fun and I had been talking about starting a business together to give some real potential to the money I had sitting around in the bank. Money that seemed to waft away from me monthly leaving nothing to show for it. Our business would be an investment, something to provide an income for us both. We threw ideas around like a ball in a ping pong tournament.

At first he talked of doing something in music, and I threw out the idea of a cupcake business and a t-shirt company, or a this or a that. The bantering between us went on for months, then a year. Each idea was flushed out, the company named, a domain was purchased, but each time something wouldn't feel right, and we waffled. Waiting for the right idea to come.

It was 2008 when we felt fairly certain about our business idea, and I told my daughters about the impending launch.

My oldest looked at me, rolled her eyes and said, **"Mom, stop, we don't believe you anymore."** She was fourteen.

Jesus.

See, I had been sharing the ideas with my daughters, and each time they became excited to help with the cupcake business, the T-shirt company, etc. Each time it got closer, I had pulled the plug on the idea, and she was right to call me out on it. I think back sometimes and wonder where she got that immense bravery to call her own mother out on something. How pathetic I must have appeared to her for her to stand up and say that to me. She was still a child.

But her statement put a fire under me like nothing else ever had. It was exactly what I needed to finally commit to doing something. I could not have my kid not believing in me. No way in hell.

Even if I didn't believe in myself, even a little, I would force myself to fake it. Prod myself to follow through on what I said this time. In as much for me and our future, I had to prove to myself that I was capable of doing something- anything-for once.

We decided on a small-scale store, one geared towards earth-friendly prod-

ucts. There was another one in a neighboring city that was doing quite well, and Mr. Fun had been visiting them a lot just to see how they were set up.

We signed a lease to rent a space in an old building close to home and started gathering what we needed to show clients: Samples, products and displays. We painted the walls and laid floors and had an open house event that my daughters attended. They brought a couple of their friends. It was something that actually happened rather than just something we'd only talked about and gave up on.

My parental credibility got a bump that day, and Mr. Fun and I did our best to make it work. But 2008 wasn't the best year to start a business, especially one based solely on discretionary spending.

We added bigger ticket items in order to be able to see bigger payouts. When we had a commitment, the potential client would have a loss in the stock market, or was suddenly in danger of losing their job. Every possible project turned into an improbable sale, but the rent was still due, and there were bills to pay at home for both him and me, and more expenses to advertise in hopes of getting more business.

At first Mr. Fun manned the store and I stayed at my prior job to have some regular cash coming in. But when the business didn't come, I thought it might be him that was the issue so I started going in there every day and left my other job.

I soon discovered that he and I liked to do the same things when it came to the business. We both liked helping people and finding the perfect products for them. Neither of us liked the accounting side, so the taxes, contracts and licensing fell to me to figure out. I did fairly well once I got it all set up. What choice did I have?

When he and I were on- we were on. We shared in the successes, and felt together the failures.

The seesaw of our relationship ran parallel to the seesaw of the business. If things were good that month, we got along, but with every month of low or no sales and more money drained from my personal bank account in order to sustain us, we fought.

My safety net- my nest egg- got smaller and smaller until it was barely there at all anymore. Something needed to change.

~

$$\sim 2 \sim$$

Hazel sat at her desk overlooking the vast copies of the *Sunny Days Gazette* newspapers that had been published for the residents about the other residents. She often thought of the book that had inspired the idea, but as many times as she would go looking for it in the library, she hadn't seen it in years.

Thankfully she had made copies of a few of the excerpts to help her remember something about her own life or to use as a format for a new story about one of the residents. But oh, how she wished she had made copies of the whole thing. If she had, she could make a new book to continue to inspire the people coming in and out of this place.

Where could the traveling book have gone?

Maybe it had escaped with a family member visiting and was either well on its way back to the owner or, better yet, it had been delivered to her already?

That is the thought she chose to hold onto about the little book that had given her and others so much in its visit to Sunny Days.

~

Guilt Can Consume Sometimes, Me, 2008

Throughout the years I have apologized to my daughters over and over for divorcing their father. If I had stuck it out with him, they would have had a more stable, ideal suburban life like most of their friends did.

Regular vacations. One house, not two. Never having to pack a bag or cross town to be with their parents. Easy holidays in the same spot. Same rules to live by. More money. Or at least no money issues. Same schedule, certainty instead of uncertainty.

I remember the time when we were talking and they both told me it was okay.

It was because of the divorce that they had more real life experiences than their other friends had. They had experienced living in an old house and an apartment, and they had learned to be more self-sufficient than many of their friends because they had to participate more. They understood more about what life could be like. They met people they might not have met in their other realm.

They felt that they might have seen more because with me they lived in the city. They took drama classes at the local theater downtown. We had walked to the Saturday market often and made memories of trying new foods, and bringing farm bouquets home to enjoy for the week. There were road trips to other people's family reunions, and getting In-N-Out burgers in California. They had two worlds from which to pick their daily activities.

The one constant being the three of us.

Them saying that was a gift to me, as it smoothed over some of the guilt I felt about how it all went down. As much guilt that could be dissuaded without them actually knowing the full story. I knew that the realization of my having an affair would come someday, but hadn't yet. Neither my ex or I could see the point at the moment as there was enough going on as it was.

Even with the secret still kept from them, I carry the weight and full responsibility of my choices. I tell myself I would never make that type of exit *again no matter how bad any relationship gets.*

Them sharing a bit of understanding was a reminder that some good can come from mistakes after all.

~

$$\sim 2 \sim$$

Hazel stopped to visit with Deidre at the front desk one morning.

"How's things with you?" Hazel asked. She liked to visit with everyone and keep her finger on the pulse of the place. Her job kept her busy but sometimes she needed to make herself slow down.

Deidre answered back, "I am juggling quite a bit right now. I have to check in with my doctor real quick about a test I need to take tomorrow, and this afternoon we are having officers of the bank come and tour the facility. We are hosting their entire team and springing for a luncheon after the tour in the second conference room. So much going on today. I'm overwhelmed."

"Sure, take your time, I can work my way back to my office after you get back."

Hazel sat and looked out over the desk, everything was neat as a pin. The paper calendar sat square in front of her chair, each event was color-coded to some time of Deidre-quantified specification. Hazel could tell she liked things in place.

The outgoing mail was to the left of the phone. A purple envelope lay on top, with some words scribbled across with red pen.

Return to sender. Addressee is deceased.

Seemed like a pretty cold way to hear that someone was dead. She squinted to see which tenant it was meant for.

Ned Coggins. A return address of Montana. The handwriting was beautiful, the envelope simple. Hazel sniffed, was it scented?

This was a new wrinkle. The sender had missed reaching him by months. Ned had never mentioned anyone in Montana, come to think of it, he'd never mentioned anyone, anywhere.

The phone rang. Someone couldn't reach accounting, so they asked to be transferred. Hazel fumbled with the phone and lost the call; they called back miffed. The second time she was able to connect them.

The postal carrier came in through the big lobby doors. "Hi, you're new!

Got anything to go out today?" The man was young and full of energy.

Hazel reached into the wire bin to hand him the mail, sliding Ned's letter onto the hidden desktop before handing him the rest of the pile. *

Hazel wasn't sure what the law said about opening a dead person's mail. She knew it was illegal for her to open someone else's mail when they were alive but the rest was fuzzy. There was no way to tell the person about his death properly with any heart or empathy unless she took on the responsibility herself.

How traumatizing it would be to just get their letter back with no explanation. Nothing to say about what had happened to Ned. The sender could be a friend, maybe even some long lost family? She owed Ned that courtesy at least.

~

1

---

1. *See Hazel Opens the Letter- *an After-story link at end of the book*

Medicating Again, Me 2009

*P*retty shut down right now. On my third set of antidepressants. I am feeling like I don't believe in love anymore. I don't think I believe in Mr. Fun anymore. He doesn't do what he says he will. I am tired of his broken promises. I feel I have given all that I am willing to give. I no longer believe in us.

Mr. Fun and I started counseling to work out our problems. After two sessions with the same counselor I had used in my previous marriage- the one who walked me down the hallway and planted me in a nondescript chair in front of the lawyer- I decided that the counselor was no longer a good fit for me.

I was complaining about Mr. Fun and suddenly he got real animated and clapped his hands in a eureka moment saying, "Actually, I think you two are perfect for each other."

Him saying that was like a total kiss off. He didn't want to listen to me or hear me anymore and his whole walking me down to the lawyer that day had been his attempt to get me off his plate.

I lay with Mr. Fun that night imagining being alone. I am sure I would be lonely. I thought I wanted to love him again. But now I am not sure.

The idea of being with someone new. What a drag. At least I know what I have with him. Is it enough? Am I certain I even know what I want?

~

S.M.

I had a crush on you from the moment you came onto my scene in fourth grade and then all the way through high school. The longest crush of my life.

Early on, you intrigued me with your game show host smile and dazzling personality. I did love myself a Chuck Woolery type from "Wheel of Fortune" and "Love Connection" back then.

You always wore the most up-to-date fashions for a guy. Your multiple Izod shirts with the spiked-up collars were on point- why did we wear multiple shirts back then anyway? So uncomfortable. Polos, Levi shrink-to-fit jeans. Your butt.

You were Mr. Cool wherever you went, popular but not over the top.

I don't actually ever remember you talking to me, more like you talked while you were around me and I was always pretty invisible.

I never got to know you, or tried to be noticed by you either but you probably caught me staring at you whenever we were in the same proximity.

Maybe you felt my eyes on the back of your neck in class? Sorry, that must have been awkward but you never said anything so maybe I had hid it pretty well?

Or maybe you were just being kind to not embarrass the little mouse of a girl who never came out of her shell?

~

It Will Kill Love, Me 2009

Years ago in my first marriage, we had settled into a precarious spot. I was at home with our daughters, completely dependent on my husband for money, shelter and everything. We knew something wasn't working. We were snarly towards each other, or quiet which often felt worse. Unsaid words hung like stalactites across the room, when we were supposed to be on the same side.

We'd stopped having fun with each other and doing things where we were both in an even status with each other, two adults working to accomplish something. Playing golf, working out, whatever, we'd stopped trying and everything was off.

I can't remember if it was our first trip to marriage counseling or if it was for something else, but when we both shared where we were at with each other with the therapist, she said something that blew both of our minds at the time.

"Yeah, I mean you don't have sex with your kid. Or at least healthy people don't. Like Oedipus and his mother, this type of relationship cannot be in romantic relations. If you don't get out of this routine and away from the resentful feelings of one of you being above the other, it will kill your love for each other forever."

Somewhere in the mess we had fallen into a place of more of a child/parent relationship. In his eyes, I was another child, needing to be cared for, and he was the parent, doing what he saw was everything.

We were able to fix things once we had the knowledge of how our relationship was broken and by taking the necessary steps to build back the even keel between us.

It wasn't until years later when I saw the other side and understood how my ex-husband might have felt all those many years before.

It was with Mr. Fun and I was the parent this time.

We didn't have the parent being home with a child aspect, as the kids were grown enough not to need us in that way, but soon after our relationship began, I found myself taking up the gap for him. In doing things around the house, the money, the business and basically everything ran through me with little effort and contribution from him, I felt I was in the mother role.

It gave me some extra understanding of my ex-husband's feelings, and I called him up to let him know that I now understood more of what he was dealing with back then, now that I was having a realization myself.

In sharing those feelings with him, I coincidentally gave him another chip on his shoulder towards Mr. Fun, which frankly was not super helpful in my world, but I understood it anyway. Maybe I should have listened to him a long time ago.

Okay, so if I knew that I was feeling "motherly" towards my love interest, and it would "kill the love," could I fix it? Did I even want to?

That would become the bigger question.

Maybe I was already tired of babysitting grown ups.

~

On the Razor's Edge, Me 2009

*M*oney problems, lack of business and two separate families to support. I am under the most stress of my life! Mr. Fun has been writing checks to himself without telling me, so I have to keep selling more assets to cover the accounts. My credit cards are almost maxed. We've been fighting a lot.

I just want him to go because there isn't enough business for us both. One of us needs to get a job. I have been paying for everything so far; it's not fair that I walk away and leave everything to him. He wants to be bought out, but there is nothing to split. He won't go. I'm so stuck. We are barely keeping the lights on anyway.

I could blame the economy, as many businesses have struggled right now. People are losing their jobs left and right, and it's hard to find work, let alone customers. I could blame it on the location, and the timing, but in the end, it doesn't matter. I am in trouble, and I really thought I was hiding it well until...

A visit from my friend L.C. She has been the biggest outside supporter of this business, and she came in to see me. She made sure I was alone and sat across from me at the big desk.

"Remember that first day we met?" she asked.

"Of course. You came in full of energy and told me how much you liked this idea and you wanted to help make us successful."

"Yes, and I have helped," she said.

"Yes, you totally have, I agree. You got us our first big customer. Thank you."

"Yes, but now, I'm worried about you. You have tried very hard to make this work, and it's not working."

"Yeah, it's hard right now. A real mess, but I'm sure it will turn around."

"Do me a favor, close your eyes, I want to tell you a story." she said.

I did as I was told.

"I want you to imagine that you are very small, a tiny little person. And a giant has grabbed you by the butt. He is trying to pull you through a knothole

in a fence and you are struggling, desperately trying to hold yourself on the one side you're on."

I see it all, just as she describes it.

"You are trying with all of your might to fight the giant. So you don't get pulled through. You've stiffened your arms and your legs, and you are doing all you can to hold on to where you are. To everything that you have around you."

"Yes." I sniffle.

"Now, I want you to imagine that you grow so tired of fighting, that your body falls limp in his hand, and he pulls you effortlessly through the hole with ease. You are through the fence now and the other side is so much better and brighter than you could have imagined. This is what is happening to you right now. You are fighting to hold onto things that are doing nothing but taxing you and taking from you. You are fighting to continue to hurt, to be stressed. You cannot keep going on like this, it's time to let it go."

Now, I am bawling.

"You are right, I have been fighting so hard to keep going, to stay here in this place because this is what I know. It's so hard, but at least I know what this feels like. I do not know what might come next."

"What if it's wonderful? You tried, we all saw it, you tried so hard. My friend, you cannot keep going on like this, you have to stop. This is not good for you to carry this much pressure, and it's not good for your girls to see you like this."

I let out a deep breath and agreed and she came around the desk to hug me. She's right and there would be a lot of work to do to unravel things. To get out of this place where I am, to get out of the toxic relationship I am in. But the first step was to acknowledge that I couldn't do <u>this</u> any more.

I told Mr. Fun that I couldn't do us anymore either, and I wanted him to leave my house and the business, he needed to go. He wanted half, or he'd buy me out with no money. He kept making attempts to stay in, and months went by with us fighting at home and acting like we liked each other at work. Lying every damn day.

Finally I laid it all out, that I had helped him with purchasing his fast car, and often helped him make child support payments or his student loan payments when he was low on funds. I had given him a rent-free place to stay for over a year. It was enough. I added up all the money I had handed him over the last three years, and he finally agreed to bow out of the business so we could both move on.

I helped him one last time with some first and last month's rent money so he could move out.

It was a step in the right direction. I asked my mom to move in with me and the girls, and together we could consolidate our bills, and work towards a plan. She had been struggling, too.

Three generations in the same house was fun, but it wasn't perfect. Mom manned the store during the day, to try to squeak through the final days of the lease, and I went and got a job, it was the only thing I could do.

With all that had gone on, I was now in jeopardy of losing the house. I was going to have to fight for all of it. Harder than I ever had in my life.

And I am tired. Worn out from bad after bad happenings in my life, work and in love.

~

L.W.

We met in fourth grade. I remember you were so popular and oh-so-cool.

We lived close to each other, so often we would walk to school together. We would hang out after school, sitting and talking at your house so you didn't have to be alone while your mom worked late. With you I found myself pushing the envelope. You were a tiny bit older but so much more worldly. You even had boyfriends in junior high, while I was a total goob who couldn't even talk to boys 'til way into high school.

Sometimes I wondered why you wanted to hang out with me when you had a crop of way more interesting people to hang out with. I wonder now if maybe you kept me around so with me you could let down your always hip exterior?

During the summer months I'd walk over to your house on the lake side and climb into your hammock that hung between two massive fir trees. You'd tell me to wrap the ropes all the way around myself to hold it closed and then you would push me harder and harder until I was spinning all the way around screaming. It was terrifying and thrilling just the same. What a rush.

With you I got to experience different things as your family always had something big going on: The entire U.S. Olympic ski team over to your house; your family owning a restaurant; everything about your life was so much more exciting than mine. You traveled around the world, and took the big city bus downtown to get your allergy shots. I would have been way too afraid to do that. You were so brave, always, or maybe you didn't have a choice.

You gave me my first sip of alcohol. We slipped some gin out of your Mom's liquor cabinet and mixed it with grape juice, in our inexperience. It was pretty awful, I remember. I cannot even remember if we felt buzzed or got drunk. Perhaps we split one glass since it was so bad, and neither of us went back for more? I'm not sure it was your first time getting into the cabinet, but it was mine.

You were the friend who exposed me to things I wouldn't maybe have known about.

The first time I got pantsed by a boy. I was wearing orange-and-white striped, Dolphin brand nylon shorts. They were the ones that had a panty lining sewn into the inside. *Typically,* the cool kids didn't bother wearing underwear with them, but no one had told me. Thankfully, in my dorkness I *was* wearing undies on the day when P.H. thought he was being funny and pulled down my shorts. My drawers saved me from being more embarrassed than I could have been.

You gave me my first experience with weed. I'd watch you take a pop can and smash a dent in it, adding a couple of holes with a small pin, one to cover up as a valve while using the opening to take in the smoke. The first time I tried it, I coughed and coughed. My second chance to be cool was sitting with you and a couple friends in your VW bug. Everyone else was smoking on their own bong. Hoping for a second hand high that never came, I joked later, *"I didn't inhale."*

I remember the day you got married. I had arrived a little late and was trying to find a spot to stand as the music started. There was torrential rain and your family had rushed to put up tents. You stood with your stepfather on the wrap around porch of your lake home, overlooking the grassy expanse of onlookers and the lake churning with the storm beyond. You looked beautiful.

Ready to walk towards your groom, we locked eyes. You looked terrified.

I felt it. I felt your fear and that you needed something from me, some courage to go through with it. I smiled, and gave you a thumbs up. Your eyes misted a little, you smiled softly and then you married him.

Over the years, he made choices that were not in your best interest. Actions that made you doubt yourself and your worth. Ones that maybe made you seek out shallow connections so you wouldn't get hurt like that again.

Forever after that moment, I have wondered about that day. And that maybe when you looked at me the way you did, that I should have stolen you away instead?

~

A Tornado of Misters in One, Me, 2009

*M*r. Fun had become Mr. Shared Car Loan and Mr. Living With Me and Having All the Bills Paid. Then he's Mr. Quitting His Job to start a record label, with the help of my divorce settlement. Soon enough I looked around and it's four years later and I've gone through all the money and I am sitting up to my eyelashes in debt, wondering what the hell happened.

After a lot of drama which I would just as soon forget, Mr. Fun is now Mr. Moved Out and Mr. Impregnated a Former Customer- or Mr. IAFC for short- but he is out of my hair forever.

I realized that there could be no middle ground with him. We had gone back and forth so many times, the only way to remain free of him was to entirely shear us off from him and his family.

I sat with the belief that I could have warned the woman carrying his child about him, potentially saving her some upheaval, but when I talked to a friend who had also dated him. She said, "Hold your tongue and let her find out for herself."

She copped to using me in the same way to escape his attention and needs. Thank God I listened to her and was rid of him at last.

I remember having another conversation about him with her.

I knew they both came from the same city and both had abusive parents. She had become successful in all that she did. Rising to the top of her field, and becoming a leader with many degrees and a ticket to anywhere she wanted to go.

Mr. Fun on the other hand had given up on his most amazing talent because he didn't believe in himself to achieve success. He stayed small and let others tell him how the world would treat him.

"What was the difference between the two of you?" I asked, begging to know why it was.

She either did some therapy or was just knowing enough to share it with me, "Yes, we both came from abusive families, I think the only difference was that when my family told me I was shit, I didn't believe them."

Mic drop.

I do hope that Mr. Fun gets his shit together someday and becomes all that he can be. Happy even. I just know that the combination of the two of us wasn't going to get either one of us there, so later, tater.

~

~2~

"Find Me" two of five lay in a box in storage at a warehouse on-site at the Sunny Days rest home. Mice had infested the building, which was inspected only once a year or opened to put away or retrieve final belongings of the deceased.

Sunny Days' policy was to keep a resident's personal items for up to ten years after the death. After that any items left were sold to better the lives of the other residents if it had any monetary value at all.

Ned Coggins' life mementos sat in the bottom of a box with his name and date of passing on it. A marking of "Keep for relatives" was written in red permanent pen.

Many boxes and memories sat together in this building, waiting to be shared with someone, anyone who might care.

On inspection day, the boxes are rotated, those closer to their toss date are moved closer to the exit door.

A mouse jumped up and sniffed at the tape holding the box closed. Will there be anything left in ten years to see?

No one knows, and no one cares. All inquiries are addressed. There have been no queries on this box.

The mouse scampers away after hearing a fellow squeak, leaving a small amount of excrement on the top of Ned's box.

Safe for now, but, what will become of Ned's memories, his life in the box?

~

Dad

I look like the female version of you. Same color eyes, same color hair. Same blood type. Same astrological sign. Alike in so many ways.

You were often there for me, being the coach for my softball team. You helped me with math and schoolwork when you could.

After the divorce, you took us on a lot of road trips, ones that were agonizing as a kid, sitting in the back seat with my brother who was always trying to bug me. We camped out and ate "Dinty Moore Stew" and had s'mores every chance we could get.

When you showed me the letters and photos of the women who wanted to date you from your personal ad, I know you didn't mean to make me feel inadequate with my looks. You couldn't help that you had preferences, and you wanted to share something you were excited about.

I think it was just the timing of all of it, my tender age of just starting into womanhood, and my lack of confidence in myself anyway that really set that feeling of being ugly in me. Eventually I got over it, and realized the beauty that I held inside and out.

In the bigger picture you were always there for us, even when things were rough.

When I was failing my math class again and kept being put back into the same class I had already failed at, you went to the school and said, "Look, this kid needs a win," and had them put me in general math, the most basic arithmetic class in the school at the time. And I aced it, bolstering me some, from the midst of my rancid high school career.

The time when I was living away from home with the idea of attending a community college close to my university boyfriend, but I couldn't seem to drag myself to class. I'd sit home every day. Planning on going but every day, my depression and lack of confidence in school kept me home. Finally you came and got me and brought me back home. You'd be the person to make the decision for me to leave, rather than have it be for me to make the call not having the strength to decide while continuing to fail every day, feeling lower and lower or not trying.

It was good, and I went back to work at the place I worked at before. I was building a sense of purpose and gained experience in the world again. Each time I faltered you were there to pick me up, always sharing a similar story from your own life for me to gnaw on.

Even with your well-to-do upbringing, you had some really crappy things happen to you. With your father dying in your early twenties, your family was suddenly afloat in an uncertain space. Your mother wasn't allowed access to the finances since your father didn't trust her, and everything was a mess. Years of upheaval, and thousands of dollars wasted in probate court because your Dad never thought he would die.

You were drafted into the services and went off to Vietnam, leaving your brand new wife- my Mom- at home not knowing if you'd be back.

It was your first time away by yourself. Your time of potential self discovery was tainted by the guilt and shame put on you that never should have fallen on you and your fellow servicemen. Bullshit United States politics, somehow you all were to blame rather than the responsibility being held by the United States leadership. You saw some horrendous things there and came back to a country that didn't welcome you back as the heroes, unlike other wars, but as a massive part of the problem.

Back home, you tried to figure out your place in the world. Married, then with one child, when your mother became ill. You hadn't had the opportunity to look around and heal yourself, you just had to keep going.

A family move didn't turn out as lucrative as you'd hoped. Opportunity wasn't knocking. Your degree wasn't one that was easily transferred into a position, so you dove into the restaurant business. With your inheritance whittling away, you tried again, finally landing a job as a manager at a tech firm. You stayed there for many years successfully until a layoff set your world spinning again.

I think that was the first time I ever saw you cry as you sat down with my brother and I and told us. Then came months of looking for jobs, and finally landing at a startup, collecting no pay until the product was launched. You continued to show hopefulness, even finding me a job at the same place, but in the end the payout never came.

Reinvention again. Finding your place again, pulling yourself out of the repeated disappointment again and again. You'd land somewhere in the nick of time.

Romantic relationships for you were sparse. With your certain ideals, there weren't many who measured up. You'd fancy some but they would go away because you weren't all the way in, or you didn't want to be a stepdad to their kids.

The one you talk about most left for that reason, and I think you regret your decision still. Maybe not regret but wonder about. What if you would have chosen differently?

Maybe she will come back when this happens or that, but it's been years. Jobs didn't stick and you had to take jobs much lower than your experience to pay the bills. After a while you stopped expecting good things to happen to you, and sat back waiting for the next ball to drop.

There was a hard moment in my life when I thought that the things I did not like about myself were attributes I also saw in you. Maybe I had picked them up from you.

Your black-and-white thinking, not of a racial nature but of an either/or. There was no space in between what you thought was right or incorrect and there was only one way to do something and it was your way.

Your quick temper was another I battled with, easily angered with no hope of calming down. There was your yearly battle with the Christmas tree stand and the one time we were at the dump with a borrowed trailer that you couldn't back into the spot when you finally got out and I had to do it.

Anticipating the worst of any situation prior to anything happening at all was another curse that kept me always on edge. When was the next horrible thing going to happen?

The last one seems to be the worst of the bunch and it is something I feel in myself to the bone.

The fear of trying new things. This one showed itself with always going to the same restaurants to staying at the same hotels anytime travel was involved. Doing the things you've always done gave you the safety but led to very little change and an extreme dislike of being forced to switch gears.

If I had a magic wand and could change anything in your life to help you navigate the rough stuff that came, it would be to grant you the courage of a lion.

I wish you would have chased your dream of being a pro baseball player, that you would have taken that chance despite your father's insistence not to. I wish you hadn't played it safe all your life because of your lesser beliefs in what you could do. Sometimes it feels like you ended up with the scraps of what your life could have been.

You have always been there for me and my brother to listen, or to hand out cash when you had it and we needed it. Sometimes you'd voice your limitations and setbacks onto us, based on your own life experience. Not out of trying to keep us down or trying to make us live smaller, but out of a love or protection of some kind. You didn't want us to suffer as you had. At least that is what I tell myself.

~

Something Had to Give, I Guess It Was Me, Me 2009

Hello autoimmune disease. As the business floundered and I struggled to get my partner out, the stress was unlike any stress I had ever been under. Everything I had was threatened. I hoped I could figure it all out.

I remember spring was coming, and I got very sick. Trying to manage, I took cold tablets and waited to feel better. It was a weekend day, and I was home alone.

I walked outside to look at the flowers that were coming up in the yard. The smoke tree that I planted was in full bloom, puffy wafts of pink clouds. My Shasta daisies were waiting to pop and the California poppy volunteers lined my short white picket fence. My curly willow tree was like a child's wild hair after the best nap ever.

I had painted the house myself last summer, and I loved the color- a deep otter skin hue paired with the natural, honey-colored pine door. I dreamed of cutting the door in half to make it a dutch door. I would've if I could have. I stood proud of this house that I had loved and made pretty for us girls, The Ladies' Lounge crew plus Mom.

Another look around to see and take in the beauty of the garden I'd tended, my face warmed by the sunshine and then lights out. I keeled over in my front yard. I woke up laying in the grass that thankfully softened my fall. Something was wrong with me.

I ended up in the hospital that day getting fluids while they ran some tests. Mono, pneumonia, and the flu all tested positive at once.

A trifecta of serious illnesses in which any one of them would have kicked any badass's butt on a good day. I was given some antibiotics to heal the pneumonia and some antiviral meds for the mononucleosis, and a hefty hospital bill to take home.

I needed bed rest and time to heal. I put a sign up on the door of the shop. Closed due to illness. I rallied some but still didn't feel great, and was *searching for answers and a new plan.*

A friend recommended a women's health specialist, so I went to her, "Something isn't right."

She checked my women's hormones and she ran more tests. Ones I really didn't know anything about. After a week, I went back and she said I needed some progesterone cream to balance out my higher estrogen and that I had Hashimoto's thyroiditis.

"You can NEVER EAT GLUTEN AGAIN." I hadn't ever heard of gluten.

"Okay," I remember thinking, "that's weird."

She was so adamant about her findings that I listened. It was as if Dr. Hashimoto (who the autoimmune condition was named after) was standing right beside her, diagnosing me too, fingers shaking at me like I had better listen.

"I mean, never, no cheating," she said.

She didn't elaborate or go into the why, but I listened to her, a little afraid that she might come after me somehow if I ate a donut or something. I would need to take thyroid hormone, and I would need to for the rest of my life. I changed my eating and listened to her advice. Over time, I started to feel better.

I'd eat very similar things each day: oatmeal or a couple of scrambled eggs for breakfast, either a chicken salad or clear type meat and veggie soup for lunch, and the opposite at dinner. Maybe an energy bar in between meals, always making sure to avoid gluten.

I continued to work towards a better resolution to the debt and the house situation, and signed up to get a loan modification from my mortgage bank. Baby steps. I even signed up to have a third party consultant come and check my paperwork to make sure I had everything, I was dotting every fricken I and crossing every T.

I got in the best shape of my adult life, but I often sat and wondered why I had to limit my diet. Why had this disease picked me?

Yes, in the beginning it was an absolute pain. Eating differently than everyone else. My kids, the holidays, my favorite foods- gone. I felt like a freak.

I stayed true for a while. Even telling the men I would date about my special diet. At first they were understanding. I was able to stay in my house, and take care, even with the hardness of life all around me.

Would I be able to sustain this? Would I take good care of myself? I guess I would see. Would I find a way to stay here, in my little house and make it work?

The Loan modification, third-party document checker lady said that I had

everything I needed, now I will just wait.
I am hopeful that things will turn my way.

~

$$\sim 2 \sim$$

Dora Alberts
Wife, Mother, Sister, Nag
1929-2009

S hari Burley of Brockton, Massachusetts, put her mother to rest today. She had spent the last two years caring for her, and with her smoking, diabetes and morbid obesity, it had been a chore. How had her mom let her health get so bad?

Shari's rounded hips teased that she could follow in her mother's footsteps fairly easily. She dreamed of having enough money for a personal trainer, like the movie stars have to get in shape. That would be perfect. Maybe her trainer would be good looking, too.

Her kids were grown now and, with her Mom gone, Shari could start thinking about herself. For her, the monthly manicures and makeup parties weren't enough. She wanted to be pampered all of the time. She dreamed of mansions and riches.

After her mother's service and the aluminum tub casserole buffet at her home, Shari began to think of how she could score some money. Big money.

As her family milled around her, her mental Rolodex spun open to her Uncle Ned.

Yes! Now was the perfect time for her to get to him and schmooze him up and reel him in. He didn't have any kids, at least any that she knew of. By showing up, she would naturally become his favorite, and she must be his next of kin. Getting a crack at that money was her right, wasn't it?

She broke into a grin as wide as the Grinch's.

Finally it was time.

Shari drove to her Mom's place and started rifling through all of her mother's scattered papers in her office. She threw ream upon ream of mail and letters into garbage bags, tossing them into the burn bin next to the fireplace. She chucked anything that didn't have Ned's name on it. Moving on to one of the many junk drawers in the kitchen, she ran across her mother's hand-scrawled note.

Sunny Days retirement home. There was the first part of a phone number scribbled on it. She could double check the area code to make sure she had the right place.

"That's it!" she squealed. "Sunny Days will be my Salvation!"

She flipped off the light in the kitchen and locked the door behind her, leaving the key under the back door mat. Best not to keep a key. She didn't ever want to have the chance to walk in on her Uncle Stan naked. She grimaced.

Uncle Stan was moving into the house tomorrow, and she hadn't bothered to clean it up for him. Stan wouldn't care what the place looked like anyway. He'd been living in a practical shack for the last five years, Mom's place would be a palace to him. She couldn't believe that Mom left the house to him, after all she had done to help her. But Mom had given her the car, so that was something.

A 1992 Toyota Corolla in Lite Blue Mica, with the back bumper half ripped off from the time her mother backed into a concrete parking post at the picnic grounds last summer. Insurance had paid her mother out, but she had kept the money, and didn't bother fixing the car. Lloyd had drilled a screw through the body of the car in a few places to make sure everything stayed together.

Back at home, Shari looked up Sunny Days Retirement Home on the internet. Shari lay next to her husband Lloyd rotating in bed like a rotisserie chicken. She kept going over her plans in her head. She got up a few times to write things down.

It was decided. She would trade in her mom's car in the morning and use that money to buy a plane ticket to go see Uncle Ned. She could get it all done by eleven and catch an afternoon flight, hitting him up on the day of the Lord.

"Who could say no to a long lost relative on a Sunday?"

Shari woke and showered late morning. She glued on her eyelashes and penciled in her brows to look like two solid arches of deviousness. Her polyester pantsuit would have to do until she had something nicer to wear. She could go shopping with Ned's moola.

"Old people love polyester anyway," she smirked, turning around slowly in front of the cracked full-length mirror.

She packed her bag, gathering up some old family photo albums and knickknacks to show her Uncle to help reintroduce him to the family since he was last around.

Shari muffled a goodbye to her still sleeping, unemployed husband and drove her Mother's car to the "Quick and Cheap" car lot by the airport. That was the name of it.

Wiggling her hips a bit, she was able to rid herself of the car for an even three hundred bucks. She batted her eyelashes at the heavy-set mechanic named Danny, and hitched a ride with him to the departures gate. She blew Danny a kiss as she sauntered inside. She still had it- Shari felt invincible.

She placed her luggage up on the carry on scale, and the bag was over by a pound. She'd have to check it.

"Dammit."

"That will be ten dollars," the attendant said.

"Dammit." She stewed, then relaxed, believing in her heart that this would be the last time she would ever bitch over ten bucks.

Shari climbed into her Coach Class middle seat and buckled up her belt. She closed her eyes and imagined herself flying in First Class.

"Champagne, Madam?" She heard the stewardess say.

"Don't mind if I do," she imagined saying back. The man next to her pulled up his sleeve and accidentally elbowed her in the boob. She winced but didn't come back to reality, she was in the zone.

In her imagination the pilot announced her name over the loudspeaker.

"Hello, Folks. Today we are all fortunate to be able to fly with the great Shari Burley, she is riding with us before her next leg to Rio De Janeiro, where she will be launching her upcoming film about how great her life is. It's a great honor for us all to be in her presence."

The entire plane rose to their feet in applause. All in her head again, of course.

She drifted off, snoring loudly all the way to her destination. The people seated next to her asked to move to empty seats throughout the cabin, and the flight attendants didn't bother waking her for peanuts or drinks.

The airplane landed with a thump. Everyone rushed to get off the plane, often cutting in front of Shari, any chance they could get.

She had time, and soon-she would have the moola.

Ned and Mom hadn't gotten along, but that shouldn't affect *her* chances at getting some of that money. After all, she had just made this trip to see him. She could tell him all about how she took care of Mom in her last days. Shari would try to explain that Mom was mean to him because of her meds or the ailments she had. Mom hadn't meant it. She always talked so lovingly towards him around her.

Now he had a whole big family to come visit from now on. Or she could just stay in town with him. Whatever Uncle Ned wanted.

~

A Rulebook For Life, Me, 2010

I ran across a list. A gift from beyond. It is a list of things I and everyone else is not responsible for. The list magically appeared while going through some papers sent to me in the form of part of the story I was writing with my Uncle. It was from years ago; I just found it while I was looking for something else.

This list now sits on top of my journals so I will read the rules often, one by one over and over until I have them memorized.

If I would have found them and read them consciously before all of this, it might have saved me some time and a helluva lot of money with Mr. Fun.

***

IT IS NEVER YOUR RESPONSIBILITY TO:

1. *Give what you really don't want to give*

2. *Sacrifice your integrity to anyone*

3. *Do more than you have time to do*

4. *Drain your strength or resources for others*

5. *Listen to unwise counsel*

6. *Retain an unfair relationship*

7. *Be anyone but exactly who you are*

8. *Conform to unreasonable demands*

9. *Be 100% perfect*

10. *Follow the crowd*

11. *Put up with intolerable situations*

12. *Please unpleasant people*

13. *Bear the burden of another's misbehavior*

14. *Do something that you cannot really do*

15. *Love unlovable people*

16. *Endure your own negative thoughts*

17. *Feel guilty toward your inner desires*

18. *Submit to overbearing conditions*

19. *Apologize for being yourself.*

20. *Meekly let life pass you by.*

Number twenty was especially poignant, as it was the reason I left my marriage and started again. But in my time with Mr. Fun I see that I had broken many more. Ones I hadn't really thought about in this way.

Truth be told, I have let many of them happen all over me. I avoided hard conversations, and avoided possible circumstances that could lead to those conversations.

I just want to be alone with my girls, my own thoughts and my home.

I resented the times when Mr. Fun needed me, wanted me to do something or asked for a favor. I felt taxed unfairly with my energy, as well as my money. With children you do for them, not because you expect something in return. You teach them, they learn to look out for themselves and they grow up. I felt at the age of thirty-nine that I became the mother of a forty-five-year-old man.

Of course he wanted to be in a relationship with me, duh. I did everything. I handled stuff when it got hard. I pulled out my checkbook and made it better. Well, this Mama's tired. Real damn tired.

He was in our lives for four years, and although we had some fun times, ultimately he whittled me down beyond my limits. It was messy, ugly, and hard, but when I didn't think I had the power to move forward, to get past him, I reached in and found the energy to save myself, to start again, again.

I believe I have learned what I needed to learn to move on and to not allow that path to happen to me, to us again.

~

$$\sim 2 \sim$$

Shari

S hari Burley got off the plane and headed to the nearest car rental desk. She handed the employee credit card after credit card until one worked.

A mid-sized sedan would do fine until she could afford to drive off in a shiny Corvette or maybe a Mercedes. A Beemer?

She would have to think about that. Once inside the car, she flipped down the visor to take a look at herself. No mirror.

"Cheap car!" She slammed it shut, breaking a nail.

"Dammit!" She chewed the nail off to get rid of the snarl. Well, almost.

She grabbed the rear view mirror and positioned it so she could see most of her hair. Okay, well some of it. She poked at it until she felt it was right.

"There."

Shari started up the car and the air conditioning turned on full blast in her face, blowing her hair over to one side. Her face crumpled. She stabbed at the buttons on the dash until the gust subsided and then started all over with her preening again.

Shari found the closest freeway, and could feel her fortune starting to change as the miles ticked by. She kept her eyes on the road, but mostly on the prize that she imagined would be waiting for her at her destination.

Less than an hour later she pulled into the parking lot of the Sunny Days Retirement Home in Gurley, Alabama.

The Sunny Days home facility manager Justin stood at the front desk.

"May I help you?"

"Hi," she smiled wide, and her makeup cracked. "My name is Shari Burley and I'm looking for my dear, dear, Uncle, Ned Coggins."

"Ned Coggins as in the Coggins Pool and Spa building here at Sunny Days?"

"Pool and Spa building!? He bought you a building?"

"Well, yes, Ma'am. He sort of left all of his money to us. We put an ad in the local paper to find his family but were unable to locate any."

"Well, I'm his family. Are you telling me he's dead?"

"Yes, Mam. He died right around six years ago."

"Six fucking years ago?" her voice was not calm anymore, not even civil anymore. She had had it.

Justin led her into a private conference room. He sat her down and gave her a glass of water. Her lipstick left a print on the edge of the glass; it was mixed with spit and dry lip skin.

"We are so sorry for your loss. Construction on the building started a year after he passed. I'd be happy to show you. Really it's no trouble, I can show you around, it is absolutely breathtaking."

Shari was deaf to the news. She couldn't live off a pool and spa building. Couldn't drive a pool and spa building! Couldn't have a personal trainer with a pool and spa building!

"Is there anything left?" she stammered.

"Yes Ma'am. I'm sending someone for it right now. The pool and spa building will be lovely. We are so grateful for his gift. We have a really nice picture of your Uncle to put on display there. We were able to have one of his photographs retouched and enhanced by a local artist; I think he did a marvelous job. Your uncle was such a kind and generous man."

"You knew him?" Shari asked.

"Well, actually no. I've only been here a month, but many of the staff here did, and some of the residents here have him to thank for adding to their nest eggs."

"He gave them money?" she stammered, her eyes nearly popping out of her head, her left eye started to twitch.

"In a sense, he had a gift with the stock market and held little classes here to help teach others. He's the reason that many can still afford to live here."

Shari slumped down into the chair.

"This must all be a real shock hearing about your Uncle's death."

The door opened and a brown cardboard box was placed, the hand-drawn arrow facing up on the table.

Justin quickly flicked a mouse turd off the top, before motioning to Shari in a *Vanna White*-style flourish.

"It's a little dusty, but here are his effects. Would you like to be alone?"

Shari nodded, unable to speak.

Justin closed the door behind him. This was one of the hardest parts of his job: Giving people bad news and handing them the last articles from the deceased. This lady had no clue that her Uncle had passed. Seemed pretty indifferent to the pool and spa building, too. Maybe looking for a handout.

"Shameful, and such language." he mused.

Justin stood outside the door to the conference room to compose him-self, "Phew." He walked back to the front desk and his station, winking at a couple of older divas on his way. He liked his job and it showed.

~

$$\sim 2 \sim$$

Shari looked around the near empty room. Cheesy beach-themed wallpaper border wound around the top of the walls. The wall color was a sullen blue, like the ocean on a winter day or the tears she'd shed for the rest of her life having missed out on big bucks because of a lousy six years.

Shari stared at the taped up box that was covered with dust. She tapped at the tape with her hand, then slipped her finger under one of the edges, subsequently breaking another nail.

"Shit!" her face pulsated with the act.

She reached under the tape, pulling with all of her might as two other fingernails flung off in different directions. Finally it popped open.

A spreadsheet sat on top announcing the contents.

1 scrapbook, misc. old photos

1 check register from Bank of America

1 savings book with savings slips (200)

1 book, Find Me 2 of 5

1 phone number of unknown importance

1 copy of handwritten note leaving all assets to Sunny Days

"Here it is, the note that screwed me."

Leafing through the pages of the scrapbook, she glanced at the photos of a young man and a young Asian woman.

"Yuck, get a room." She slammed the scrapbook shut. Flicking the side of the spiral- bound blue book, she set her eyes on the bank notes.

"All these savings slips and the account book; he was worth millions." Shari cackled as she slowly went insane.

All of her hopes and dreams of getting out of that dump of a house. Away from her belching fat husband Lloyd and her sucky job at the beauty salon, gone. Shari threw the spiral bound book into her fake alligator bag, and clipped it shut.

"Maybe there is something in this book. The rest is crap."

She left the box on the table and walked out into the lobby.

"Would you like to see the Pool & Spa building now, Mrs. Burley?

Justin followed as she headed for the front double doors.

"No!" She barked back.

"Come back for a swim anytime. Our two year anniversary party is next month." Justin waved to Shari's back, smiling, as the other tenants looked on at the commotion.

Shari used her middle finger with the broken nail in an unladylike way as she stormed out. She wished she could have slammed the doors but they were on hydraulics, so no dice.

She slid into the driver's seat of the sedan and plunked her head against the steering wheel, sobbing until her fake eyelashes fell off and poked her in the eyes.

~

Lessons from Mr. Fun, Me, 2006-2009

*H*im filching on that bet he'd made with my daughter at her soccer game, I have wished so many times later that I would have booted him then.

It was a totally obvious and unapologetic view into his real character. I ended up paying my daughter the hundred bucks, telling her it was from him. It would be just one of the many times I would cover up or make excuses for him over the next few years.

Looking back I had been a fool in love. In my efforts to fix him, and turn him into something I could be proud of, I lost my power and ended up making excuses for him for the next four plus years.

Starting a business in the worst economy since the Great Depression was probably not the best idea in hindsight. But we kept it alive for three years. We met many new people. I gained many friends and learned a lot about myself and what I was capable of.

Over time, my doing the lion's share of the work wore on me. It is much better to be in business with someone who fills your gaps. We were both good at sales, but the ghastly economy quickly leveled the playing field and sales were hard to come by.

When money did come in, he had been quick to take a share regardless of what bills needed to be paid. Me and my divorce settlement, plus my credit cards kept us afloat.

At times, I would gain strength and tell him to leave, but he kept me imprisoned with guilt and his hollow threats for years. He once threatened to commit suicide if we split.

All this happened, and here I am now. Alone. Again.

Not wanting to blame others for my own mistakes or trusting ways, but wanting some guidance, I went to a lawyer with the story.

He explained that I'd probably have to buy him out of the business to get him to leave. "Even if it was only a dollar, you two have to agree."

"But, I've bought him a car, supported him, and looked after his kids?" I said, screaming at myself inside, but saying it softly, and pathetically, I'm sure, to the lawyer.

"I should sue him!" I exclaimed.

"Does he have any money? "he asked.

"Well, no."

"Then," he clapped his hands together, **"Then, it's a lesson."**

He stood up to walk me out.

"I won't charge you for today, I don't think you really need any more to worry about."

No truer words were ever said.

He said it was a lesson just as simply as I suppose it was. I had to just accept it. He was right.

It was a lesson, and no fighting or claiming unfairness or sitting in a victim mentality of who did what to whom would change any of it. My kind, wanting-to-believe-in-people nature had severely screwed me over on this one, and I stood at the crossroads of a lifetime of bitterness, or sucking it up and moving on.

After that, everything fell like dominoes around me. With the house in jeopardy, I had to have conversations with my creditors. I borrowed money from Mr. Stability as a last ditch effort to keep the business afloat. With thousands of dollars worth of work bid out, and my business partner finally out of the picture, I put the business to part time, put on my accountability-big-girl pants and went out and found myself a job.

I was hopeful to get back on top, and wonder if love will find me again.

~

$$\sim 2 \sim$$

Shari arrived home by taxi with her small bag in tow. It had been one hell of a day. The initial excitement of potentially coming into some serious money had made her very excited, but this was another level of let down.

She knew there would be a risk in trying to connect with Uncle Ned. But she could be very persuasive and he was super old, most likely senile. Older than her Mom was, he could have been finessed into doing whatever she might want.

The one thing she hadn't figured on was that he would die.

Shari's husband Lloyd got up from the couch and came over to help her with her small bag.

"Where have you been all day? Did you have to work? I was really hungry and I called for you. You didn't come, so I made myself food. Twice."

"I went to Sunny Days Rest Home, in Gurley, Alabama, to see if I could score some money from my old Uncle Ned. Lord knows, Mom didn't leave us anything."

"She left us the car," Lloyd said, trying to be positive.

"I sold it to buy the plane ticket to get there. I didn't figure we would need it anymore with all the dough I was going to get from Ned. But go figure, the old guy died and left all of his money to the old folks' home. Dead Ned. All I got was this stupid book."

"Shit. We don't have the car anymore? I didn't even get to drive it. You've been hogging it the whole time."

"Do you understand, numbnuts? I didn't get anything. We don't have Mom's car, Ned's money or anything."

"What's the book?" he asked, still hopeful.

"Our fucking inheritance."

Shari pulled off her polyester jacket and threw it over the couch. Her pants were next, having left a thick visible line across her stomach, she let out a sigh as she unzipped. The button- down shirt was untucked and opened, baring her bra which was old and tattered and let fat bulge out from all sides.

He reached for her, suddenly in the mood.

"Right." She snarled.

Lloyd pulled his hand back and slunk into his well-dented spot on the couch. He stuck his hand down his pants and held his member as he took a long swig of his beer. At least his beer wouldn't reject him.

~

Words Are Always There for Me, Me 2010

I'm trying so hard to stay positive, waiting for news on the house, believing every day that the answer on my loan modification will be a yes, and that I will have a chance to keep our home.

As I wait, I find little wisdom nuggets everywhere. They pop up from the most interesting of circumstances.

I read an online blurb about Paolo Coelho's life that talked about how he had written one of my favorite books, 'The Alchemist,' when he was forty years old. At the time he told the universe that he needed a sign in order to write the book that he imagined in his head. A sign came to him in the shape of a single white feather.

As I am now in my fortieth year and still eking out my first novel, I felt lifted and inspired to keep writing after seeing my own white feather on my way to work this morning.

Since then, I have seen so many. All since I read the story about him.

Later that day as I sat at the gym in the massage chair after my workout, I read in a magazine how another woman had not become a novelist until her own fortieth year.

Again, a nudge that inspires. Maybe it's not too late for me?

These notes tell me that I'm not alone in wanting to achieve something. I am not alone in the unintentional procrastination. Sometimes there just isn't much to say until you have lived through more. Sometimes you don't have the best ending until you live it?

I feel no need for apologies, I feel no guilt, only the immense urge to get it done just because it's time.

I celebrated those mid-life author's moments, and later shared them with a friend.

We are all on this journey called life. Some are more engaged than others in the why of it all but we are all somewhat seekers of understanding in one way or another.

Some seek fame or incredible wealth in their lives. Some seek adventure or dangerous thrills. Some seek family or the perfect piece of pie.

Others like me just seek a feather. To carry on with our dreams when we stumble or pause.

A bonus gem in the kid's movie tonight: 'Kung Fu Panda' Disney movie.

The past is history. The future, a mystery. Today is a gift, that's why they call it the present.

~

~2~

Shari Burley had spent the last year smoldering over her lack of luck in life. Her husband Lloyd had lost six more jobs, and was getting fatter every single day. She was also growing wider, as he liked to remind her under his breath.

The holidays were coming again and times were tough. The family decided to give elephant gifts that weren't worth much instead of going deeper in debt.

Shari shuffled through her closet for something to give to her sister-in-law Shayla. Her hand caught on the belt loop of her old polyester pantsuit, crumpled into a pile on a shelf. She had not seen it or thought of it since she got back from trying to see Uncle Ned. It might fit Shayla. As she pulled, something else came along with it.

It was the book that she took from the Sunny Days retirement home after finding out about Uncle Ned's death. "Find Me" 2 of 5 fell splat onto the floor.

"That's perfect! That crappy book that used to belong to Crappy old Uncle Dead Ned!"

Shari wrapped the book in the Sunday comics and set it by the front door. This would be a sure hit at the family dinner.

Two of Five would become the default elephant gift of the family. It was the most Ned's presence had ever been celebrated.

~

Wondering About My Books, Me, 2010

No matter what, my books are out there. I did it. They are children that cannot be taken. Children that may outlive me. If my book never reaches me it's okay because through them I have adventured, lived, loved and grown through them at least in my imagination.

As an adult, I really feel like I do not know what I am doing. Every day. It's a total guess. Did I make the right choice there? Did I say the right things? Ugh.

Life for me is about the journey, not the destination. It isn't a race to get anywhere. From point A to point B. To figure out what's next in this extraordinary/ordinary life that I have been given.

Constantly in thought I search for answers. It is the never ending quest of a crusading soul. Many had been inspired by my wish for an extraordinary life, spurred on, to ask more from themselves and their own lives. I revel in the ones that inspired me, churning her need to expand her horizons.

It is my desire to feel life fully, and pay attention. I ask it not only of myself but of the others who joined on the tour. I have been writing mental postcards for most of my days. Photos on one side, sentiments or moments on the other. I mail them to myself to collect them in the mailbox of my mind.

Someday when it is time- my time- I will pull the box out and relive the memories. Maybe when my body decides not to be pliable and capable any longer. That time comes if one is lucky enough to live past the age of demands, and live into the time of just being.

All of these memories, plus the dream of seeing a certain five would have to carry me through.

~

~2~

Shari's sister-in-law gave the little blue book back to Shari's family household the following year as a Christmas present to her big brother Lloyd. It was wrapped in "Depends" undergarments, as if Ned had wrapped it himself from the nursing home. She had spread melted chocolate-hazelnut butter on the inside of the pad to emulate poo. It smeared into the cover and dulled the embossed writing, filling in more of the imprinted gold with its mess.

After dinner the family took turns reading excerpts from the book out loud to each other. Each using different mocking style voices. Some chose whiny voices, while others played up the very slow and old cadence of someone who was elderly. Some braised over the words stuttering as they knew Ned had been afflicted. Each member of the family tried to outdo the other in making fun of the book, and however they could mock the stories inside, they did.

At the end of the book, what could have been a nice moment of togetherness or growth for the family, instead settled into a sick and twisted joke on Ned and the author herself. A new family tradition was born.

The author's quest was stopped cold, and may well be trapped in this crazy, dysfunctional family forever. Kept as a pawn of shame, jealousy and envy, brought out sneering and laughing at old Ned's expense.

Shari tucked the book under some junk mail in her wooden antique baking cabinet to pull out for next year. She hadn't yet picked the next recipient, but the night of entertainment had been more than she ever dreamed it could be. She would for sure bring it out again and see if anyone could outdo their old performances.

Shari would be working on her next act, too.

~

P.P.

My most ghastly memory from junior high was being placed into three classes with the exact same teacher, one who actually hated me although people say teachers never do.

I had her for Typing, Language Arts and Computer Science. Every day of seventh grade. I saw her three times a day, every single day.

I say she hated me because I have physical, documented evidence in my 7th grade yearbook. I had really tried in her classes. I did. I tried to type fast, but it was hard.

Computer class was kind of cool, but doing programs with lines that started with 10- then a bunch of symbols, like this @#@^%^& or whatever then 20- and more symbols, like this &*%%^$ or whatever to make something happen was less than exciting to a girl who plain suffered when it came to numbers and remembering things.

Do not get me started about Language Arts. I love to write, but I did not read. Ever. I couldn't sit still long enough or be engaged in a book just because someone told me to.

One time I was supposed to do a book report on Ray Bradbury's, "*Something Wicked This Way Comes*" and I had a full three months to read the book. Did I? Nope, I flipped open the book on my way to school on report day, and choked out the first scene where some voice is mysteriously whispering to the boys in a terrifying way.

This scene was acted out loudly by me standing in front of my class reading from a blank page. It was an utter disaster as I tried to change my voice to be creepy in order to sound more like I read it.

I got an F. Which I most likely turned into an A before the paper came home, because the letter A is easy to do that with, just by adding another line if one is creative.

Back to my evidence of her detest. It was the last day of school and we were finally going to be free for the summer: I had waited the whole year for it. "Stay cool" and "H.A.G.S." populated everyone's class books- all day long.

It was my favorite day of school. I stood in line at Mrs. P's desk awaiting her signature in my prized and hard-won book. It would be something I could look back on for the rest of eternity, as I saw it.

In front of me, S.H. stood giddy as Mrs. P took her yearbook and wrote a practical novel in it about how great she was. She finished and then they exchanged a warm heartfelt hug.

My turn. I stepped forward and handed her my book to sign, I stood before her in great anticipation. She paused, let out a palpable sigh and wrote, "Keep smiling," and handed it back to me. See, she totally hated me.

Total proof.

~

Royally Screwed, Me, 2010

The bank finally got back to me and said even though the third-party double-checking person agreed that I had everything I needed to do a loan modification on my house, the bank wanted one more document. A goddamn Schedule M.

As I do all the taxes and books for my business, I needed help to be able to populate such a document, and an accountant wanted hundreds of dollars. I am exhausted with this process.

Call every four days, send documents, wait. Call in two days, call in four days, never talking to the same person twice. In the meantime the default letters still come, as if I am doing nothing to prevent this.

Call, send more documents, call. Fax this, fax that. Wait.

It is killing me.

In the end, I gave up and kissed my down payment goodbye and the bank sold my house to the highest bidder who just happened to be an old client of mine who I already offered to sell it to. They will benefit from the equity and updates I put into the home, and they will be the reaper of the wealth when they run a train station right next to it, and build up commercial buildings all around. I will try not to be bitter.

The mortgage protection insurance I paid for in my monthly payments made sure that the bank got their money back, but I left with nothing.

No place to live, a ding on my credit and no glint of any money from the equity I added to the house. It was a big eff you from the banking system, and I wasn't even close to the only one.

Where were the watchdogs to help the people manage through this time, with people losing their jobs left and right? Having to sign up for Cobra insurance at a thousand dollars a month for a single person to keep their medical care?

It wasn't just me who was struggling, I had bonus stuff like being self-employed, but I played along, I did the work and got them the documents. This last second request with its attached waiting and phone calls and waiting again, was the point where I finally acknowledged that~

Nothing I do will ever be enough for this to work out for me, I have to just stop. These people do not give a damn about individuals; it is and will forever be about money and the corporate bottom line and how much benefit they can give to their investors.

I was just one of the many millions who lost their homes and would have to figure it out. Millions of people were upside down in their houses having spent more than the properties were suddenly worth. Many of those people just walked away from their mortgages, my brother included.

I was looking at a cataclysm of three. Losing my business with 290K of promised work sitting in estimates, with all of those people excited to move forward. Everyone seemed to be waiting on something to pull the trigger to start their projects : Confirmation that they still had a job, that their investments held, whatever it was.

Number two of the cataclysm was losing my home that I had plunked 80K down on, and would not see any of it coming back in my direction. Number three was that I could not pay the debts I had incurred, so my only answer was bankruptcy.

Was this just a karmic payback from the carnage I left behind in my marriage? Was it because I often trusted individuals that I shouldn't? Was it because I hadn't had a proper financial education or decent role models growing up when it came to money?

Everything I learned about being a grown-up were basics from a life class in high school. A class I don't even know if they still teach.

I keep trying so hard to make it all make sense.

Why? Why me? What could I have done better, or who should I have listened to? Should I have just stayed to make sure I was safe? Will I ever recover from this? It tears at every bit of belief in myself that I thought I had. Total breakdown.

My brain asks the why in everything; sometimes it just is, and there isn't any more I can do about it. Regret does nothing to change the outcome, it only makes the person feel like shit.

The worst economic downturn since the Great Depression. Why in the world was that called "Great" anyway? It pretty much sucked for everyone.

This time there were bailouts, left and right, for big business and the banks- everyone except small businesses and regular people. No forgiveness or help there.

Will I die from this? Most likely no, but it feels like I could.

This monetary hole is such a shameful place to be in. It's an agonizing thing to go through or watch someone you love go through. I didn't want to stand in front of a judge and say I had given up, but I didn't have a choice anymore. It was all too much, and I am beaten down into hardly a person anymore.

I'm sick, I'm broke, and I am tired.

~

~2~

It was the day before Christmas at the Burley household. Two of Five lay wrapped under the artificial tree again this year, addressed to Albert.

A recent addition to the Burley household, Albert had been thrown out of his childhood home by his mother, Shari's sister.

He had landed with Lloyd and Shari somewhat accidentally, and now they were used to his presence and the fact that he fed the cat and mowed the lawn for them. He was skinny and didn't eat much and he never ate the last bit of anything helping him remain invisible food-wise. Maybe some paste went missing from the office or a few slices of bread from the freezer from what Shari could determine.

The tradition of the book being gifted at the holiday had been going for three years, and Uncle Ned had become the joke of multiple generations, even though the majority of the family at this point had never met him.

The book was rarely read anymore, but sat as the only holiday tradition the Burley family took part in. It was given, then put aside to give to someone else the following Christmas.

Its pages were worn, and the cover was stained and ugly from being used mostly as a coaster. The gold lettering had started rubbing off the front cover.

It had been a long time since anyone cared for any of the items in the home. The couch, a Naugahyde burgundy leatherish fabric, had wear spots where butts often frequented. Where Lloyd sat was torn through. Straps of brown and gold houndstooth fabric were stretched and hung limp on the sides of the arms, often grabbing the sweaters or clothing of any sitters nearby.

The handmade and once beautiful knotted rag rug made by Shari's grandmother out of old clothes from her ten children growing up, had worn through in spots and had never been cleaned- let alone vacuumed- since entering this house. No one actually knew what colors it had in its design. Now a gunky brown tone, most likely held together by the dirt particles themselves.

Lamplight is all that remains in the room since the overhead can lights need new bulbs put in place. The box of new bulbs sits on the kitchen counter collecting dust. No one in the house even sees it anymore.

A navy blue recliner is Shari's favorite spot to give her relief from her bunions after standing in the salon all day, washing the rich people's hair. She kicks off her shoes at the door and slips on her flip-flops that don't pinch into the sides of her feet. A half-ripped shawl is flung over the back, and Shari often naps there before or after dinner.

Supper is often a tray of individual "Hungry Man" dinners for each of them: macaroni and cheese or meatloaf. Shari is a million miles away from attaining her goal of health and a taut body. Frozen lasagna is a particularly sought after family treat, only attempted on Saturdays because it takes three hours to cook in their late 1970's oven. That is if someone remembers to preheat and put it in there. Sometimes they eat as late as nine, because of forgetfulness. It's been years since they ate a salad.

This Christmas many of the family had decided not to get together. There has been a great downturn in the economy, and the war in Afghanistan continues to rage on.

An almost-Depression has hit not only the country but this family as well. Presents are plain off the table this year, as every dollar coming in will go to bills. Juggling bills artfully to avoid the shut-off dates of the water, electricity, and gas, and waiting until the last minute to pay other bills, all nudging mighty close to a collection notice.

There are mornings when Shari wakes up after dreaming of gaining access to Ned's money. The Pool and Spa building are out back of her new and luxurious house and she barks orders at her many personal assistants to take care of the grounds. A hot pool guy also comes with the place. She admires him often and he returns her glances with a kissy face.

But every day she opens her eyes to her bad-breath afflicted, snoring husband Lloyd, and she scowls- or maybe that is the permanent placement of her facial features. At least she can count on him being there, not asking for much; another body to keep the bed warm when they turn off the furnace at night to save money.

Albert, even though he is mostly a freeloader, smiles and is appreciative for what they have. He is grateful for a halfway warm house in the middle of winter instead of sleeping out in the barn at his Mom's.

A stray, the family's new cat Rascal hasn't been neutered out of laziness and money issues and he sprays all around the house constantly. On the carpet and the corner edges of the couch, marking his territory. The family is aware of the smell and his habit but none of them have the gumption to try to stop him, or try to clean the area to remove the smell. Rascal is particularly cute and purrs on command so he gets away with murder.

They had put up the artificial tree as usual and set three gifts under the branches. Lloyd and Shari have wrapped items of their own that they haven't seen in awhile; they will open them and will act as if they are so surprised. Acting has become a hidden pastime for the family since the cable TV was shut off last month. They often exchange clothes and do skits in the low light of the house or make up stories about big things that happened to them that day that are a total farce. There is a growing competition for the biggest, most outlandish lie. No prize for the winner, but the contest is real-nonetheless.

Both Shari and Lloyd were out all day, toiling for their weekly check. Albert tinkered in the garage with something he found in there: an old toaster he believed was just broken that he hoped to fix for the family, to place another gift under the tree.

Like everything else in the house, the Christmas lights are low quality and old. Big bulbs that run hot, someone had forgotten to turn them off for the day. It is quiet, as Rascal awakens from a nap on the blue recliner feeling mischievous in the large and open space alone.

Rascal knocks the lights around trying to climb up into the tree. Suddenly, there is a spark. No one is there to see it, to maybe stop a catastrophe. The tree catches fire, then the presents, and soon everything else around it. The curtains, the rug and the couch. The cat runs out the cat door to avoid the heat and hides in the neighbor's bushes.

Miscellaneous items around the house act as accelerants. Lloyd's remote control car batteries, his *Mad* magazine collection piled high. Shari's old softball trophies melt into the mantelpiece as the walls catch fire.

Seeing the smoke, the neighbors make desperate calls to Shari's workplace; she is yanked away from her duties at the sink and barrels off down the road to get home.

Lloyd's cell phone was turned off as he was just finishing his second beer at the bar, out celebrating his new job as a security guard at the mall with a couple of buddies. The two of them arrive home at the same time.

~

Going Down in Flames, Me 2010

*T*he house is going away soon. I have no way to keep it anymore. My life is crumbling around me. Projects that were promised to start were again delayed, just enough to ruin any chance I had at saving the business. Not enough money coming in, the bank required yet another form to save the house. I had filed for bankruptcy and taken the classes that showed my efforts to not let this happen again.

At the bankruptcy hearing, my Mom sat next to me. We were two in a room full of people. Regular people like me, all with different stories and circumstances. Broken, distraught, needing relief. A young family with a baby in a car seat. An older man and woman, their faces worn down from stress.

I never felt so low, pathetic, and ashamed in my life.

I listened as the judge explained how this would go. He didn't need to hear all about the issues, excuses or things people might have tried to keep this outcome away. He was kind in his speech and clear in his delivery. People were called alphabetically or by case number, I cannot say; only that I wasn't the first to stand in front of the judge.

I saw people walk up and say their say. When they were done, and walking back to their seats, I kept my eyes low avoiding eye contact as the only courtesy I could think of to empathize.

Finally it was my turn.

The judge asked me about my debts, and if I had a way to pay them. I answered no.

"Since you have taken the classes that were required by the state, completed them and done all that you can to work with your creditors, your debts are hereby, dismissed."

As we left, I remember feeling as though God himself had scooped me up, looked me in the eye and told me that I would be okay.

Thankfully, my daughters were insulated for most of this hardship, be-

cause their Dad was in a good place financially. They did see me struggle though: they saw me cry, and be depressed. But I am not sure if it was always a bad thing.

I had read somewhere that often parents in their own pursuit of perfection, hide their failures and challenges from their children. Those kids walk the world seeking perfection in themselves and often fall short. Those children are more in danger of committing suicide.

In my first marriage I had developed a penchant for Afghan rugs. We had many throughout the house and each had its own pattern and brilliance. One in particular came in with a more visible flaw and I reached out to the seller and he shared their intention.

"These artisans work hard, often sitting on the ground for weeks on end completing their masterpieces. If the rug is nearly completed and there are no imperfect stitches, the weaver adds a mistake on purpose, because to them only God is perfect."

Lest we forget, everyone struggles some time or another, and if we can show our children that we can hit a pothole now and then come back from it, we are teaching them how to be resilient, too.

I learned a lot in that time period.

I learned that "stuff" doesn't matter. Stuff can always be replaced, but the main thing to take care of- the only thing that counts- is your kids.

You can't always trust people who say they care about you. Mostly I learned that the proverbial "they" could take literally anything that I owned, but if they couldn't take my kids from me, I would be fine. Knowing that, helped me through a lot of days when I didn't think I could get out of bed.

It felt like the life I had made was burning down around me. I prayed I would magically turn into a Phoenix and rise again, like my Father had so many times in his life.

My perception of myself is in the toilet. I am bruised and battered and hanging on by a thread. Not much else could go wrong, I figured.

I wasn't the only one to lose everything in the greatest economic downturn in U.S. History since the 'Great Depression'- the Great Recession."

Not even close.

~

~2~

S hari and Lloyd stood in disbelief with everything they owned aflame. It was cold outside and the snow fell lightly, but not enough to help snuff the flames. Albert sprinted out from behind the garage. He was yelling and waving something at them.

The flames reached further up into the sky, lighting up the night with the blaze.

"I've saved it! Aunt Shari, I saved our inheritance!." He is holding Ned's little blue book, still partially wrapped. "I ran in and grabbed it when I saw the smoke."

Shari whipped that book out of Albert's hand so fast, it made his eyes blur. She clenched it in her right hand and flung her arm back as if she was deep in a major league outfield throwing a ball home to save the game in the World Series. Thrusting her arm forward, made the pages in the book whiz in speed.

Something had come over her, something neither she nor Lloyd had ever seen. Breaking one of her fake nails on her wig on the follow through, the blue book flew towards the house, and plunged deep into the fire.

"I don't ever want to see that stupid book again!" she raged crazily, as large chunky snowflakes fell into her open gape.

Shari continued to pace and scream, firing off swear words like a drunken sailor. Her wig tipped back and held on for dear life by one off-colored bobby pin. She feels nothing; not the cold, the wet or the immense heat coming off of her home or what was soon to be left of it.

No one said a word.

With all three of their cell phone batteries now dead, she, Lloyd and Albert step back and together the family watch the rest of their house burn all the way to the ground.

"You paid the homeowner's insurance, right?" Shari asks Lloyd calmly as the embers of their home smoked into one last coil towards the sky.

"Uh, I thought you did," Lloyd said.

***

*Find me
Two of Five
is Lost.*

Book Club Discussion Questions

1. Could you relate to any of what the author went through in this book? How?

2. How did you feel about the author throughout this volume?

3. Which character who found the book was your favorite and why?

4. Did you feel pulled to learn more about any of the U.S. Historical tidbits you learned about in this book?

5. Did reading about the seniors at Sunny Days make you want to ask questions of any elders you know?

6. Did any scenes make you emotional? Angry, sad, happy?

7. Did the book turn out like you thought it would?

8. Who was your favorite character to dislike? Why?

9. Did this book make you want to write down some of your experiences?

10. What advice would you give to the author?

Mentions and Places Listed in this Book

For diving deeper

*H*ave fun going down the rabbit hole :)

Mariel Boat Lift Operation-mass exodus from Cuba to U.S. *https://www.history.com/news/mariel-boatlift-castro-carter-cold-war*

Pop Shoppe soda-*https://www.thepopshoppe.com/*

Lupus autoimmune condition-*https://www.lupus.org/*

Rosie the Riveter-*https://www.history.com/topics/world-war-ii/rosie-the-riveter*

Lockheed Burbank Operation Camouflage-*https://www.lockheedmartin.com/en-us/news/features/history/camouflage.html*

Millerette's women's baseball team Wisconsin.-*https://www.mnopedia.org/group/minneapolis-millerettes*

Author George Sand-*https://www.georgesandassociation.org/*

Sexsomnia-*https://www.healthline.com/health/sleep-sex#causes*

Tybee Island GA. Pavilion history- *https://visittybee.com/article/get-to-know-tybee-islands-fascinating-history*

Black History Tybee Island- *https://tybeemlk.com/tybee-black-history-trail* & *https://storymaps.arcgis.com/stories/3f4508b00beb456fa95b663057e62d79*

Executive Order 9066 Japanese American internment-*https://www.archives.gov/milestone-documents/executive-order-9066* & *https://www.nps.gov/subjects/worldwarii/confinement.html* & *Documentary Film-For the Sake of the Children by Joe Fox & Marlene Shigekawa*

Rh incompatibility in blood during pregnancy-*https://my.clevelandclinic.org/health/diseases/21053-rh-factor*

James Harrison- "The Man with the Golden Arm"- *https://www.lifeblood.com.au/news-and-stories/stories/james-harrison*

The Secret-*https://www.thesecret.tv/*

Korean War rebuilding after the war with U.S. Army Corp of Engineers- *https://www.usace.army.mil/About/History/Historical-Vignettes/Military-Construction-Combat/098-Korean-War/*

Union Streamliner—Union-Pacific passenger train-*http://streamliner memories.info/UP/UP66Map.pdf* & *https://www.up.com/heritage/history /passenger_trains/index.htm*

Kansas City A's Baseball team-*https://missouriencyclopedia.org/groupso rganizations/kansas-city-athletics*

Rocket City- Huntsville Alabama-*https://apnews.com/article/d4c8b31a d3d245d8b5a71b2b4eaa9a21*

Sheriff Coltrane & Cletus- *Dukes of Hazzard characters*-*https://www.warnerbros.com/tv/dukes-hazzard*

Mont Blanc Meisterstuck gold pen- *https://www.montblanc.com/en-us/ discover/company/about-us*

Gurley Alabama-*https://www.townofgurleyal.com/* & *https://www.town ofgurleyal.com/community/page/history-gurley*

Oedipus in Greek mythology-*https://www.britannica.com/science/Oedi pus-complex*

Kung Fu Panda movie-*https://www.dreamworks.com/movies/kung-fu-p anda*

Mad magazine-*https://www.dc.com/mad*

The Author takes no responsibility for the information, upkeep or details shared on these websites, these resources are meant as a place to start with your own research and learning.

These are just the beginning.

When we search out the experiences of others and try on their point of view, we become closer to calming the waters in the turbulent sea of our world.
With Love, H.H. Rune

About the Author

My need to impart wisdom

It all started when my two daughters were little. The words *'Imparting wisdom'* came and suddenly I was sharing nuggets with them as often as I could.

Little things like opening a bag of sugar in the sink or not mixing bleach and ammonia while cleaning. Through the years there would be hundreds of things I would share with them.

I'd start with the intro- "I am about to *impart some wisdom,*" and they would stop what they were doing and gather around. It might have started as a game but even now I send my grown daughters messages with imparted wisdom. Funny is now- they do it with mc too.

As in life I feel that the answers to life's questions come in the nick of time. When you might be at your wit's end and uncertain as to your next step. This book series is my *"Imparted wisdom"* for the world at large, sharing each lesson, each resource that came into my life at just the right time.

I do hope you will find some wisdom that may be helpful in your current moment. Wishing you all the answers you seek.

~H~

Newsletter, updates and more

After-stories

*W*hy an After-story?

I know, I miss them, too. If you want to hear more bits about the characters in this book who left too soon, sign up for my newsletters to hear more about them and other pondering thoughts.
It's been a pleasure.
Sincerely,
H.H. Rune

Check out this after-story from the series...

hazel's after-story

click here to see
that and sign
up for more

If you enjoyed this story~ I would love a review!

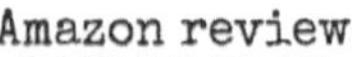

Goodreads   Amazon review

Find Me-2   Find Me-2

For news and the latest from the Extraordinary Life Seeker series...
and to watch the travels of the limited edition trackable versions of Find
Me
please visit

hhrune.com

Stay Tuned for the next book in the Extraordinary Life Seeker series, Find
Me, Book Three, currently slated for Winter 2024.
H.H. Rune's books are brought forth by:

heartfinder media

If you choose to pass this
book along

Date	Name	Location

Date	Name	Location

Date   Name   Location

Date	Name	Location